Also by Camilla Läckberg
Available from Random House Large Print

The Golden Cage

Also by Camilla Läckberg
Available from Random House Large Print

The Golden Cage

SILVER TEARS

SILVER TEARS

CAMILLA LÄCKBERG

Translated by Ian Giles

RANDOM HOUSE
LARGE PRINT

Translation copyright © 2021 by Ian Giles

Published in the United States of America by Random House Large Print in association with Alfred A. Knopf, an imprint of Penguin Random House LLC, New York. Originally published in Sweden as **Vingar av silver** by Bokförlaget Forum, Stockholm, in 2020. Copyright © 2020 by Camilla Läckberg.

Front-of-jacket photograph by lambada / E+ /Getty Images
Cover design by John Gall

The Library of Congress has established a Cataloging-in-Publication record for this title.

ISBN: 978-0-593-41454-5

www.penguinrandomhouse.com/large-print-format-books

FIRST LARGE PRINT EDITION

Printed in the United States of America

10 9 8 7 6 5 4 3 2 1

This Large Print edition published in accord with the standards of the N.A.V.H.

For Karin

For Karin

PART ONE

PART ONE

Two inmates convicted of murder escaped early this morning from their prison transport. When their prison guard stopped at the Gränna motorway services on the E4, the men seized the opportunity and fled into the forest.

Several police patrol cars were summoned to the scene, but the search for the fugitives has as yet been fruitless.

According to the Swedish Prison and Probation Service's press spokesperson, Karin Malm, the men are not considered to pose a threat to the public.

Aftonbladet, 5 June

Faye switched on the Nespresso machine. While it made her an espresso, she looked out of the tall window in the kitchen. As always, the view blew her away.

The house in Ravi had become her paradise on earth. The village itself wasn't all that large—it was home to just two hundred permanent inhabitants. It took all of five minutes or so to walk around the entire village, if you dragged your heels a bit. But in the center of the small piazza there was a restaurant that served the best pizza and pasta she had ever eaten. And it was packed to the rafters every night. Sometimes a few tourists would trickle in, and now that the end of May was approaching their number was increasing. Enthusiastic French cyclists or American retirees who had rented a motorhome and were now fulfilling their dream of seeing Italy, while their grown-up children wondered despairingly why their parents insisted on having their own lives instead of being on call as babysitters for the grandkids.

But no Swedes.

Faye hadn't seen a single Swede here since she had bought the house. That had been a deciding factor in the choice of location. In Sweden, she was famous the length and breadth of the country. In Italy, she wanted and needed to be anonymous.

The beautiful old house she had bought wasn't actually in the village—it was some twenty minutes' walk beyond it. It was high on a hill with vines climbing the slope toward the house. Faye loved to stroll up and down the steep village streets buying bread, cheese, and air-dried prosciutto. It was the ultimate cliché of life in the Italian countryside, and she was enjoying it to the fullest. Over the last two years, while her ex-husband languished in a Swedish prison, she'd made a safe haven here for the two people she cared about most in the world: her daughter, Julienne, and her mother, Ingrid. This week they'd been joined by Faye's closest friend and business associate, Kerstin, who doted on Julienne as if she were her own and had spent her visit competing with Ingrid to spoil the child.

The espresso was ready. Faye picked up her cup and went into the living room at the rear of the house, where the sound of splashing and happy childish cries divulged that there was a pool before it came into view. She loved the living room. It had taken time to decorate the house, but her own patience and one of Italy's most talented interior designers meant it was exactly the way she wanted it. The house had thick stone walls that kept the heat out and made it cool even in the hottest summer months, but it was consequently rather dark indoors. They had remedied that with large, light furniture and plenty of discreet lighting. The large windows at the back also helped to let in the light. She loved how almost imperceptibly the living room faded into the terrace.

The white drape caressed her as she stepped outside. She tasted the espresso and watched her daughter and her mother without them noticing her at first.

Julienne had grown so big, while her hair— bleached by the sun—was almost white. She got new freckles pretty much every day. She was beautiful, healthy, and happy. Everything that Faye wanted for her. Everything that had been made possible by life without Jack.

"Mommy, Mommy, look! I can swim without armbands!"

Faye smiled and made an expression of amazement to show her daughter how impressed she was. Julienne was swimming in the deep end of the pool, doing a tortuous doggy paddle but completely independent of her Bamse the bear armbands, which were lying on the edge. Ingrid was watching her grandchild nervously, half sitting, half standing, ready to throw herself into the pool if need be.

"Relax, Mom. She's got this."

Faye took another sip of the espresso, which was almost all gone, and wandered farther out onto the terrace. She regretted not having made a cappuccino instead.

"She's insisting on staying in the deep end," said Faye's mother, looking despairingly at her.

"I think she takes after her mother."

"Thank you very much, I can see that!"

Ingrid laughed and Faye was struck—as she had been on so many occasions over these past two years—by how beautiful her mother was. Despite everything life had put her through.

The only people who knew that Ingrid and Julienne were alive were Faye and Kerstin. As far as the rest of the world was concerned, both were dead, Julienne murdered by her father—a crime for which Jack was now serving a life sentence in Sweden. He had come so close to crushing Faye. Her love for him had made her a victim, but in the end she'd seen to it that he paid the price.

Faye went to her mother and sat down next to her in a rattan armchair. Ingrid continued to watch Julienne, her body tense.

"Do you have to go away again?" she asked, without shifting her gaze from her granddaughter.

"This is a busy time for us. Expanding the Revenge brand into the American market means negotiating our way through a lot of red tape. And then there's the Italian acquisition, which will give us a foothold in Rome. Giovanni, the owner, wants to sell, but, like all men, he seriously overestimates his own value. It's just a case of making him realize that my price is the best offer he'll get."

Her mother looked anxiously from Faye to Julienne.

"I don't understand why you're still working so much. You've only got a ten percent stake in Revenge now, and you'll never have to lift a finger again given the fortune you made selling your shares."

Faye shrugged, drained the last drops of espresso, and then placed the cup on the rattan table.

"Sure, there's part of me that would really like to hang out here with you two. But you know me. I'd die of boredom after a week. And no matter how many shares I have, Revenge is my baby. And I'm still chairman. What's more, I feel a tremendous responsibility for all those women who came on board and invested and are now shareholders in Revenge. They took a chance on me and the company, and I want to carry on repaying that. In fact, I've been thinking about buying a bigger stake, if there's anyone willing to sell. It would be a good exit for them, at any rate."

Ingrid sat up slightly as Julienne turned at the far side of the pool.

"The sisterhood," she huffed, then caught herself

and apologized. "I'm afraid I don't have quite the same perspective on women's loyalty that you do."

"We're in new times, Mom. Women stick together. Anyway, Julienne is okay with me taking a quick jaunt to Rome—we talked about it yesterday."

"You know I think you're incredibly smart? You know that I'm proud of you?"

Faye took Ingrid's hand.

"Yes, Mom, I know. You take care of the kid and make sure she doesn't drown, and I'll be home again soon."

Faye went to the edge of the pool. Julienne was snorting, switching between strokes and swallowing mouthfuls of cold water.

"Bye, sweetheart, I'm off now!"

"Bye, b—"

The rest was drowned out by another gulp of water as Julienne tried to wave while swimming. From the corner of her eye, Faye saw Ingrid hurrying toward the pool.

In the living room, her stylish Louis Vuitton case was packed and ready to go. The limousine to take her to Rome had probably already arrived. She lifted the case to make sure the wheels didn't scratch the dark wood floors and headed toward the front door. As she passed Kerstin's study, she spotted Kerstin absorbed in something on the computer screen, her glasses on the tip of her nose as always.

"Knock knock—I'm off now . . ."

Kerstin didn't look up—there was a deep worry line between her eyes.

"Is everything okay?"

Faye took a step into the room and put down the bag.

"I don't know . . ." Kerstin said slowly, without looking up.

"Now you're making me worried—is it something to do with the stock issue? Or America?"

Kerstin shook her head.

"I don't know yet."

"Do I need to worry?"

Kerstin took her time to reply.

"No . . . not yet."

A car honked outside and Kerstin nodded toward the front door.

"Off you go. Seal the deal in Rome. Then we'll talk."

"But . . ."

"It's probably nothing."

Kerstin smiled reassuringly at her, but as Faye went toward the heavy wooden door, she couldn't shake the feeling that something was going on. Something threatening. But she would deal with it. She would have to. That was the person she was.

She got into the backseat, waved at the chauffeur to drive, and opened the mini bottle awaiting her. As the car purred off toward Rome, she sipped the champagne thoughtfully.

Faye examined her face in the elevator mirror. Three men in suits were eyeing her appreciatively. She opened her Chanel bag, puckered her lips, and carefully applied Revenge's own lipstick to them. She tucked a strand of blond hair behind her ear, and replaced the cap with the engraved **R** just as the elevator reached the lobby. The men stepped aside to let her exit first. Her footsteps echoed on the white marble floor, the night air making her red dress flutter as the doorman held open the glass doors.

"Taxi, **signora**?" he asked.

She shook her head, smiling without slowing down, and turned right when she reached the pavement. The traffic beside her was at a standstill. Cars were honking and drivers were swearing through wound-down windows.

She reveled in the freedom of being a solo visitor to a city where she knew almost nobody and where no one could demand anything from her.

Free from responsibility, free from guilt. The meeting with Giovanni, the owner of the small family-owned cosmetics firm that was going to supplement Revenge's existing line of products, had gone splendidly. As soon as Giovanni had realized he couldn't use mastery and male dominance to convince her to agree to his terms, the meeting had been turned to her advantage.

Faye loved the game of negotiation. The opposing players were usually men, and they always made the mistake of underestimating her expertise simply because she was a woman. Later, when they had to admit defeat, there were two types of men. There were the ones who left the meeting boiling with rage, their hatred of women even more firmly entrenched. And then there were the ones who loved it, who were turned on by her commanding presence and know-how, who left the meeting with a hard-on in their trousers and an inquiry about whether she was free for dinner.

As Faye walked through the balmy evening, the city buzzed around her and she felt it drawing her in with everything she had longed for. Her walk had no objective. Some opportunity would arise, all she had to do was let the pulse of the city take over her body.

It wouldn't be long before she had to put the mask back on again—play the role that had become hers in her home country. But tonight, she could be who she wanted to be. She continued to walk until she came to a beautiful cobbled square. She wandered deeper into the labyrinth of winding lanes.

You have to lose yourself to rise again, she thought to herself.

A man disengaged himself from the shadows and offered her his wares in a hoarse whisper. Faye merely shook her head. A large door bathed in the yellow hue of the streetlights opened softly and two people—a man and a woman—who had been waiting outside stepped through it.

Faye stopped and looked around before changing tack and heading for the door, which had closed again. There was a small doorbell. A camera above her. She pressed the button, listening for the sound but hearing nothing. Eventually, the lock clicked and the door slipped open. An enormous room filled with beautiful people and the sound of clinking glasses opened up before her. Directly ahead of her there was a glass wall and beyond it a magnificent terrace. The illuminated ruins of the Colosseum shone like the wreckage of a spaceship in the distance.

A large mirror with a gilded frame allowed her to see well-dressed, faceless shadows chatting in groups behind her. The women were young, beautiful, and tastefully made up, wearing elegant short dresses. The men were generally somewhat older, but also looked good—radiating the calm and self-confidence that wealth so often gave. The small fragments of conversation that reached her were in Italian. Glasses were being refilled, drained, refilled.

Not far from her, a couple was kissing. Faye scrutinized them with fascination, unable to tear her gaze away from them. They were young—perhaps twenty-five or so. He was tall and handsome in that Italian way, with stylish stubble, a powerful nose, and dark hair combed into a side part. She was wearing an expensive bone-white dress that fit tightly around her hips and emphasized her slender waist. Her dark brown hair was up in a simple arrangement.

They were clearly so infatuated that they couldn't keep their hands off each other. Again and again, his long fingers would slip up the inside of her tanned thigh. Faye smiled. When her eyes met those of the woman, she didn't lower her own gaze—instead, she calmly contemplated the couple. She raised her drink—a whiskey sour—to her mouth. Once upon a time, she had been in love like that. But that love had suffocated her, turning her into an inert thing with no will of its own, contained within a gilded cage.

Faye's train of thought was interrupted by the young woman, who suddenly came over to her.

"My fiancé and I wonder whether you'd like to have a drink with us," she said in English.

"You don't look like you want company," Faye said with amusement.

"We'd like yours. You're very beautiful."

She was called Francesca and had been born in the city of Porto Alegre, near the Atlantic coast in Brazil. She worked as a model and was also a painter. He was called Matteo and his family owned a hotel and restaurant empire. He painted too, although he wasn't as good as Francesca, he explained with a slight smile. They were friendly, polite, and made her laugh. Their zest for life and unconcernedness were infectious. Faye became caught up with them and had another two drinks. She was dazzled by their beauty, youth, and love for each other without feeling any envy. She didn't miss having a man. She wanted to control her own life without thinking about someone else all the time. But she loved seeing these two together.

After an hour, Matteo excused himself and departed in the direction of the men's bathrooms.

"We're about to leave," Francesca said.

"Me too. I'm traveling home tomorrow."

"Would you like to come back to ours for a while and continue the evening?"

Faye weighed up the offer without dropping her gaze. She could catch up on the lost sleep on her way home. She didn't want the evening to come to an end—not yet. She wanted to see more of them.

. . .

The taxi pulled up outside a looming, stately looking building. Matteo paid and they got out of the car and were let inside by a liveried doorman. The apartment was on the top floor and had huge panoramic windows and a balcony facing a pretty park. The walls were covered with black-and-white photographs. When Faye examined them more closely she realized that some of them were of Francesca. Some kind of Italian pop was playing from the speakers. Behind her, Matteo was mixing drinks from a selection of spirits on a drinks trolley. Francesca told a story that made Faye laugh harder than she had in a long time.

Faye sat down on an enormous cream-colored couch beside Francesca. Matteo passed them their drinks before sitting down on the other side of Faye. Her head was spinning pleasantly with intoxication. The murmur from the street below had a calming effect but at the same time she was filled with tense expectation and excitement.

Francesca put her drink on the coffee table, leaned in slowly, pushing down the thin shoulder strap of the red dress with soft fingers, and kissed Faye on the collarbone. Waves of warmth raced through her body. Matteo twisted her head toward him, his lips getting closer before he feinted away, grazing his mouth across her throat and nuzzling her neck before kissing her. Francesca's hand softly caressed her thigh, moving up, stopping at the last moment and appearing teasingly at the small of her back. It was like being in a dream.

They undressed her first, then themselves.

"I want to see the two of you," Faye whispered. "Together."

Jack's face appeared in her mind's eye—she thought about the time he had talked about inviting a woman to join them. Faye had refused. Not because she found the idea unappealing— but because it had always been so apparent that it was for his sake. It was different for Francesca and Matteo. Faye was there for both of them. It wasn't because they'd grown weary of each other, but because their love and attraction was so strong that it was brimming over and there was enough for one more. And she was taking delight from the entire situation.

Faye groaned when Matteo bent her over—across Francesca—and pushed into her from behind. Faye stared into the Brazilian's wide eyes as her fiancé thrust into her. Francesca's mouth was half-open, her eyes inquisitive, intense.

"I like seeing you fuck her, baby," Francesca whispered to Matteo.

She was a means for them to strengthen their solidarity, although she was also included.

When Faye was close to coming, Matteo pulled out of her. The deep couch was a tangle of their naked, sweaty bodies. Faye had never experienced anything as intimate as becoming part of these beautiful, infatuated people's pleasure. Her body trembled as Francesca moved closer to her. They exchanged a look as they got onto all fours at the end of the couch and curved their backs. Matteo stood behind them, first penetrating Francesca and then Faye, before moving his cock between them. Finally, Faye reached climax. She cried out loud. Matteo couldn't contain himself any longer; his breathing was becoming heavier.

"In her," Francesca panted.

Faye felt him get harder before he exploded.

Afterward, they moved still entwined and lay down in the big bed in the adjacent bedroom— all three of them. They passed a cigarette between themselves, still breathing deeply. Faye set the alarm clock on her mobile to make sure she didn't oversleep, before trying to drift off. After half an hour, she gave up. She carefully disentangled herself and clambered out of bed without waking the couple. They stirred slightly in their sleep, wrapped their arms around each other, and crept closer in the warm patch where Faye had been lying.

Naked, she poured a glass of champagne from an open bottle and then took both out onto the balcony. The city was filled with sound and light. Faye sat down on a lounger and perched her feet on the rail. A warm summer breeze caressed her naked body, making it tingle and tickle. But what should have been a perfect moment was marred by thoughts of Kerstin's expression as she had looked at the monitor in the study just before Faye had left the house the previous day. Not much upset Kerstin. She was a rock against which other rocks crumbled into dust. Something was up.

Faye sipped the champagne thoughtfully while her thoughts careered away. There was so much that could go wrong in a company as big as Revenge, especially given the sizable investments they had made. Big money, big investments, big profits—but also big risks. Nothing was certain. Nothing was unshakable. Faye of all people knew that much.

She turned around and saw the beautiful couple lying in bed inside. She smiled at them. Right now, she didn't want to think about Kerstin's troubled face; right now, she didn't want to think about everything that lay ahead. She wanted something else.

"Mommy!"

Julienne came running toward Faye and gave her a wet hug.

"Don't run on the paving stones!" Ingrid called out from over by the rattan sofas.

"Now you're wet, Mommy," Julienne said with concern once she had disengaged from the hug and saw that the front of Faye's blouse had a damp patch on it.

"It doesn't matter, sweetheart. It'll dry out. But what's this? Haven't you got out of the pool since I left?"

"Nope." Julienne giggled. "I slept in the pool and ate in the pool too."

"Fancy that—I thought I had a little girl, but it turns out she was actually a mermaid!"

"Yes! Like Ariel!"

"Just like Ariel."

Faye stroked her daughter's wet hair, which had begun to shimmer a slightly greenish shade.

"I'm going upstairs to unpack, be back down soon," she called to Ingrid, who merely nodded and returned to her book. She had clearly begun to trust Julienne's capabilities in the pool a little more.

Faye climbed the stairs and carried her bag into the bedroom. She quickly wriggled out of the wet blouse and the other clothes she had been traveling in and changed into a soft cotton loungewear set. She stowed the wheelie bag in her walk-in closet. Her Girl Friday, Paola, would unpack it later.

The bed looked so inviting that Faye lay down on top of the covers with her hands clasped behind her head, allowing herself to relax. The thought of what had happened in the bed in Rome made her smile to herself. She yawned and could feel how tired she was—she had literally not slept a wink during the night. On the other hand, she had slept all the way home. She didn't want to risk nodding off now, but over the years she had learned the art of taking a few minutes' absolute rest before getting up with more energy. The trick was to resist the impulse to close your eyes, so she looked around and let her eyes linger on both the details and the big picture.

The bedroom was her oasis. There was also a light color palette here—crisp white and a soft shade of blue. Sleek, elegant furnishing—nothing too heavy. Nothing like the enormous, solid desk that she had bought as a gift for Jack, solely because it had once belonged to Ingmar Bergman. Jack had loved that kind of thing. Big gestures. Major bragging rights. Being able to show visitors around the house and casually mention that this desk they happened to be passing had belonged to the great director.

Faye contemplated her own neat white desk with satisfaction. It had never been owned by any autocratic, self-satisfied lecherous old bastard who had conned and exploited the women in his life. It had only ever belonged to her. Without the weight of what had gone before. Just like Faye. She had disentangled herself from her own story. Reshaped herself.

She sat up and swung her legs over the edge of the bed. The anxiety about what Kerstin had said was beginning to make itself felt again. It could no longer be postponed. Kerstin's study had been empty earlier, so Faye assumed she was in her bedroom. Kerstin often liked to take a siesta, but Faye always tried to avoid thinking about the fact that she was no spring chicken any longer—that she had seen both sides of seventy. The very thought that Kerstin wouldn't always be there at her side was enough to give Faye palpitations. The loss of her best friend, Chris, to cancer had brought home to her all too clearly that nothing and no one could be taken for granted. And besides, death had been a part of her life for far too long.

She tapped on Kerstin's bedroom door.

"Are you awake?"

"I'm not asleep."

Kerstin sat up drowsily when Faye came into the room. She reached for her glasses on the nightstand, her eyes clouded with sleep.

"Did you sleep well?"

"I wasn't sleeping," said Kerstin, standing up and smoothing her trousers. "I was just resting my eyes for a moment."

Faye wrinkled her nose slightly at the scent of patchouli in Kerstin's spacious bedroom. After she had met Bengt, who was posted to the Swedish Consulate in Mumbai, on a flight, she had begun to spend an increasing amount of time in India. She had gotten involved with an orphanage and always traveled out with great quantities of necessities for the children. The only thing was, she would return with gaudy gold-tasseled souvenirs to "brighten up" the muted color palette of Faye's lounge. Paola was under strict instructions that any such items were to be returned to "Ms. Karin's room." They had quickly given up all attempts at teaching the irascible Italian to pronounce Kerstin the Swedish way, so they had settled upon the rather more simple Karin by way of compromise.

"Do you miss Bengt?"

Kerstin snorted and put on a pair of slippers that were neatly stowed at the foot of the bed.

"At my age, you don't miss each other. It's like . . . something else when you're a little older."

"Oh, that's bullshit," Faye said with a grin. "Paola has been gossiping about how 'Ms. Karin has much nicer underwear now.'"

"Faye!"

Kerstin blushed all the way down to her neck and Faye couldn't resist the impulse to wrap her arms around her.

"I'm so happy for you, Kerstin. But I hope he's not planning to claim you on a full-time basis. We need you here too."

"Don't worry. After a while over there, I get sick of him." But Kerstin's smile didn't quite reach her eyes. "Come on, let's go down to the study. I've got something I have to show you."

They descended the stairs in silence. Faye could feel her heart sinking with each step they took. Something was wrong. Very wrong.

Kerstin sat down behind her desk and switched on the computer, which began to whir. Faye settled down in one of the two large Chippendale armchairs in front of the desk. Although the ban on gaudy trinkets extended to Kerstin's study, Faye had decorated it with Kerstin in mind. In addition to her recently discovered delight in all things Indian, Kerstin had one great passion in her life: Winston Churchill. So Faye had ensured her study was done out in a classic English style with a modern twist.

The pièce de résistance was a huge framed photograph of Winston Churchill in pride of place on the wall above the desk.

Kerstin turned the display toward Faye, who leaned forward and tried to bring order to the figures flickering past on the screen. She was most certainly knowledgeable in the financial aspects of the business world, but Kerstin had proven herself to be the true expert. Winston stared down at them sternly, but Faye avoided looking at the picture. Right now, she didn't need the judgmental gaze of a man.

"I've been looking after Revenge's shareholder register since you've got so much on your plate with the American expansion and the new stock issue. Before you left for Rome, two shareholders had sold their holdings. And now another three have gone."

"To the same buyer?"

Kerstin shook her head.

"No, but I can't shake the feeling that they all seem to be synchronized."

"Do you think someone is trying to take over Revenge?"

"Perhaps," said Kerstin, looking at her over the top of her reading glasses. "I fear that may be what we're facing."

Faye leaned back in the armchair. Her body was tense and every one of her veins throbbed with adrenaline. She forced herself to remain calm, even though her thoughts were running away with her. It was too soon for speculation. What she needed more than anything right now were facts.

"Who's selling?"

"I've printed a list for you."

Kerstin pushed a sheet of paper over to Faye. Kerstin knew her well. Faye always wanted critical business information printed instead of just reading it on a screen. She would have to save the trees by other means.

"I don't get it . . . Why are they selling?"

"There's no time for sentimentality right now. First we need to evaluate the situation—you need to get up to speed with everything while I keep digging. We can be pissed off later. But not now. It takes energy we can't afford to waste right now."

Faye nodded slowly. She knew Kerstin was right. Nevertheless, it was hard to refrain from speculating about which of the women she had trusted was selling her shares in Revenge. Behind her back.

"I want us to go through everything together. Line by line," she said.

Kerstin nodded.

"Let's get started."

Faye looked at her and then returned her gaze to the sheet of paper. Something turned over anxiously in her gut. She hadn't predicted this. And that worried her more than anything else.

The house was silent. Everyone had gone to bed. Everyone except Faye. She was still up with the list, going through it over and over. Trying to collect her thoughts.

The figures danced before her eyes. She was tired and dejected—the latter an emotion she hadn't felt in a long time. Not since Jack. And it was one she disliked intensely. Forbidden thoughts began to creep up on her. What if it was already too late? What if they could no longer save Revenge? What if she had let down her guard so much over the last two years that enemies had been able to sneak up behind her unnoticed? She would never be able to forgive herself. Weakness was something she had left behind. With Jack. He was the carrier of her weakness, and he bore it as close to himself as the ill-fitting prison clothing.

Faye put down the sheet of paper. The prospect of betrayal stung. The names on the list of women who had sold their shares were very familiar to her.

Their faces flickered by—women to whom she had presented the idea behind Revenge. Women she'd persuaded to believe in Revenge. To believe in her. Why had no one said anything? Had all that talk of sisterhood meant nothing to anyone but Faye?

She rubbed her eyes, which were prickling with tiredness, and swore when she got a flake of mascara in her eye. Faye blinked frenetically and hurried to the bathroom to remove her makeup. She was much too tired to do any more this evening. The escapades of the night before were still making themselves felt, and she realized that without a good night's sleep she would be no use to anyone. Not herself, not Revenge.

Just as Faye was pulling back the covers to slip between her crisp Egyptian cotton sheets, she stopped. She looked toward the door and felt the impulse throughout her body. She padded slowly into the hallway. The door into Julienne's room was open—she didn't like sleeping with it completely shut. Faye carefully opened the door wider and slipped inside. A small rabbit-shaped night-light shone gently inside the room. Enough light to chase off all the ghosts. Her daughter was sleeping on her side, her back to Faye. Her long fair hair was spread across the pillow. Ever so slowly, Faye settled down beside Julienne. She pushed her daughter's hair off the pillow and laid her head behind her. Julienne whimpered a little in her sleep and stirred slightly but didn't wake up—not even when Faye put an arm around her. Millimeter by millimeter, she moved closer to Julienne until she had her nose buried in her hair, which smelled of lavender and chlorine.

Faye shut her eyes. She felt the tension slowly dissipate as sleep took over. Right there, with her arm around her daughter, she knew she would have to do everything she could to save Revenge. Not for her own sake, but for Julienne's.

FJÄLLBACKA—THEN

Even though I was only twelve years old, it felt as if I already knew everything about life. My existence in Fjällbacka was predictable. The same transitions between ten months of complete tranquility and two months of summer chaos. Everyone knew everyone—in the summer the same tourists came year after year. Nothing changed at home either. It was as if we were running on a hamster wheel, around and around, without any chance of moving on. As if nothing was ever going to change.

So I already knew when we sat down to eat dinner that it was going to be one of those nights. I'd caught the whiff of booze off Dad as soon as I got home from school.

I both loved and loathed our house. It was Mom's childhood home. She had inherited it from my grandparents, and everything that I loved about that house had to do with her. She had done the best she could. It was cute cozy—everything that was associated with a happy, thriving home. The shabby wooden table from Grandma and Grandpa's day. The white linen curtains that Mom had made herself—she was good at sewing. The framed cross-stitch sampler given to Grandma as a wedding present by my great-grandma. The crooked, warped staircase with a thick rope as a handrail that bore traces of the footsteps of several generations. The small rooms and their white transomed windows. I loved all this.

What I loathed were the traces of Dad. The knife marks on the kitchen counter. The dents on the wooden door to the living room, a reminder of the occasions when Dad had kicked it in an outburst of rage while drunk. The slightly bent curtain pole from the time Dad had pulled down the curtain to wrap it around Mom's head until Sebastian had finally plucked up the courage to pull Dad away from Mom.

I loved the open fireplace in the living room. But the pictures on the mantelpiece were a downright insult. The family photos Mom put there, the dream of a life that didn't exist. A smiling picture of her and Dad, of me and my big brother, Sebastian. I wanted to tear them down, but at the same time I didn't want to upset Mom. It was for our sake that she tried to keep the dream alive. One time, she put a photo of her brother there. But when Dad caught sight of the picture of Uncle Egil, he went mad. While Mom was in the hospital, Dad made sure the photograph disappeared.

I had a tummy ache while waiting for it all to explode. Like always.

Dad had spent the hours after I'd come home from school in his shabby armchair in front of the TV, which wasn't even switched on, while his bottle of cheap Explorer vodka emptied faster and faster. Mom knew it too. I could see it in her anxious, flapping movements. She took extra care with the food and cooked a dinner that included all of Dad's favorites. Big pork chops with baked brown beans, fried onions, and potatoes. Apple pie with thick whipped cream.

None of the rest of us liked pork and beans, but we knew that we should still eat all of it. At the same time we knew that none of it would help. The critical juncture had already passed—like a seesaw that had tipped past the point where down was the only possible direction.

No one said anything. We laid the table in silence, picked the good crockery, set out napkins, which I folded into fans. Dad never cared about things like that, but we always let Mom think that it might help. That he would see how nice we had made things, how tasty the food that Mom had cooked was. That something inside him would be moved by the consideration and he would let it be. Just let it be. Let the seesaw tip back to its original position. But there was nothing within him that could be moved or touched. It was empty in there. Desolate.

"Gösta, dinner's ready."

Mom's voice trembled slightly as she tried to sound cheerful. She carefully touched her hair. She had made herself nice. Put up her hair, put on a blouse and a stylish pair of trousers.

Before long we were all in our seats. Mom served up exactly the amount of pork onto Dad's plate that she knew he would want. In precise proportion to the beans, potatoes, and fried onions. Dad looked at the plate. For a long time. For far too long. All three of us knew what that meant. Me, Mom, Sebastian.

We were frozen mid-movement, frozen in a prison that Sebastian and I had lived in since birth and Mom had been in since she had met Dad. We were frozen to the spot while Dad stared at his plate. Then, slowly—as if in slow motion—he took a full fist of food. Pork, beans, onions, and potatoes. He managed to get a little bit of everything from the plate in his huge fist. With his other fist, he firmly grabbed Mom's hair—the do that she had spent ages struggling to put in place. Then he pushed the food into Mom's face. Slowly, carefully, he mashed it around her face.

Mom did nothing. She knew that her only option was to do nothing. But both Sebastian and I knew that tonight it wouldn't help. His gaze was too cold. The bottle was too empty. The grip on her hair was too firm. We didn't dare look at her. Or each other.

Dad stood up slowly. He yanked Mom out of her chair. I saw the residue of pork and baked brown beans on her face. The scent of sugar and cinnamon in the apple pie was wafting from the oven. Dad's favorite. I went through all the possibilities of what Dad might do now. All the body parts he could choose to target. Perhaps he would return to a well-frequented area. The arms had been broken in five places. The legs in two. He had cracked ribs on three occasions. The nose once.

Dad was apparently feeling creative on this particular night. With all the might of his muscular arm, he pushed Mom's soiled face down toward the table fast and hard. Her teeth struck the edge of it. We heard the sound of them shattering. The shard of a tooth almost got me in the eye, but my eyebrow caught it and it tumbled down onto my plate. Right into the baked brown beans.

Sebastian jerked back but he still didn't look up.

"Eat," Dad hissed.

We ate. I used my fork to push Mom's tooth aside.

"Coffee?"

"No thanks. But we'd love some more bubbly and red wine."

"I'll have a coffee, please."

Kerstin accepted a paper cup filled with coffee from the flight attendant, who then went to fetch Faye's order.

"Who do you think it could be?" Faye said in a troubled voice.

"It's impossible to tell. And it would be wasted effort to try and guess before we know more."

"I don't understand how I could have been so naïve. I never gave a moment's thought to the idea that the other co-owners would be able to sell their shares without talking to me first."

Kerstin raised her eyebrows.

"I warned you it was a risk selling such a big stake in the company."

"Yes, I know," Faye said in frustration, craning her neck to look for the flight attendant bringing her bottles. "It felt like the best solution at the time. In the middle of the whole thing with Jack and Julienne, the trial, the media. And Chris dying. I secured the capital and I believed I'd be able to retain control as chairman."

"You should never believe in business," said Kerstin.

"I know you love saying I told you so, but can you drop it for a bit? We're talking about something else at the moment. I'm stressed out about being stuck on a plane unable to do anything or find out any more until we're in the meetings tomorrow. It's bad enough that I've been thinking about this all day."

The flight attendant returned with a miniature bottle of sparkling wine and a miniature bottle of red wine. Faye picked up the two empty bottles on the table in front of her and passed them over in exchange. She opened the bubbly first and placed the chilled bottle of red between her thighs to warm it up.

"You could always drink something," Kerstin said dryly, sipping her coffee while Faye drained the sparkling wine from her glass.

"Like I said, we don't have any meetings until tomorrow. So I fully intend to drown my sorrows in booze with a clear conscience. Anyway, shouldn't you be drinking something? Given you're scared of flying . . ."

"Thanks for the reminder. I had just managed to

stop thinking about it. No, if I'm going to die then I'm going to die sober."

"Sounds completely illogical. And unnecessary. When I die I want to go completely hammered. Preferably with that pilot between my legs . . ."

Faye raised her eyebrows and nodded toward one of the pilots who had emerged from the cockpit to exchange a few words with the flight attendant. He looked to be in his thirties, had dark hair, a charming smile, and an ass that divulged many hours spent in the gym.

"You know what, I think it's probably best if we let the **pilot** focus on flying the plane instead of potentially pursuing an encounter in the onboard lavatory."

Kerstin looked nervous and Faye laughed.

"Calm down, Kerstin. That's why God invented autopilot . . ."

"So that the pilot could sleep with the passengers? Seems doubtful."

Faye downed the last of the bubbly, opened the bottle of red wine, and poured it into the glass.

She loved Kerstin, but she was often reminded that they came from different generations. Chris would have understood exactly what Faye meant and laughed with her—maybe even challenged her to make good on her talk about the pilot. Ever since they had made friends at the Stockholm School of Economics, Chris had been there for Faye. Guided her, protected her, been her biggest supporter—and her most honest critic. Now Faye always wore her **Fuck Cancer** wristband as a reminder of Chris and what she had lost.

Kerstin patted Faye's hand. As usual, she could tell when her thoughts had wandered to Chris.

Faye cleared her throat.

"It'll take a couple of days before the rental apartments we looked at are available," she said. "We'll have to stay at the Grand Hôtel for the time being."

"I'm sure we'll manage there," said Kerstin dryly.

Faye smiled. They most certainly would.

"I sometimes think back to the early days after the divorce," she said. "When I was your lodger. Sitting there after dinner drawing up the plans for Revenge."

"You were an amazingly inspirational woman," said Kerstin, patting her hand. "And you still are."

Faye was forced to blink away tears and turned once again toward the cockpit. The pilot had come out for another brief chat with one of the flight attendants. Faye held her glass midair in a toast and received a faint smile in reply.

A few minutes later the pilot announced on the PA that it was time to prepare the cabin for landing. The crew roamed up and down the aisle collecting trash and checking that all the tables were stowed, all seats upright, and all seatbelts fastened.

Kerstin gripped the armrests so hard that her

knuckles went white and Faye took the hand closest to her. She stroked it gently.

"Most accidents happen during takeoff and landing," Kerstin said breathlessly.

Before long, the plane's wheels bounced against the ground and Kerstin squeezed Faye's hand so hard that her rings cut into her skin. But Faye kept her expression neutral and calm.

"We're down now," she said. "It's over."

Kerstin exhaled and smiled weakly at her.

When the plane came to a stop, they gathered together their hand luggage and moved forward along the aisle. The crew was standing by the exit saying farewell to all the passengers. The pilot met Faye's eye and she discreetly passed him her business card. He smiled warmly at her and she hoped most sincerely that they were allowed to take their uniforms home from work.

Once they had checked in at the Grand Hôtel, Kerstin went up to her room to rest. Faye contemplated heading down to the spa to book a treatment, but realized she was far too restless to do that right now. Instead, she headed for the Cadier Bar.

She sat down at the long bar and looked around. The Cadier was as full as ever. The majority of the clientele were businessmen in expensive suits, with receding hairlines and business-lunch bellies. The women were also expensively dressed and Faye browsed the labels she could see from a quick glance: Hugo Boss, Max Mara, Chanel, Louis Vuitton, Gucci, and a few intrepid souls who were out and about in Pucci.

Emilio Pucci signaled "expensive but rebellious," and Faye herself had a large number of garments from the collections of recent years in her wardrobe.

Today, however, she had opted for something more sober. Slacks from Furstenberg and a silk blouse from Stella McCartney. Cream. Dry-clean-only clothes. Love bracelets from Cartier. She shuddered when she discovered that next to her **Fuck Cancer** wristband she was still wearing a bracelet that Julienne had made for her. Colorful beads strung together with no coherent pattern whatsoever. She quickly took it off and slipped it into her pocket. For a moment, she had forgotten that everyone in Sweden thought that Julienne was dead.

"What can I get for you?"

A young blond bartender was looking attentively at her. She ordered a mojito—one of Chris's favorite drinks. She could picture her friend moving the stirrer around in her glass with that playful look in her eyes before telling Faye about her latest adventure—whether it was in the world of business or with a hot young guy.

The bartender turned away and began to deftly mix the drink in a tall glass. Faye got out her laptop, opened the screen, and switched it on. There was nothing more to be done about the share sales until tomorrow, so she might as well carry on with the American expansion as if nothing had happened. It would help her to remain calm.

Work had always had that effect on her. With hindsight, she couldn't understand how Jack had managed to get her to give up her studies and her career. To wander about within the four walls of their home like a lost soul, or to spend countless hours on boring lunches with meaningless conversations. Had she ever been happy with that existence before the cracks had started to show? Or had she merely persuaded herself that she was? Because she'd had no other choice? Because Jack had cornered her?

Jack had worn her down in a way that no one else had managed to do. But she had taken her revenge on him—built a successful company and crushed his.

Jack's best friend and companion, Henrik Bergendahl, had also fallen and had started over from nothing. Well . . . A couple of million kronor in the bank and a big house out on Lidingö that was paid off wasn't exactly what most people considered "starting over from nothing."

In the beginning, Faye had felt sorry for him. He had always been pretty decent to her, and he had suffered only because he was Jack's colleague. But she knew he had been constantly unfaithful to his wife, Alice, and in practice there was little difference between him and Jack. They had both treated the women in their lives as consumables.

Henrik had gotten back onto his feet again, so the damage had been only temporary. His investment firm was doing well and his fortune was now significantly greater than it had been during his years with Compare. She didn't begrudge him his success, but she didn't wish it on him either. If he hadn't treated Alice so badly, she might have felt a pang of sympathy for the fact that she had trampled over him in passing. But as it stood, she wasn't losing sleep over him.

The bartender set down the mojito in front of her with a smile and she paid.

"What's your name?" said Faye, sipping gently through the straw. This taste was one she associated so strongly with Chris.

"Brasse."

"Brasse? Short for . . . ?"

"Nothing. I was christened Brasse."

"Okay, I think you need to explain that. Where does the name come from?"

He shook a cocktail while answering.

"It was Dad's idea. The Sweden–Brazil game during the 1994 World Cup."

"Nineteen ninety-four? Let's see, that makes you . . ."

"Twenty-five," a man next to her interrupted.

Faye turned toward him, quickly taking him in from head to toe. Gray suit: Hugo Boss. White shirt, well pressed. Platinum Rolex with a blue face—about three hundred thousand kronor—on his left wrist. Thick, fair hair. It was either good genes or a discreet visit to some clinic. Pretty commonplace appearance but looked like he kept himself in shape. The SPR Athlete Factory in Östermalm was her guess. He seemed the type who went in for martial arts training.

"I know, I look younger," Brasse the bartender said while pouring a cocktail into a Russian matryoshka doll.

"Old enough," said Faye.

The man next to her laughed.

"Sorry," she said. "Can I help you?"

"No, no, don't let me interrupt . . ."

Brasse escaped to the far end of the bar and began to take orders. Faye turned toward the man in the gray suit, who proffered a hand.

"David," he said. "David Schiller."

She reluctantly took his hand.

"Faye."

"A lovely name. Unusual."

She could see it in his eyes when he made the connection.

"You're . . ."

"Yes," she said curtly.

David seemed to get the message, because he didn't say anything else about it. Instead, he nodded at her laptop.

"You're working hard—I assume that's what's behind all the success. Myself, I've got a meeting with a good friend in a bit."

"Okay, so what line of work are you in?"

Faye pushed the laptop aside. Brasse was better flirting material, but she couldn't focus on work now. She might as well pass the time talking to a stranger.

"Finance. Cliché, I know. Finance bro sipping a G&T in the Cadier Bar."

"A little clichéd, I suppose. Well. Very clichéd."

"Pathetic, to be completely honest."

He smiled at her and something happened to his appearance. For a second he was almost good-looking.

"Incredibly pathetic," she said, leaning forward. "How about we play finance-dude bingo? See how much I can get right?"

"Go for it," he said, amused, a twinkle in his eye.

"Okay, I'll start with a few easy ones." She frowned slightly. "BMW? No, no. Alfa Romeo."

"Bingo."

He smiled again and Faye couldn't help smiling back.

"Hmm, you dine at the Teatergrillen restaurant at least once—no, twice—a month?"

"Bingo."

"Now we come to the question of whether you live in an apartment or a house. Östermalm or Djursholm. Or what about Saltsjöbaden . . . Well, I reckon it's a house out in Saltis."

"Bingo again. You're amazing."

"Yes, I am. But thus far it's all been obvious. Now it's a little trickier . . ."

Faye finished the last of her drink and David flagged Brasse over.

"Same again?"

"No, I think I'll try out one of those matryoshka cocktails."

Brasse nodded and set to work.

"I hope I didn't ruin what could have been the beginning of a beautiful love story." David tilted his head toward Brasse.

"Oh, I'm getting tired of twenty-five-year-olds," Faye said. "They're too smooth and enthusiastic."

"Smooth and enthusiastic . . ."

David laughed. Faye really did like his laugh.

"Well, keep guessing. You've knocked it out of the park so far. It's only slightly worrying that I'm apparently such a cliché."

"Mmm, let me see. You clearly work out. Martial arts? SPR?"

"Yep. I'm kind of impressed by that one, actually."

"Which discipline?"

"Brazilian jujitsu."

"Naturally. Okay, what else? You've tried out paddle tennis in the last year and now you're completely smitten?"

"Bingo."

"But your wife still practices at the Royal Tennis Hall. When she's not riding."

David raised his eyebrows slightly.

"Bingo. And bingo. Ack, that's enough." David shook his head and hid his face in feigned shame.

Faye grinned and took a sip of her drink. David's phone lit up as a text arrived.

"My contact is here—he's out on the veranda. Nice to meet you . . . Faye."

When he had gone, she turned back to the laptop and pulled it closer. David had put her in an unexpectedly good mood and she was able to focus on work again.

A message popped up on her screen. From Kerstin. Faye had been about to put her cocktail to her lips but stopped mid-movement. Another share in Revenge had been bought. She shut the laptop and requested the bill. The good mood was gone without a trace.

The coffee was weak and acrid, as usual at AKV Accounts. The offices themselves were small and dark, with bookcases everywhere groaning under the burden of binders stuffed with papers. So much for a paperless society. Nevertheless, Faye and Kerstin had chosen to hold the meeting at AKV's office instead of their own rather slicker one. For the time being, it wasn't smart to show anyone outside the company that anything was brewing. Faye looked up at the illustration pinned to the wall of Revenge's accountant, Örjan Birgersson: a duck swimming placidly above the water's surface but paddling like mad beneath it. That was exactly how she felt.

"More coffee?" Örjan offered, but both Faye and Kerstin shook their heads emphatically.

It had seemed polite to accept one cup, but neither of them felt able to subject herself to two.

"So what do you think?"

Faye leaned forward and tried to read Örjan's

expression. He was a small, gray-haired man who wore thin steel-rimmed spectacles. His eyes were alert and he was always disproportionately enthusiastic about everything to do with numbers, key figures, and debits and credits.

"Well, this is complicated," he said cheerfully, and Faye could feel herself grinding her teeth.

For her, this was a matter of life and death. For her, Revenge was a living thing—something made from flesh and blood, something breathing. Alive. Chris lived on in Revenge. Julienne was in Revenge. Kerstin. All the women whose wounds and scars had formed the basis of Revenge—they were all living parts of the company. But they were also the ones who were now threatening its existence.

"Kerstin was quite right. When you look at these acquisitions, it's possible to discern a pattern. So there's much to suggest that it is one and the same buyer."

"Can you see who's behind it? Is there a common denominator?"

Faye took a sip of the coffee and pulled a face. She set the cup aside to avoid making the same mistake again.

"Not yet—it's going to take time. Whoever's buying up the shares—whether it's an individual or a corporation—knows what he's doing. The best way I can describe it is as a ball of yarn. A muddle of companies and acquisitions—if it hadn't been for the fact that all of them follow the same pattern it would have been hard to spot that it must be the same single buyer behind them all. The pattern gave them away. Which, as I said, Kerstin very deftly identified."

He fluttered his eyelashes at Kerstin, and Faye looked at him resignedly. Kerstin didn't look in the slightest bit amused.

"Do your best to find out what you can. As quickly as possible," she said in her most professional tone.

Oblivious, Örjan carried on twinkling his eyes at her. "Of course, Kerstin. Of course. Here at AKV, we always do our best. If I may say so, I'm one of the very best in the business. For instance, the army recently called us in to assist—"

"What's our situation?" Faye said, interrupting him. She'd listened to enough of Örjan's war stories from the battlefields of accountancy to know that she couldn't endure sitting through another one.

"It doesn't look all that promising."

"We know that much, but we need details."

Faye heard how sharp her voice sounded, but stress and impatience were merging into one. She was a woman of action—she wanted to act. Until she was in possession of all the relevant facts, she was powerless. If she was to strike back, she needed to know how and against whom.

"My impression from the new share purchases

made yesterday is that the buyer no longer cares about concealing that a takeover is in progress. They're now operating on the assumption that alarm bells have gone off."

Faye muttered and Kerstin placed a placatory hand on her arm. No one was going to come and take what was hers. No one was going to come and take what she had risked and sacrificed so much to build.

And she wasn't the only one who'd made sacrifices. When Chris died, she'd left Faye the hair-care empire she'd built up from scratch—her life's work. That company had been merged with Revenge, so if the buyout succeeded it would destroy Chris's legacy. If she let that happen, Chris would probably rise from the grave to strangle her with her bare hands. Faye would have to sleep with one eye open for the rest of her days.

"Find out who's behind this. And give us a printout of everything you pull together. We'll take it from there."

Faye got up and Örjan looked disappointed. He looked at Kerstin, who also stood up, took her bag, and smoothed her skirt.

"I realize you may have a lot to do just now, but we all have to eat nonetheless, so I was going to ask whether . . ."

He looked once again at a panic-stricken Kerstin, who nudged Faye with her elbow.

Faye cleared her throat.

"We don't have time to eat right now, but you have my number. Call me as soon as you know something."

"Of course. But I think it may be tricky for you girls to straighten this out. Maybe you want to bring in a team from McKinsey? They've got some good guys over there."

"No thanks."

Faye slammed the door behind them.

"I'm going to replace Örjan," she said, once they were in the taxi. "We'll have to find someone new."

Kerstin nodded.

"I realized it the moment he called us girls."

The taxi pulled up outside the gilded revolving door of the Grand and they got out.

"Lunch?" Faye picked up her handbag and coat, glancing at Kerstin.

"I've got a couple of things I want to check up on right away. Do you mind eating lunch alone?"

"No, I'll manage. I have some things I need to attend to as well. But let's meet at two o'clock, shall we? In my room? Then we can roll up our sleeves."

"Yes, two's fine."

Kerstin went through the revolving door and Faye made to follow her, throwing her coat over one arm so that she could pull the key out of her bag. She came to an abrupt halt when someone tugged at the coat from behind. She turned around and saw that the coat had gotten caught in the doors.

"For fuck's sake!"

She tugged at the coat, but it was completely jammed. The clerk behind the lectern in the lobby hurried over to help her, but he had no luck either. He made an apologetic expression and rushed upstairs for help while Faye continued to pull at her coat.

Someone tapped on the glass. It was David, the man from the bar the day before.

"If you take a step back, I'll push the door from my side. You won't be able to open the door by pulling the coat."

"No, I'd got that," Faye said dryly.

She took a step back. Carefully, David pushed the door and it created a bigger crack, allowing her to release the coat. The clerk who was coming back down the stairs with the concierge looked relieved.

David smiled at her.

"Good thing that worked."

"Off for some lunchtime paddle tennis?" Faye said petulantly.

She knew she ought to be grateful, but he looked so insufferably pleased to have been able to play the knight in shining armor.

"No, I thought I'd have a solo lunch somewhere nearby. Have you eaten?"

"No," she replied before immediately biting her tongue.

"Are you going to eat?"

"Yes. Well, no. I really need to do some work and thought I'd get—"

"Well, then. Let's eat lunch together. Do you want to eat here or shall we go somewhere else?"

"Eat here."

Faye bit her tongue again. What the hell was wrong with her? She didn't even want to have lunch with this man. But she supposed she would struggle to focus on work after the meeting with the accountants, so she might as well have something proper to eat.

"The bistro. Lunch is on you," she said.

He flashed that smile again.

"Naturally."

"I warn you, I'm expensive to run. I eat like a lumberjack and drink champagne like a trophy wife whose husband has just left her for the secretary."

"Don't sweat it. I can afford it."

He began to climb the carpeted stairs and turned around to look at her quizzically. She sighed and followed him.

"Actually, no. No fucking way you're buying. Lunch is on me."

David shrugged.

"You're the boss. But I warn you, I'm expensive to run too."

"And I can also afford it," Faye replied.

The only question was how long that would remain true.

"Come on, aren't you going to try an oyster? Just one?"

Kerstin looked at Faye in disgust.

"I don't know how many times you've asked me that, and do you ever get anything but the usual response? No."

"It's delicious—I promise."

Faye squeezed lemon over an oyster and added a small teaspoon of chopped red onion in vinegar.

"I mean, you have no idea what you're missing."

"I prefer food that's cooked. Like this lobster, for instance. No one insists on eating that raw."

Kerstin reached for one of the half lobsters on the large seafood platter in front of them. The Sturehof brasserie was vibrating with the sounds of guests laughing loudly and cutlery clattering. Staff in elegant white jackets with gold detailing smoothly maneuvered between the tables.

"You like herring, don't you?"

"But it's not raw, it's . . . Well. What the hell is herring? Cured? Pickled? At any rate, it's not raw."

"Well, if you say so . . ."

"Shush now and eat your shellfish. Otherwise I'll eat your half lobster too."

"You can have it—I'm still full from lunch."

Faye leaned back in her chair and sipped from her glass. To the barely suppressed horror of the waiter, she had ordered a bottle of Amarone. Apparently you didn't drink Amarone with shellfish. The staff was well drilled enough not to say so. The customer was always right. But she was certain that the sommelier was in the kitchen in tears right now.

"Oh yes, lunch. Did you . . . enjoy it?"

"Pfft, it wasn't like that. I just happened to get to talking to him in the hotel bar yesterday. Exactly the kind of man you'd expect to find in the Cadier Bar."

"But it still sounded as though you had a nice time? You've mentioned him several times this afternoon . . ."

"Now you're being annoying."

Faye reached for a prawn and began to peel it skillfully. When you came from Fjällbacka, you knew how to peel shellfish in your sleep.

"Yes, well, no, well, we had a nice time. He's easygoing and generally well informed without being overbearing. Always a pleasant attribute in a man."

Kerstin raised her eyebrows and Faye shook her head.

"Enough about my lunch. So, we have a plan?"

They had spent the afternoon in Faye's hotel room thrashing through everything they knew and discussing their options for taking action. There were fewer of them than they had hoped. They had brainstormed the names of companies and individuals who they thought might be behind the acquisitions, but no one name had emerged as a more likely candidate than the others. Faye simply couldn't work out who was trying to take Revenge away from her.

Worse still, she couldn't understand how her co-owners could go behind her back. These were the women she had shared Revenge's growth and success with. There hadn't been any dissatisfaction. Her leadership style had been met with nothing but praise. There had been articles in the press paying homage to her and she'd had the distinction of being named businesswoman of the year. No one had come to her with complaints. There had been nothing to set the alarm bells ringing. She simply couldn't understand it.

"You can't leave the body like that," Faye said in outrage, pointing at Kerstin's half lobster. "That greeny-brown stuff is lobster tomalley—it's the tastiest part. And you know you can suck the meat out of the small legs, and there are tiny thin slices of meat in the tail if you separate the sections of shell . . ."

"Let me eat my food my own way," Kerstin muttered, returning her lobster shell to the ice on the platter and helping herself to a fistful of prawns instead.

"Perhaps you should ask for some tinned lobster next time, so you don't have to bother with all that palaver with the shell . . ."

Kerstin shook her head in laughter and brushed her bangs aside with the back of her hand. Faye took a mouthful of Amarone while contemplating Kerstin, who was clearly struggling with the shells on the prawns. She was once again struck by how grateful she was that Kerstin had come into her life. Things had been so different when they had first met. When Faye had rented a room in Kerstin's house in Enskede, Kerstin had been living alone after her bastard of a husband had ended up in a care home after a stroke. This was something Kerstin had not been grieving over, given that he had made her life hell both physically and mentally. They had slowly become a family and now they were there for each other through thick and thin. Faye had difficulty trusting people, but she had absolute trust in Kerstin.

A distinguished gentleman with white hair and a well-groomed mustache let his gaze linger on Kerstin for slightly too long. Faye kicked her under the table.

"Over there. At two o'clock. The guy who looks like he's stepped straight out of colonial times. He can't take his eyes off you. Have you started bathing in some kind of musk oil? What's it all about?"

Faye wagged a finger at Kerstin, who blushed all the way up to her ears.

"I'm not even going to answer that. Order me a glass of Chardonnay, then we can go over the plan for tomorrow."

Faye waved the waiter over and ordered what Kerstin had asked for. The man with the mustache smiled at Kerstin, who did her best to try to ignore him.

"You'll have to set aside some time to prepare for your appearance on **Skavlan,** so we won't be able to get started until you're back from the TV studios. In the meantime I'll get busy drawing up a list of shareholders who haven't sold their shares yet. Soon as you're free, we'll divvy them up and speak to as many as possible."

Faye took a prawn from the large silver platter. "Whatever we do, we can't let on that trouble is brewing. We don't want everyone to know that the company is under attack."

"I get that, but our top priority must be to prevent any more women from selling."

"From the gentleman over there."

The waiter set down a bucket containing a bottle of champagne beside their table and placed a long, elegant champagne flute in front of each of them before opening the bottle with a pop.

Faye raised her eyebrows meaningfully. Kerstin snorted.

"I knew it," said Faye. "Musk oil."

She guessed it was the happiness Kerstin had felt since she had met Bengt that made her so irresistible to men.

Faye nodded toward the colonial grandpa, who raised his glass in a toast, a wide smile stretching from ear to ear. She kicked Kerstin under the table again.

"Behave yourself. Raise your glass and thank him. You never know what it might lead to."

"Faye!"

Kerstin blushed again. But she raised her glass in an obedient toast.

The studio lights were blinding. Faye had lost track of time. She had no idea how long the interview had been going on for or how long was left. The audience was seated in rows on banked seating— a hungry, amorphous mass, on the alert for every word, every shift in her facial expression.

Usually, she thrived in these situations. There was a little diva inside her who liked sitting in front of an audience, feeling the nerves of recording for TV. But today she felt strained and anxious.

Thinking about the shares being bought had kept her awake most of the night, tossing and turning. She had gone over the conversations in advance— conversations with women she would need to persuade to keep their shares without revealing in any way that something was happening. No easy task—it would take both tact and finesse.

A slightly too long silence wrenched her away from her thoughts. She had been asked a question and was expected to answer.

"The plan is to expand in the USA," she heard herself say. "I'm here in Stockholm for a month or so to meet potential investors and put together the final details. And I want to personally oversee the new issue of stock."

It was horribly warm. A trickle of sweat ran down the small of her back.

Fredrik Skavlan, the Norwegian talk show host, sat up straight.

"But this hunger . . . What is it that drives you? You're already a billionaire. A feminist icon."

Faye strung out the silence. The other guests were an American Hollywood actor, a female professor of linguistics who had just published a nonfiction best seller, and a woman who had climbed Mount Everest with prosthetic legs. The Hollywood star had been flirting ceaselessly with Faye ever since she had arrived at the studio.

"Before my best friend Chris died, I promised her I would live life for both of us. I want to see how far I can get, what I can build. My biggest fear is dying without achieving my full potential."

"And Julienne, your daughter, who was murdered by your ex-husband. What does her memory mean to you?"

Fredrik Skavlan leaned forward and the tension in the studio increased.

She didn't answer right away, letting the temperature rise even further. Reach boiling point. The answer was learned by heart, but it was important it sounded natural.

"She's with me in everything I do. When the longing and pain get too much, I bury myself in my work. I'm running Revenge, trying to make it grow, so that I don't lie down and die myself. So that I don't end up as just another woman silenced in the shadows of a man's actions. So that he—the man I once loved but who killed our daughter—doesn't succeed in killing me too."

Faye pursed her lips as a tear slowly ran down her cheek and fell toward the glossy black studio floor. It wasn't hard. Her pain was always so close to the surface that it was easy to visit it.

"Thank you, Faye Adelheim, for coming here today to tell us your story. I know you're needed elsewhere and have to leave us."

The audience rose to their feet and the applause rattled the rafters. It was seemingly never-ending. It continued as she stumbled across the studio floor, past the seating, and into the backstage area.

On the way to her dressing room, she summoned a young woman with an earpiece and asked her to call a taxi. A little way down the corridor she heard the Hollywood star calling out her name. She ignored him and shut the door behind her. There was a fan whirring in the dressing room. A shabby, mustard-yellow couch stood neglected in one corner. Faye stopped. She leaned against the wall and tried to smile at her own reflection. Mission accomplished. Everything had gone well. The jigsaw pieces of lies, truths, and half-truths had come together into the picture of herself she had wanted to share. Yet she was still missing the adrenaline rush she usually got after a good TV appearance. She couldn't shake off the anxiety that was enveloping her like a wet blanket. She had made the mistake of taking the future for granted. She had been afflicted by the same pride that had made Icarus fly too close to the sun with his waxen wings. Now she was paying the price as the wax melted and her wings fell apart.

FJÄLLBACKA—THEN

I was raped for the first time on my thirteenth birthday. It was a day like any other, really. It was mostly chance that it happened on my birthday. There hadn't been any celebrations. Dad always said that kind of thing was a waste of money and what was more, he had no interest in getting up before work to sing.

We also sat in silence at dinner, which was fish gratin. Me, Sebastian, Mom, and Dad. Mom attempted small talk—a couple of run-of-the-mill questions to start a conversation, to create a few seconds of something akin to normality. But after Dad had roared at her to shut it, she too had sat there in silence, poking her food. I still appreciated her trying. Maybe it wasn't true, but I believed that she had made a little extra effort because it was my birthday. Beneath the table, I briefly caressed her hand in a soundless thank-you, but I don't know whether she noticed it.

When Dad was finished, he got up and disappeared, leaving his plate on the table. Sebastian put his on the drainboard. Mom and I had no problems dealing with the washing up. Quite the contrary. Mom would usually mess around as much as she could in the kitchen while cooking and clearing up dinner to make sure the time we got to ourselves would last for as long as possible.

The TV in the living room was switched on and we smiled at each other, relieved to be alone. Protected by the clatter of dishes and the running tap, we began to tell each other about our day in whispers. I usually invented and added things—things that sounded fun—so that she wouldn't get upset. I think she did the same thing. That time in the kitchen was our breathing space. Why ruin it with something as depressing as reality?

"Come with me."

Mom took my hand and left the water running so that Dad would think we were still doing the dishes. I crept after her into the hallway. She put her hand in her coat pocket—carefully, so that the rustle wouldn't be audible—and handed over a small package with a ribbon around it and a rosette on top.

"Happy birthday, darling," she whispered.

I carefully removed the rosette, pulled off the paper, and quietly removed the lid of the box inside. Within it was a silver necklace with a charm in the shape of silver tears. It was the most beautiful thing I had ever seen.

I hugged Mom. I put my arms tight around her, drawing in her scent, feeling her heart beating anxiously in her breast. When we separated from our embrace, she took the necklace out of the box and put it around my neck. Then she patted my cheek tenderly and went back to the dishes. I touched the tears. They seemed fragile between my fingers.

Dad coughed in the living room. I let go of the tears, quickly tucked the necklace inside my top, and went to help Mom with the washing up.

When we were done, I went up to my room, which was next door to Sebastian's. I quickly did some homework. Even though I was in sixth grade, I was already using the eighth grade math book. I had tried to protest—I knew it would only antagonize my classmates, ramp up the war against me. But my teacher insisted and said it was important to make an effort if you wanted to get anywhere in this world.

My desk was old, wonky, and crooked—and it was covered in marks from when my pen had missed the page. I had to adjust the folded piece of paper under one of the legs at regular intervals so that the table didn't wobble.

I put down my pen and craned my neck. As it so often was, my gaze was caught by the bookcases.

Thumbed, well-read books. Sometimes I had to sort through it with a heavy heart to make space for new books I had picked up at rummage sales or been given by Ella, the kind librarian, whenever the public library in Fjällbacka was clearing old stock.

Some of the books were ones I'd never get rid of. **Little Women. Tess of the d'Urbervilles. Lace. The Life and Loves of a She-Devil. Kristin Lavransdatter. The Thorn Birds. Wuthering Heights.** Not only were they books I had inherited from Mom, they were memories. They were moments when I had been able to climb into another world. To escape my own. To become someone else.

Where the walls weren't covered in bookcases, I had put up pictures of my favorite authors. While the other girls in class had Take That, Bon Jovi, Blur, and Boyzone, I had Selma Lagerlöf, Sidney Sheldon, Arthur Conan Doyle, Stephen King, and Jackie Collins. Once upon a time they had been my mom's idols. Now they were mine. My heroes. They lifted me out of my own reality and transported me somewhere else. I knew it was nerdy. But no one ever came around, so who would see them?

I moved to the bed, skipping brushing my teeth. I could hear Sebastian moving back and forth across the floor in his room. Downstairs, Dad was yelling at Mom. She was silent, no doubt gritting her teeth. I assumed she would promise to mend her ways, hoping that would be enough to avoid being beaten to a pulp today. So far this year, she had been to see the doctor four times. They must surely have seen through her excuses about doors she had walked into, stairs she had fallen down. The interior fixtures and fittings of a whole house seemed to have it in for her, like some mighty enemy made from wood. No one could have believed it. Yet no one did anything. In this little community, they let people keep their secrets to themselves. It was easier that way when everyone was tied to one another, dependent on one another, like a gigantic spiderweb.

I lay down on my side with my head in my hands. My face was toward the wall. When we had been younger, Sebastian and I had communicated with knocks through the wall. Especially when Mom was taking a beating. The last time we had done it had been about a year or so back. Sometimes Sebastian had slept in my bed when Mom and Dad fought, looking to his little sister to keep him safe. But most often we knocked. One evening he simply stopped answering. I tried, for weeks, until the day I frenetically knocked with increasing desperation for a reply, and he rushed into my room and roared at me to stop hitting the wall.

"Fucking whore," he shouted.

I stammered an apology, shocked at his words.

It was at the same time that he stopped being

bullied. He had started hanging out with two boys who were a bit older than him—two of the popular kids. Tomas and Roger.

Tomas always caught my eye when we saw each other at school. There was something engaging about him, something brittle yet charming, that always made me slow down a little when I met him in the corridor. Part of me hoped he'd come home with Sebastian. Part of me hoped he wouldn't.

I switched off the main light, my bed becoming a small island of light in all the darkness. Since I'd finished the Agatha Christie novel while waiting for dinner and hadn't been to the library to borrow anything new, I picked out **The Adventures of Huckleberry Finn.** It was one of the books I would never get rid of, and that I was reading for what must have been at least the tenth time.

My eyes were gritty with tiredness, but I had a lot to forget, so I read to avoid a confrontation with my thoughts. The more tired I was, the quicker I fell asleep and the less time I spent lying there awake.

It must have been just before midnight when a door suddenly opened. I expected to hear the creaking of the stairs as someone crept down to the toilet. But they didn't. Instead, my bedroom door glided open. To begin with, I was happy, because I thought this meant Sebastian and I were finally going to start talking to each other. I had missed him so much lately.

The Cadier Bar was half full. Tourists and business-men were scattered across the sofas, holding drinks in their hands. Swift-footed waiters dashed back and forth. Faye pushed away the plate that had been picked clean and a waiter speedily appeared and asked whether she wanted anything else. Faye shook her head, leaned back, and looked at the illuminated royal palace across the water. A group of Americans in the party next to her were put out by the Swedes' idea of what a palace was and were talking loudly about their disappointment. According to them, the palace looked more like a prison. She guessed that all the Disney castles had given them unreasonable expectations.

She was completely shattered after an intense day. First **Skavlan**, then several conversations with shareholders—some by phone, some face-to-face. But it had gone well. Her assessment was that she'd gotten her message across—they had to keep their shares—without creating any suspicion. She and

Kerstin had come up with a strategy that seemed to work, hinting that there were big things on the horizon due to the American expansion and that it would be wise to hang on to their holdings.

A voice that was getting increasingly loud made her turn around. A table or two away from her there was a man in his fifties sitting opposite a woman in her twenties. They might have been father and daughter, but it slowly dawned on Faye that it was a job interview. The young woman was trying to keep the conversation professional and present her work-related skills. The man was countering by asking her in an increasingly inebriated way whether she had a boyfriend and whether she liked to party, harping on about how she should have a drink and "relax."

Faye shook her head. She felt the rage growing inside her.

"Are you sure you don't want a G&T?" the man asked. "Or maybe you prefer sweet drinks? Perhaps you'd like one of those mojitos?"

The young woman sighed.

"No thanks, I'm fine," she said.

Faye felt sorry for her. It was clear that the man, who judging by the discussion owned a public relations company, was distracted by thoughts of something other than a potential new hire.

Faye got up and carried her wineglass across to their table. The man had been in the middle of a monologue about his boat and had just invited the woman to it. He fell silent.

"I couldn't help overhearing the fascinating account of how you built your company. Well done."

It was obvious that he recognized Faye. He licked his lips and nodded.

"Hard work pays off," he said.

"What's your name?"

Faye reached out with her hand.

"Patrik Ullman."

"Faye. Faye Adelheim."

She smiled at him.

"But there's one thing that's bothering me, Patrik. So I'll just come out and ask it: Do you hold all your job interviews in hotel bars at this time of night, or only when they're with young women?"

Patrik Ullman opened his mouth and then shut it again. He reminded her of a perch gasping for air on a sun-warmed jetty.

"Because it doesn't feel like a sensible way to find out about a person's skills—filling her up with alcohol and asking her about boyfriends and then in the next breath inviting her to your boat. But then, what do I know?"

The young woman's lips twitched. Patrik Ullman's face grew even redder. A whimper began a long way down in his throat, but Faye beat him to it.

"What was it you had again? A Galeon 560? Sweetheart . . . I wouldn't even go out fishing in a plastic tub like that."

The woman could no longer contain a laugh.

"You fucking wh—"

Faye raised a finger in the air and leaned forward so that their noses were almost grazing each other.

"You what?" she said in a low voice. "What was it you were going to say, Patrik?"

The man pursed his lips. Faye straightened her back.

"I thought so."

She smiled at him, took a swallow of her wine, and turned to the woman. She pulled a business card out of her clutch bag and placed it on the table in front of her.

"If you want a real job—or a trip on a proper boat—get in touch."

She turned on her heel, went back to her table, and sat down.

Patrik Ullman's face was bright red. He muttered something to his companion, paid the bill, and stormed out of the place.

Faye waved at his back as it disappeared, drank a little more of the wine, and got ready to go up to her suite. She was longing to sink into a hot bath, wash off the TV makeup, and then slip into bed.

Her train of thought was interrupted by a throat being cleared. When she turned around she discovered David Schiller behind her. Laughter was twinkling in his eyes. She hadn't noticed their color before. Azure blue. Like the Mediterranean. He was holding a dry martini in one hand.

"I just wanted to thank you," he said.

"For what?" said Faye, defensively.

"For what you just did. You made me think about my two daughters. I want them to grow up with the belief that the world is at their feet, the same way I did. That young woman could have been my Stina or my Felicia in a few years' time. So I'm glad there are people like you on their side."

Her chest tightened in response to his words. Faye raised her glass in a toast.

"What's the point of having a fuck-load of money if I can never tell people to fuck off?" she said.

David, whose mouth had been full of dry martini, laughed so hard that the clear liquid began to seep out of the corners of his mouth.

"My best friend Chris always said that."

"Well, here's to Chris," said David.

He hadn't noticed that she had expressed herself in the past tense and she didn't draw attention to it. The pain was still too palpable. She hadn't even been up to staying in touch with Johan, the fine man who Chris had married on her deathbed. He was far too much of a reminder of everything she had lost.

Faye looked at him again. She shrugged—she didn't know what about. Her previous objections, possibly.

"Want to join me?" she said.

They ordered fresh drinks: another dry martini for David and a G&T for Faye.

"How long have you been staying at this hotel?" she asked when she had set down her glass. "Because I assume you're staying here. If not, you have an unhealthy weakness for hanging out at the Grand."

David grimaced.

"I've been staying here for two weeks."

"That's a long time. Is there any particular reason why? Seems pretty unnecessary when you've got a house in Saltis."

He sighed.

"I'm in the middle of a divorce from the girls' mother."

He picked the olive out of his drink and put it in his mouth.

"Things could be worse," he said, making a sweeping gesture around himself. "I am staying at the Grand Hôtel, after all. There are homeless people sleeping on the pavement just a stone's throw from here, because they can't afford even the most modest accommodation. You have to see things the way they are. Johanna is a significantly better mother than I am a father, no matter how much I try. So it's only right that she's at home with the girls. But Jesus, I miss them."

Faye took a sip of her G&T. She liked the way he talked about his ex-wife-to-be. It was a sign of respect—not depicting the other party as an evil monster.

David laughed. Thinking about his daughters seemed to have triggered something inside him.

"Stina and Felicia are coming here on Saturday. We'll do the theme park at Gröna Lund and then a Harry Potter marathon. And, tragically, I think I may be looking forward to it more than they are."

He waved an imaginary wand in the air and Faye couldn't help smiling.

"We've already established that you work in finance," she said. "What exactly is it you do?"

Faye realized reluctantly that David sparked her interest. There was something disarming—open, even—about him that appealed to her.

"I . . . well, I suppose I'm what they call an angel investor. I find interesting new companies and invest in them—preferably as early on as possible."

"And what's your most successful investment been to date?"

David named a company in the biotech sector that Faye was very familiar with. It had been meteoric on the markets. The founders were now good for hundreds of millions of kronor and heading for even more.

"Nicely done. Congratulations. How early did you get on board?"

"Gosh, it was so early that the boys weren't even out of school. They were still at Chalmers University of Technology and it all started as a degree project. But they got a bit of press for their innovation, I happened to read it, got interested, got in touch, and, well . . . the rest is history. Above all, it's the people behind a company you invest in. It's more about having a good feel for people than being hot on your key figures. Some people just have that certain something that means they're going to succeed, that they won't give up until they do. It's vital to find those people. A lot of people who pitch to me are privileged rich kids who've never had to fight for anything in their lives, and who think being an entrepreneur is a piece of cake."

"Oh yes. I was at the Stockholm School of Economics with some of them."

David pointed at her G&T.

"No matryoshka today?"

"No, I'm usually a creature of habit and mostly stick to the classics."

"There's a reason why they're classics," he said, raising his dry martini into the air.

"True."

She contemplated David over the rim of her glass. She was impressed by his drive. Being an angel investor demanded competence, intuition, know-how, and major capital.

"But it must still be risky, right?"

"Drinking a dry martini?"

"Ha ha. No, investing in companies with your own cash. I've seen a lot of companies go under, no matter how good an idea or product they had. There are lots of pitfalls in business, plus a fickle market."

"Yes, you know all about that. But I have to say that I'm incredibly impressed by what you've done with Revenge. It's a textbook example of how to elevate a company into the billions in a relatively short space of time. Very impressive."

"Thanks."

"But to come back to your question: Sure, it's a risky business but I love every minute of it. If you don't dare take risks then you don't dare live."

"True."

Faye ran her finger around the rim of her glass, considering. Around them, the Cadier Bar was beginning to fill up with patrons and the hubbub was rising toward the ceiling. Brasse the bartender nodded quizzically at their almost-empty glasses. Faye looked at David, who shook his head.

"I would love to stay and have a drink with you. Or two. Or three. But it just so happens that tonight I've got a business dinner I have to suffer my way through. And yes, it's at Teatergrillen . . ."

Faye returned his smile. To her surprise, she felt disappointed. She enjoyed his company.

He waved to Brasse.

"Chalk the lady's drink up on my tab."

He took his coat and turned toward Faye.

"No protests. Just buy the next round."

"I'd be happy to," said Faye. And she meant it. As he sauntered through the room heading for the exit, she watched him for a long time.

Faye finished the contents of her smoothie glass while in her seat on the terrace and then wiped her mouth with a napkin. She reached for her phone. She knew she ought to check how many emails had arrived overnight, but the ache in her stomach was making itself felt again—the longing for Julienne. So instead, she pulled up the number and waited impatiently as it rang.

Her mother answered and, after some small talk, Faye asked her to pass the phone to Julienne. There was a warm feeling in her chest when she heard her daughter's voice so close—she shared Julienne's delight as she explained that she could now swim to the bottom of the pool.

Then the unavoidable question.

"Are you coming home today, Mommy?"

"No," she said, feeling her voice grow thick. "I have to stay a little longer. Soon—I'll be home soon. I love you so much, miss you loads, and I'm sending you so, so many kisses."

After Faye had ended the call, she wiped away a few stubborn tears. Her stomach ached again; the longing was lodged there like a thorn. But she reassured herself that her daughter was having a good time in Ravi with her grandmother. Now she had to push aside thoughts of Julienne and once again adjust to a world that thought her daughter was no longer alive.

She went into her room and over to the closet, where she selected a blue pantsuit.

The sun was shining and the heat was oppressive, despite it not yet being midday. When she had leafed through the newspapers, she had seen that the weather forecasters had promised an unusually hot summer.

On Monday she was finally going to get the keys to the apartment.

"Things could be worse," she muttered, smiling when she remembered the previous evening with David Schiller.

His charm had come as a surprise. What he had said—that if you didn't dare take risks then you didn't dare to live—had set her thinking. When it came to Revenge, she could take big risks without blinking, but in her personal life she surrounded herself with high walls that it would take a ladder to scale. It had been a long time since a man had said something that had made her reflect on herself. But there was something different about David Schiller.

She turned on the laptop to prepare for the meeting with Irene Ahrnell at Taverna Brillo on Stureplan. She had deliberately postponed the meeting with Irene until she had warmed up with some of the other investors. Irene had been her first investor. And her biggest. She was a legend in the world of Swedish finance—and over time they had also become firm friends.

Irene was one of the few people that Faye turned to for advice, but in the last year Faye had neglected to keep in touch with her. She no longer had the same grasp of what was going on in her life.

She googled Irene. Some of the articles from the last year were ones she had already read, but some of them she had missed. It had been a good year for Irene. Two important new board appointments, a much-discussed sale of one of the companies that she had made a success, and a new role as CEO for one of the most respected finance companies in Europe. There was also a new man in Irene's life: the heir to an Italian auto giant. They would have a lot to talk about at lunch.

The blue Proenza Schouler pantsuit fit Faye perfectly. It had been an impulse buy at Nathalie Schuterman and had cost a small fortune, but she needed to feel fantastic today of all days. She smoothed out a couple of tiny wrinkles. She was ready to take on the day.

．．．

Faye put on her sunglasses as soon as she stepped into the lobby. From the corner of her eye, she saw a woman stand up from one of the sofas and approach her.

"Do you have a minute?"

Faye frowned—she vaguely recognized the woman. She assumed she was a journalist and thought it was just as well she got used to being followed again.

"Now's not a great time," she said, as kindly as she could.

The woman glanced over her shoulder and produced a police ID from her jeans pocket. **Yvonne Ingvarsson.** Faye realized it was the same police inspector who had led the investigation into Julienne's murder. She shut her eyes for a second and assumed the role of grieving mother.

"Have you found her?" she whispered. "Have you found my Julienne?"

Yvonne Ingvarsson shook her head.

"Can we sit down somewhere we can talk in peace?"

She took Faye by the arm and led her through the revolving door, down the steps, and onto the quayside outside the hotel. They sat down on a bench.

"We haven't found the bo— Your daughter. Yet," the investigator said, following a ferry to Djurgården with her gaze.

Faye forced herself to maintain her composure

and let Yvonne Ingvarsson take the first step. It was worrying that the woman had looked her up, but as yet it wasn't a disaster.

"You maintain that you were in Västerås the night your ex-husband supposedly killed your daughter?"

Faye shivered. She was grateful she was wearing sunglasses.

"Yes, of course," she said quietly.

"There's an ATM at the corner of Karlavägen and Sturegatan here in Stockholm," Yvonne Ingvarsson said calmly, keeping her eyes on the water.

Faye gathered her thoughts. If the police really had something on her, they would hardly have been sitting here in the sunshine chatting.

"Oh?"

"The CCTV captured a person who bears a remarkable likeness to you. You were in Västerås though?"

Yvonne Ingvarsson finally turned her head and looked at Faye, whose face didn't change one bit.

"What are you insinuating?" said Faye. "What is it you're sitting here and implying?"

Yvonne Ingvarsson raised her eyebrows.

"I'm not implying anything. I asked a question— whether it was at all possible that you were near the presumed murder scene and not in a hotel room in Västerås."

There was silence for a while. Faye pulled her handbag toward her and stood up.

"I don't understand what you mean. Do your job instead of coming to me with ridiculous claims like this. Find my daughter's body."

She turned away and left with her heart pounding in her breast.

Faye arrived a quarter of an hour late at Taverna Brillo, with sweat sliding down her back. Irene Ahrnell stood up smiling behind a circular table situated in the beautiful restaurant's inner dining room. Faye held her head high, ignoring the whispers and the looks being exchanged among the lunch guests. She embraced the other woman before both of them sat down.

"Irene, it's been way too long. And sorry for being late."

"No problem, and I agree—but I knew you had a lot on."

"Yes, it's been an intense year, what with preparing for the new stock issue, the American expansion, and—well, the challenge of incorporating Chris's company, the Queen group, into Revenge. It's taken a fair bit of time—it's only now that it's starting to feel like one company, not two."

Irene nodded and reached for the menu. She produced a pair of reading glasses and perched them on the end of her nose.

"I know what you mean—different structure, different corporate cultures, a thousand things to be streamlined. And as far as I'm concerned, don't feel you have to get in touch with me. I've got a lot on the go too, but I'm always here, no matter how long the gaps in our communication. I know it must be hard for you, trying to rebuild your life after losing your daughter . . ."

Faye nodded and took a sip of water, then, as if the topic was still too raw to discuss, immediately changed the subject: "Talking of having a lot on, I read something about a new man."

Irene blushed and Faye contemplated her with amusement. She had never seen Irene blush—it made the sixty-year-old woman look like a schoolgirl.

"Well, we'll have to see what comes of that. But so far it feels good. Mario is amazing. It's almost too good to be true. I feel like I'm constantly waiting for the skeletons to come crawling out of the closet."

"I'm just as skeptical as you are about the male sex. You know that. But there must still be a few good ones out there. You may have found one of them."

"We live in hope," said Irene, putting down the menu. "I've kissed enough frogs over the years."

She shook her head gently and Faye leaned toward her.

"How about we have a small glass of bubbly as well?"

Irene nodded with a smile and waved the waitress over to take their order.

When the champagne arrived, Faye took a cautious sip and wondered how to start.

Before she had time to say anything, however, Irene cleared her throat.

"There's a rumor that someone is buying up shares in Revenge."

Faye had an uneasy feeling in her gut. Of course Irene already knew.

"That's right. I didn't know how much you'd heard."

Irene shrugged, took off her glasses, and set them down on the table.

"I don't know any details. It's just idle gossip."

Faye put down her glass.

"It began a while ago with small numbers of shares being bought. However, these sales are now happening with such regularity that we've detected a pattern—we think it's the same buyer behind all of them."

"And you have no idea who it is?"

"No. The acquisitions have been concealed in a jumble of buyers. But we're digging as much as we can and we will find the answer. The only problem is, that takes time, and I don't know how much time we have. I don't know what the next move is."

"And you're worried that I'm going to sell?"

A pizza arrived and was positioned on a stand in the center of the table. It smelled heavenly. Liberal toppings of Kalix löjrom, crème fraîche, and red onion. They took a slice each; it was piping hot. But Faye wasn't able to fully concentrate on her food. She was looking at the woman sitting across from her: urbane, sophisticated, still inaccessible in some ways.

"Yes, I don't understand why the others have sold, and I wanted to reassure myself that you're going to keep your holding."

Irene was the single largest individual shareholder, second only to Faye, and it would be a disaster if she too sold.

"No one has approached me. Yet. Probably because they know we're good friends and that the first thing I'd do is tell you. But I give you my word that I won't sell."

"That's a relief to hear," said Faye, taking another slice of pizza.

She took a bite and washed it down with her champagne. The taste was wonderful.

Are you really going to eat that? Jack's voice came back to her. That furrowed brow. The look of disgust. In the years after giving birth to Julienne, she'd been on the end of constant digs about her appearance and her weight. Nothing she did could make Jack happy.

Now she ate what she wanted, in moderation. The insecurity that had given rise to binge eating was a thing of the past. Instead of being ashamed of her body, seeing only the imperfections, she took pride in it. Exercise had gone from being a form of punishment she was forced to endure to something that gave her pleasure, especially when she observed the toned muscles she'd acquired.

Her self-esteem was another of the many things she had won back from Jack.

"What else are you doing?" said Irene. "Has . . . what's her name . . . Kerstin come with you to Sweden?"

"Yes, Kerstin is with me and she's working around the clock to find out what's going on. Yesterday, we spoke to several investors to persuade them not to sell."

"Without giving anything else away, I hope?" Irene scrutinized her keenly while reaching for a second slice.

"Naturally. And I think it worked. But I ask myself whether that's enough. It's a question of how focused the person behind this is. I'm worried that it's someone very focused indeed."

Irene put down her cutlery and looked at Faye.

"How are you doing?"

Faye knew that with Irene it was best to stick to the straight and narrow.

"To be completely honest, I'm surprised at how

badly this has shaken me. We've had crises in the company before in the last few years. Hundreds, maybe even thousands, of crises of different sizes. Running a company is effectively a matter of crisis management. Well, you know that. But this . . . Someone is trying to take my life's work away from me. I created Revenge with my own two hands and I'm still the one at the tiller. And it may be naïve of me, but I never considered the possibility that someone would try to take away everything I've worked to build."

Irene shook her head emphatically.

"It's not naïve. After all, how often do hostile takeovers happen nowadays? Basically never. Might it be Jack who's behind this, somehow?"

"Jack? No, he's got no capital left. And no contacts either. He's wiped out and everyone has turned their back on him. I can't see how he would be in a position to pull off something like this from prison. Especially after what he did to Julienne."

"Is there anyone else you can think of?"

The waitress came back with their main courses and placed them on the table in front of the two women. She looked questioningly at the half-eaten pizza.

"Are you finished? Should I take it away?"

"No, no, leave it. We need carbs today," said Faye, and Irene nodded. "Obviously I've picked up my fair share of enemies over the years," Faye continued once the waitress was gone. "You can't build a big company without treading on people's toes along the way. But there's no one in particular who stands out. I wish I had a clearer picture, or at least some theory about who it was. But no. Unfortunately, I have no idea."

"You can rest assured that I won't sell in any case. And I'll keep my ear to the ground. Perhaps I can find something out, and if I do then of course I'll get in touch."

Faye felt her shoulders relax. It was only now that she realized how tense she had been.

She clinked glasses with Irene. Around them, the lunch guests continued to murmur while the two women attacked their main courses with pleasure.

The water was delightfully warm against her body. Faye took long, powerful strokes and reminded herself to take deep breaths. The pool at the Grand Hôtel resembled a cave, with beautiful vaults and subdued lighting. If you spoke, it was in a low voice, and in the background there was nothing but discreet music of the kind that was typical of spas the world over.

Kerstin was sitting on the wide step halfway into the pool. Faye swam over and slid into place beside her. She straightened herself and leaned back, her elbows against a step, gently splashing with her legs.

"How many are on your list today?" Faye said.

"I've got five to seven that I think I can get through, depending whether I can get hold of them and how long each conversation takes."

"Well, as I said, there's no need to worry about Irene. She's promised us she won't sell."

"Good. Not that I thought she would, but then

again, I didn't think some of the people who have sold would either."

Faye looked down into the water at the ripples created by her legs as she shifted on the step. She thought about the dark water. She remembered screams. Saw terrified faces in front of her.

"Faye, how are you feeling?"

Kerstin's voice brought her back to the present and Faye shook her head slightly.

"There's a lot that needs doing if the American expansion is to go ahead. I need to spend the day working on that," she said. "I can't afford to devote all my time to managing this crisis—daily operations must go on, otherwise we'll end up with nothing left to lose."

"Focus on your things and I'll keep ferreting away."

Kerstin closed her eyes, savoring the water. She had been in the spa for an hour before Faye had arrived and had swum a decent amount despite the pool really being too small for swimming lengths.

"I know you've got a lot to do, but can you help me check up on one other thing?"

"Of course," said Kerstin, opening her eyes. "Something in particular?"

"Can you find out a bit more about a man called David Schiller? He's an angel investor."

"Of course I can," said Kerstin with an amused

smile. "Something tells me that it's the man here at the Grand who was definitely not your type?"

Faye splashed some water at her.

"Are you being sassy?"

Kerstin grinned.

"Not sassy. Just pointing out the fact that you want to find out more about a man that you claim to be completely uninterested in."

Faye looked down at her feet in the water again.

"Well, let's just say that he's proven himself to have some plus points. And that makes it even more important to find out all I can about him." She turned toward Kerstin. "I'm determined never to let anyone catch me unawares again."

Kerstin got up, wrapped her white bathrobe with the hotel logo on it around herself, and tied the sash at her waist.

"I'll dig up everything I can find. And you should take the opportunity to get some rest. It won't do any of us any good if you hit the wall. Have an hour here."

"You're right. I'm actually going to let myself have that."

Faye got out of the pool too and reached for her robe.

When Kerstin had left, Faye lay down on one of the loungers and enjoyed the tranquility. The lunch with Irene had dispelled much of her anxiety, and the fear she had felt after her encounter with Detective Yvonne Ingvarsson had begun to dissipate. There was a blurry image of someone who looked like her. So what? Jack had been convicted of Julienne's murder. He wouldn't be released for years. The media had helped by drumming in the message that Julienne was dead. It was now an accepted truth. Even though there was no body.

She reached for the glass of freshly pressed orange juice on the floor beside the lounger and took a sip while her thoughts wandered off to her beloved daughter, who was probably splashing about in another pool right now. Today was the first day of June and there was apparently a heat wave across Italy.

Footsteps on the tiles made her look around. David, who had come down from the gym on the second floor, glanced around without spotting her. He took off his black shorts and T-shirt, revealing an unexpectedly well-toned back, and dived into the shimmering green water wearing nothing but underpants. Faye smiled. It was probably strictly prohibited. He swam a couple of lengths and Faye discreetly craned her neck. Eventually, she grew bored of watching, got to her feet, and approached the pool.

David swam up to her and flashed that smile that changed his appearance and made him almost handsome.

"Good morning," she said. "How was the full day with your daughters?"

A flicker of darkness crossed his face. He heaved himself out of the pool and gratefully accepted the towel that Faye passed to him.

"They couldn't come," he said abruptly.

"Has something happened?"

They walked side by side back toward the loungers.

"Johanna decided at the last moment to take them to Disneyland Paris instead."

"But why?"

David sank down onto a lounger and dried his legs with the towel. He avoided looking at her.

"She's done it before," he said quietly. "She finds out from the girls what I'm planning and plays a trump card at the last moment. I don't know why, but I'm sure she has her reasons."

"I thought you were getting along well, despite the circumstances?"

"Perhaps I glossed over it when we last spoke. I don't want to be the guy who talks shit about his ex-wife."

She looked him deep in the eyes.

"You can tell me."

They looked at each other in silence for a while. Then he stretched and laced his fingers together behind his neck. Faye lay down on her lounger, facing toward him.

"She's always been jealous," David eventually

said. "But around two years ago it began to go into overdrive. I've never been unfaithful, not to her or anyone else. But I noticed that she had begun to watch me—checking every tiny thing I did. She would suddenly demand to read my texts. I didn't have anything to hide, so I let her. But then . . . She turned up at the office. Scared my female employees. Sent them threatening messages on Facebook."

David sighed.

"I tried to protect her, smoothed things over. I paid them off so they wouldn't report it to the police. I did everything to protect Johanna. To protect the girls. Sometimes she was completely absent—wandering around the house like a sleepwalker. She would forget to pick up Stina and Felicia from practice or would talk to them harshly. It was one thing when she had an outburst of rage at me, but them? She distanced herself from us. I began working from home more, so that the girls wouldn't have to be alone with her."

A tear ran down his cheek and he quickly wiped it away. His jaw was trembling.

"I feel so fucking powerless."

Faye knew everything about feeling powerless. But she rarely spoke about what had gone before. She rarely spoke about Jack.

"I know just what you mean," she said in a low voice, her gaze fixed on the tiled floor. "I felt like that for many years. Lived like that for many years.

Let myself be controlled, had my identity taken away from me. My self-confidence. Everything."

She felt David's eyes on her and forced herself to meet them. She felt naked, unprotected, but also alive. Why had she thought he was uninteresting?

David placed his hand on hers on the lounger and it was as if she'd had an electric shock.

"I'm sorry someone hurt you so badly," he said, his blue eyes not wavering from hers. "I know that if there's anyone who can manage on their own it's you, but I want you to feel that you can talk to me. About everything. You don't have to be strong by yourself."

"I'm used to it," she said, withdrawing her hand.

She could still sense the warmth of his skin.

"Do you feel up to telling me about it? I'm here. And I want to listen."

Faye hesitated. She had kept the door to her past with Jack closed for so long she wasn't even certain she could open it. Or how she would do it. David said nothing. He waited for her while she allowed her own thoughts to swirl around. Then she made up her mind.

"We met at the Stockholm School of Economics . . ."

David placed his hand on hers again. This time she let it lie there while the words came out. Slowly at first, as if every word hurt. Then more and more rapidly.

FJÄLLBACKA—THEN

I lay there shaking in the darkness, my eyes wide open.

"If you tell anyone I'll kill you."

Sebastian took a stranglehold on me, shoved his face into mine so that I could smell his sour breath, and squeezed.

"Get it?"

I nodded slowly.

"Yes," I croaked.

When he let go, I coughed. Sebastian picked up his underpants and returned unhurriedly to his room. I opened the window to let in some air and crept back under the damp covers. It hurt between my legs and I dried myself using my top. Then I sat there staring out of the window.

Memories rushed through my mind. Sebastian and me when we were little. Holding each other's hands under the table while Dad yelled into Mom's face, the tip of his nose touching hers. Sebastian curled up in a small ball next to me, seeking my warmth. My security.

All that was gone now. None of those memories was worth a thing any longer. He had taken them from me.

We had sought refuge in each other—the two of us had been the only ones who understood. Now it was just me and Mom left. And Mom was weak. I couldn't blame her for that. She was weak because she had carried us and protected us as best she could. Stayed for our sake.

I could hear Sebastian restlessly pacing across the floor in his room before the window opened and silence descended. I wondered what he looked like and how he felt sitting curled up on the windowsill seven or eight feet away from me. And then I realized that I could kill him. He was dangling his legs at a height of at least fifteen feet above the ground. If I crept out after him, opened the door to his room, and rushed over, then I'd have time to push him down. I'd tell Mom and Dad that I'd heard him cry out and that I'd run into his room to see what had happened. But I couldn't do it. I still loved him, despite what he had done.

If I had known what awaited me, what he would subject me to, I would have killed him immediately and without hesitation. It would have spared me a lot of pain. And trouble.

Faye was lying on the big bed in her suite. Her bags were standing, packed, by the door. Tomorrow she was going to leave the Grand Hôtel and move into the apartment by Östermalmstorg. Although it would feel good to be in her own space after so many days at the hotel, she realized to her surprise that she was going to miss David.

The display on her phone lit up and she saw that Kerstin had sent her a message. She clicked on it and read it, a smile spreading across her face.

Everything seems to check out. Have so far been unable to find any issues with David Schiller whatsoever. No criminal records, no defaulted payments, nothing on social media, and I've also made discreet inquiries in his business circles and haven't turned up anything that suggests he's not okay.

Faye rolled onto her stomach. She couldn't stop smiling when she thought about her time with

David in the hotel spa the day before. They had sat there talking for over an hour before they had had to part ways.

The fact that she had been able to start telling someone about Jack—what he had forced her to think and do—made her feel like she'd lost several pounds. The relief was huge. David had seen her and heard her. She felt like a person. Not just a woman, where the endgame for the man was always to get a lay.

She pulled out her phone again and called Julienne on FaceTime.

Her daughter's face on the small screen always made her forget all her troubles, all her negative thoughts. That was the only thing she felt grateful to Jack for. He had given her a daughter who was, in Faye's eyes, absolutely perfect. From the messily painted pink toenails to the blond hair that tumbled a long way down her back.

"Hi, sweetheart!"

"Hi, Mommy," said Julienne, waving cheerily.

Her hair was wet and Faye guessed that she had been in the pool again.

"What are you doing?"

"Me and Grandma have been swimming."

"Did you have fun?"

"Mmm, lots of fun," said Julienne.

"I had a swim too. Yesterday. I thought about you then."

"Oh right," Julienne said. Faye noticed that she

had already begun to lose interest in talking on the phone. Life was tempting her away.

"I'll call tonight and talk to you then. Miss you. Kiss kiss."

"Mmm, bye-bye," said Julienne, waving hastily and impatiently.

"Say hi to Gra—" Faye began to say, but Julienne had already hung up.

Faye smiled. Without doubt, Julienne was going to grow up into an independent woman.

She got up from the bed, went to the bathroom, and turned on the tap to draw a hot bath. Someone knocked on the door and Faye glanced quickly at her wristwatch. It was twenty to nine. Faye stopped the water and went into the hallway.

"Yes?" she called through the door.

"It's Yvonne Ingvarsson from the police."

Faye took a deep breath and then opened the door. Yvonne Ingvarsson looked at her with a hint of a smile.

"Can I come in for a while?"

Faye remained in the same spot, her arms folded.

"I don't think it's okay for you to just turn up like this."

"I want to show you something. Can I come in or not?"

Faye sighed and stepped aside so that Yvonne could come into the room. After three or four feet the officer stopped.

"Nice suite."

"I didn't know that visits like this were part of your job description. What's this all about?"

Yvonne Ingvarsson didn't answer. Instead she put her hand in her bag and took out a clipping from a gossip magazine. It was an old photo of Faye and Jack. She passed it over.

"I don't know . . ."

Yvonne held up a finger to shush her, then put her hand back in her bag and took out a printed photo. Faye noticed that Yvonne's nails were chewed down, the cuticles dry and inflamed. This photo was blurrier, the light was yellowish, and it seemed to have been taken in the evening. Faye saw right away that the woman whose back was visible was herself. The coat she was wearing was the same as the one in the picture with Jack.

"What do you have to say?" Yvonne asked, scrutinizing her with curiosity.

"About what?"

"It's you in the photo, Faye. You know it and I know it. You weren't in Västerås. You were at the scene of the murder."

A quick, unpleasant smile flashed across the woman's face. She squinted at Faye.

"It's not me," said Faye. "Every housewife in Östermalm has that coat—it's a Moncler. It's like having clogs if you live in the country."

Yvonne shook her head slowly, but Faye calmly stood her ground. Just like the last time Yvonne had turned up, Faye thought to herself that they wouldn't be having this conversation if there was evidence. And the fact that she had turned up on a Sunday made Faye suspect that Yvonne was acting beyond her authority.

What did she want? Money? Or could someone have bribed Yvonne to harass her? But no, something told her this was a private crusade—a vendetta aimed at Faye.

"What **exactly** is it you want?" she asked.

"The truth," Yvonne said quickly. "All I'm after is the truth."

Without taking her gaze off Faye, she took a piece of paper from her back pocket. Faye wondered how many things Yvonne was going to pull out. She was like Mary Poppins and her bag.

Yvonne held out the piece of paper between her thumb and forefinger, dangling it in front of Faye. Faye took it from her hand. It was an old article from the **Bohusläningen** local paper, one that she recognized immediately. Her stomach dropped and she struggled not to show Yvonne Ingvarsson the tumult within her.

"You seem to be bad luck for the people around you," Yvonne said, before adding in a low voice: "Matilda."

Two boys from Fjällbacka are missing after a sailing trip with their friends. The entire community is paralyzed with grief.

"I refuse to believe that they're dead," says 13-year-old Matilda, who was there at the time of the accident.

Faye swallowed hard, slowly folded the printout up without finishing reading it, and passed it back to Yvonne, who shook her head.

"You keep it," she said, turning to go. "Nice suite. Really nice," she muttered as she opened the door before vanishing into the corridor.

Faye examined the thirteen-year-old girl who was staring straight into the camera below the headline. She looked unhappy and helpless, but Faye knew that she had only been posing for the photographer. Inside her, the darkness had been rampaging.

She lay down on the bed and stared up at the ceiling. But she didn't see the white stucco of the Grand—she saw something completely different. Dark, swirling water that made her stomach turn.

A shrill sound made Faye jump. She looked around in horror. For a second, before she was able to gain her bearings, she was still there by the swirling water. Her pulse slowed when she realized it was just her phone ringing. Kerstin's name was illuminated on the display.

"I'm afraid I've got bad news." Kerstin got straight to the point, as always.

"What is it now?" said Faye, closing her eyes.

Did she want to hear the answer? Would she be

able to cope with any more? She didn't know, and that scared her.

"**Dagens Industri** called. They've heard a rumor about the buyout. If we don't manage to stop them from printing the article, the cat will soon be out of the bag."

Faye let out a sigh.

"Which will only lead to even more sales of shares. Rats always leave a sinking ship," she said.

"What do you want me to do?" Kerstin asked.

"I know a woman there. I'll give her a call and see what I can do. Leave it to me, I'll handle this."

Faye hung up and threw the phone onto the duvet beside her. If she had been the sort to give up, she would have pulled the duvet over her head now and slept for a couple of days. But she wasn't. She never had been. She picked up the phone again. The battle continued.

Faye was sitting in a huddled heap on the bed with the pieces of paper left by Yvonne and Kerstin's account of the share movements in the company. Taken by themselves, these two things were enough to worry about, but taken together they were almost too much. Before long, the serious work on the American launch would be starting—someone had called from Revenge's office on Stureplan with the news that several people who wanted to invest in the venture had been in touch following Faye's appearance on **Skavlan.** Having Yvonne Ingvarsson on her heels at this sensitive stage was risky, and Faye also needed to ensure that she actually still had a company to launch in a new market.

Her mobile phone beeped and she opened the Telegram app, where her messages and images were deleted after fifteen seconds. She smiled at a photograph of Julienne by the pool.

"My little darling," she murmured before the picture vanished.

A new knock at the door made Faye jump. She raised the throw on the bed and shoved the papers beneath it, got to her feet, and went to the door. The sight of Julienne had given her energy and awoken her thirst for battle. Yvonne Ingvarsson didn't know who she was crossing swords with, and Faye intended to move heaven and earth to find out who was attacking her company.

David Schiller was waiting outside the door. He smiled at her.

"You look like someone who could do with a walk with a friend."

Faye and David strolled over to Strandvägen— deserted on a Sunday. It was a warm evening. People were walking their dogs along the avenue and the theme park rides at Gröna Lund were sparkling, spinning, and shining across the water on the island of Djurgården. Faye had forgotten how enchantingly beautiful Stockholm summer evenings were.

"Are you feeling okay after our chat yesterday— about everything you told me?"

David sounded concerned. Faye realized she was moved.

"Don't worry about it," she said with a smile, and David's blue eyes lit up.

"Great. I was worried that you might have regretted it afterward."

"No, no, it's fine. It was . . . liberating. I haven't really talked to anyone at all about what happened, and about what life with Jack was like. Barely even with Kerstin, who I consider my closest friend. Of course, Chris knew most of it . . ."

"Who is Chris?" said David carefully. "You mentioned that name before."

He looked like he was attempting to take his first steps out onto ice formed during the night to see whether it was strong enough.

"Chris. God, how do I explain who she was? We became friends at business school. She . . . she was a force of nature. Nothing was hard for her."

"What happened? If it's all right for me to ask . . . ?"

They passed the Strandbryggan restaurant, which was in the midst of dealing with the evening onslaught. The young, beautiful, and distinctly inebriated all flocked there, surreptitiously checking out one another's designer bags and false eyelashes and the Rolexes given to them to mark their high school graduation.

"She got cancer," said Faye, raising her arm so that he could see her **Fuck Cancer** wristband. "It happened so quickly. But she had time to fall in love—with an amazing man who was perfect for her."

"That's still wonderful," said David. "Finding love before the end. Isn't that what we're all looking for?"

They'd turned left, heading up toward the Nordic Museum and Junibacken.

David gazed out across the water. The Vasa Museum was just visible behind the trees—a peculiar monument to one of Swedish history's greatest flops.

"Do you love her?" said Faye.

David looked at her quizzically.

"Who?"

"Your wife. Who else?"

David laughed in embarrassment.

"Well yes, I suppose I should have understood. After fifteen years together it feels like such a weird question. Love. Is that something you do after fifteen years, the daily grind, and kids? Does anyone?"

"That sounds pretty cynical."

"Maybe. Or perhaps we were just wrong for each other from the start. If I'm being completely honest."

He shook his head and turned away from her.

"That makes me sound so awful."

"You don't say."

Faye linked arms with him as they approached Gröna Lund. The delighted screeching from the rides was increasingly audible.

David cleared his throat.

"I don't think it was ever about love. It was . . . well, I suppose it was something more practical. It was about ticking all the boxes. But feelings? I don't know."

He patted Faye's arm.

"Are you offended?"

"No, not at all. People get together for a thousand different reasons. Few are privileged to truly experience love. Real love."

"Have you?" he said, stopping.

Part of her wanted to avoid his gaze, to avoid answering. She heard the screams from the freefall tower—where people voluntarily went high up in the air to feel the tingle in their stomach as they plunged toward the ground. That was kind of how she experienced love.

"Yes, I have. I loved Jack. More than I thought I would ever love anyone. But that wasn't enough. I wasn't enough. And then Julienne came along. And that was a completely new kind of love. And it took over . . ."

Her voice faltered and she turned away. For a moment, she was overcome by all of it. Everything that the family had been subjected to. By Jack. And by her when she wanted to rescue them from him.

"I can't even imagine what you've been through," David said, and Faye shuddered—for a moment she had forgotten that he was there. "And to lose a child? Faye, I . . . I wish I could take away all that loss, but I don't think anyone can do that."

Faye shook herself. She forced away all the emotions and memories that clamored for her attention.

If she let herself remember—or feel—she wouldn't be able to take another step.

"It's just good that you're here," she said. "That you're listening."

They continued to stand there in silence, the flashing lights of the amusement park in the background. Neither of them said anything for a long time. Then David reached out with his hand.

"Come on. Let's head back."

Faye nodded. They turned around and began to walk back toward Strandvägen. Once they had passed Strandbryggan again, David stopped and turned toward her.

"Want a swim?" he asked.

"Here?"

"Yes, it's a warm evening and we live in the Venice of the north. There's places to swim everywhere you look. For example, right there."

He pointed to a spot between two houseboats where a wooden jetty protruded into the water. Without waiting for her, he jogged over to it—the boats concealing him from Strandvägen. He bent forward and untied his shoes. Faye looked around. There wasn't a soul in sight. Traffic was sparse. David took off his linen shirt, jeans, and shoes. His socks. His underpants. His pale buttocks shone in the darkness and then Faye heard a cry that was followed by a splash. She leaned forward. Six feet below he was treading water and looking up at her.

"It's cold but it feels good," he reported. "Come on, jump in."

Faye glanced over her shoulder and saw that the coast was clear. She took off her shoes and placed her dress next to the heap of David's clothes but kept her underwear on. Then she took a deep breath before kicking through the air and breaking the water's surface. She cried out with horrified joy. It really was cold.

They swam a little way from the shore and then stopped. They were treading water beside each other as they took in the lights of the city, shivering.

"I like you," said David.

The words were intermittent, through chattering teeth.

And Faye smiled, because the whole thing was so crazy. She felt so warm inside herself that for a while she forgot about the cold. She wanted to answer but remained silent. She had promised herself she wouldn't fall in love with anyone, but she knew that her defenses were beginning to crumble. David made her laugh, and he was a gentleman without any hidden motives. On the contrary, he was a successful businessman who understood her work and he had a smile that made her heart melt—even in this cold, cold water.

When they had gotten out of the water and quickly put their clothes back on, David rubbed her upper arms to warm her.

"What should we do now?" she asked.

She realized that she didn't want to go back to the hotel room.

David looked mischievous.

"Come with me," he said, slipping on his shoes.

She followed him toward the yacht club on the far side of the Djurgården Bridge. Her hair was plastered to her shoulders and back as they jogged to warm up. They stopped at the gate. David peered into the guard's hut, noted it was empty, and climbed over the fence.

"There's a camera," said Faye, pointing.

"Don't worry," he said, once he had landed on the far side. "I've got a friend with a boat here. He won't be upset if we borrow it."

Faye tentatively raised her foot, grabbed hold of the fence, and heaved herself onto the other side, where David caught her.

He surveyed the boats.

"There it is," he exclaimed, pointing to a large motorboat moored farthest away.

The next moment, he grabbed her hand and dragged her along.

They climbed aboard and David crouched, fumbling with his hand under a white seat cushion, before holding up a set of keys with a triumphant smile. He unlocked the cabin and Faye went in, relishing the warmth. They took off their wet clothes and wrapped themselves up in large bath towels that David found.

"Whose is the boat?" Faye asked. She sat down

on a sofa while he rooted through the compart-
ments in the kitchen.

"A good friend's," he repeated, before exclaiming:
"Well, look what we have here! Whiskey!"

He poured two glasses and passed her one before
settling down beside her. The spirit warmed her
body from within. Waves lapped against the hull,
making the boat rock pleasantly. A child's barrette
with Elsa from **Frozen** and a large blue rosette
on it was lying on the side and she played with it
distractedly. It reminded her of Julienne. She loved
Elsa and liked to sing "Let it gooooo" in her best
attempt at English.

"Where did you go?"

David looked at her tenderly. Then he saw the
barrette and gasped.

"Sorry . . . I . . ."

Faye put a hand on his arm to show that it was
fine. She was touched that, sensing the barrette had
triggered thoughts of Julienne, his first thought
was to shield her from painful memories of her
murdered daughter. The warmth from his body
made her tingle.

David smiled at her.

"What is it?" she asked.

"Nothing," he replied.

She was close to saying that she liked him too—
a delayed response to what he had said to her in
the water. Somehow she couldn't bring herself to.

The words got stuck in her throat. Got stuck in her scars. The ones that weren't visible from the outside.

"Can I visit you when you move out of the Grand tomorrow?" he asked.

"If you like."

"I would."

"Me too."

He sighed with a smile.

"I don't know what's up with me, but when I'm with you I'm just so absurdly happy. I'm like a fifteen-year-old, y'know—I want to impress you. I don't even like wild swimming. And I know it's no big deal, that you like me too—even if you don't say it. And I'm grateful to you for opening up to me."

Faye nodded silently.

"I met him, by the way. A few years ago. Jack. I thought he seemed like a stuck-up, self-satisfied bastard and—"

Faye leaned toward him. She didn't want to talk any more about Jack. Not now, not ever. She pressed her lips to David's to silence him. His lips were softer than she had expected.

"We're not talking about him. We're not talking about anything other than us—at least not tonight."

"Deal."

As if by unspoken agreement, they stood up and took the bottle into the sleeping compartment. The bed was surprisingly large and made up with white sheets.

Faye sat down on the bed. She let the towel fall from her. Underneath it, she was completely naked. She looked into David's eyes. His gaze was hazy—equal parts whiskey and excitement. He moved toward her slowly, also letting his towel fall. He was already hard. He strode over to Faye, where she was sitting on the edge of the bed, his penis in her eyeline.

Without dropping her gaze from him, Faye took hold of his cock with her hand. She slowly moved her face closer and opened her mouth. At first, she simply let her warm breath envelop his glans. Then she extended her tongue. She licked away a drop of precum. David groaned deeply. He briefly closed his eyes but then opened them again and looked at Faye.

She opened her mouth a little further. Let her lips enclose the end of his cock. Her tongue teased the small frenulum and she enjoyed the gasping sounds coming from David. Slowly, slowly, she took more and more of him into her mouth. She felt a gentle gag reflex but withdrew his cock ever so slightly just before it became uncomfortable. Then in again. And out. She kept her hand around him; her saliva had made his cock wet and slippery and her hand glided with ease.

David was breathing more and more quickly,

groaning loudly, and now his eyes were shut and his hands were around her head, his fingers deeply buried in her hair.

"I can't wait any longer—I want to come inside you," he murmured.

She lay down on the bed with him on top of her, between her legs, pushing into her—he slid forward and slowly, inexorably slowly, he penetrated her. It felt absolutely incredible. Now it was her turn to groan. She felt his warmth between her legs, his hardness, his desire.

When he was almost fully inside her, he suddenly pushed in fast and hard—all the way—and she felt his weight on top of her. With his mouth at her ear, his warm breath on her cheek, he thrust into her while she wrapped her legs around him. She held his hips firmly, helping him to find his rhythm, pushing her hips against him—she wanted more, she wanted all of him.

Then he pulled out of her.

"I don't want to come yet. You turn me on so damn much. I want to taste you."

She opened her legs, and licked the fingers on his right hand. He began to slowly stroke her. She raised her head—she wanted to see him touching her. He stroked her clitoris before slowly inserting two fingers into her, then three. She gasped, groaned.

David withdrew his fingers from her. She

whimpered—she was close to coming now. He pushed her legs farther apart and brought his face closer. He let the tip of his tongue playfully toy with her clitoris. Faye tried to press her hips toward him, but he gently held her down with his hands on her legs. His tongue was gentle but resolute, applying more and more pressure to her clitoris, moving in circles. He was pushing her over the edge—she grasped the sheets hard and her back arched. When he put his fingers inside her, she felt the orgasm building—it was verging on painful, the boundary between pleasure and pain was just a hair's breadth, and she twisted her head back and forth as he brought her ever closer to the brink.

When Faye came she cried out. He continued, increasing his intensity while her entire body shook and she contracted around his fingers.

When the orgasm had finally stopped washing through her, her whole body relaxed, but Faye didn't want to rest. She wanted him inside her.

The swell outside made the boat sway. Faye turned around. She got onto all fours. At first, she hit her head on the low cabin ceiling, and both she and David laughed. She lowered herself a little and curved her back inward, turning her head so she could see him approaching her from behind. But he didn't take her right away. Instead, he caressed her ass—tenderly, lovingly.

"You're so beautiful."

"Fuck me," said Faye, wiggling her hips at him.

David stroked her buttocks again, then he took hold of her hips and pushed his cock deep inside her. Despite the fact that Faye had just come, she was still just as turned on by him—she wanted more.

"Fuck me, David," she said huskily. He didn't hold back on obeying her.

Afterward, they collapsed onto the bed and enjoyed the warmth of each other's bodies. David pulled her hair away from her neck and kissed her on her most sensitive spot, behind her ear. She giggled—it felt wonderful, but it was also ticklish. He rolled off her and lay on his back, his hand on the curve of her spine.

"I'm sweaty," she said, lying on her side so that his hand was on her hip.

He reached out and caressed her cheek tenderly.

"Do you know how amazing you are? How beautiful you are?"

"No, I think you'll have to tell me."

"I promise I will. Over and over and over again."

Faye realized she was smiling as she lay with her back to him. She blinked away tears. She told herself she couldn't fall for a man again—even if she had begun to fear it was already too late.

Faye got out of the elevator and took slow, expectant steps toward the heavy door. She didn't miss the old apartment. It contained far too many memories. Jack had managed to become a part of that too. This apartment was going to be just hers.

The keys weighed heavily in her hand. She loved the feeling of newness—how unspoiled it was. Even though she was only renting the apartment, she had been given permission to repaint.

She smiled when she put the key in the lock, thinking about the night before with David and everything they had done together.

When she opened the door, she detected the scent of fresh paint. She had never thought she would love that smell so much, but she did. The apartment was virgin territory. Hers to conquer.

Kerstin was in the apartment next door. She would still be nearby. Family. But this was hers. Just hers.

Faye unlocked the black security gate and stepped

inside, taking off her Jimmy Choos and placing them on the walnut shoe rack in the hallway. Slowly, cautiously, she walked into the apartment, which opened up before her—big and airy.

The whole place was more than two thousand square feet in size. Maybe it was a little over the top just for her, but after all those years in a gilded cage she wanted air and space around her more than anything else. She had loved this apartment from the moment she had set eyes on it on the rental site—it felt like her even if it was just a rental.

The kitchen was reminiscent of a farmhouse kitchen, but a modern version. Philippe Starck, Gaggenau, and Le Cordon Bleu created the right blend. The big wooden table with long benches made from the same weathered wood had been custom-ordered from a carpenter on Södermalm. She ran her hand over the tabletop. She loved the feeling.

When she reached the living room, she smiled at the sight of the enormous emerald-green velvet sofa. The room had been painted in light, muted colors that made for a relaxing feeling.

She went over to the window and spent a while gazing across the rooftops of Östermalm before slowly continuing her tour of the rooms in the apartment. It was going to be her home while she worked on the American expansion and saved Revenge. She now had two homes. One in Italy and one here. Both were important but in different ways. Half her heart was in Italy, where Julienne and her mother were. But half of her heart would always be here. She had made Stockholm her town from the very first moment she had arrived. Julienne had been born here, taken her first tentative steps here. Stockholm was her and Chris's town. They had shared laughter, adventures, successes, misfortune, and deepest sorrow here.

This apartment was going to be her fortress, her stronghold.

She had come home.

Faye's pulse quickened as she entered through the main street door on Birger Jarlsgatan. When she saw Revenge's logo—the ornate **R**—she forced back a wave of emotion. On her way through the open-plan office, she smiled at the young women greeting her.

Her body was buzzing when she opened the door to her office—she loved this space where she had created magic and built an empire.

And it was from here that she had orchestrated Jack's fall. Conquered him. Taken over Compare, the company he'd built using her ideas, the company she'd helped him set up, only for him to claim all the credit and cast her aside.

She placed her handbag on the desk and sat down in the chair, then opened her laptop. She glanced through the sheet of glass at the twenty employees at their desks. Ten or so new hires had arrived—she knew their names since she had been emailing with them, and she appreciated finally having the chance to see them in reality. They were women of all ages. Talented, multilingual, self-starters, and professional. Modern women, full of self-confidence.

Revenge's revenues were going to set new records, and as she sat there gazing at her employees, she thought to herself that there wasn't really any need to expand. Why risk all this? Wasn't it better to focus everything on stopping the buyout?

Financially, Julienne's future great-grandchildren's prospects were secured. But she knew that Chris would have loved to see Faye fulfill her dream of taking on America. And the **Skavlan** interview had exceeded all expectations. Their inbox was full of financiers who wanted a slice when Revenge took the step across the Atlantic. They were so incredibly close to sealing the deal with their partners in the USA. Much closer than she had let on. But she wanted to have the right investors on board. People who would allow her free rein to operate as she saw fit—and even more important, people who did good in the world. People with a good center, as Chris used to say.

Sometimes she remembered Chris's smile, heard her laugh, felt her firm hand in hers. If she closed her eyes right now, she could almost imagine that Chris was standing beside her. Her throat tightened and Faye brushed away tears. The melancholy was back.

What was the point of the money and success

if she was forced to be apart from the people she loved? While she might like those female employees out there, they hadn't been there for her when she was a nobody—before she became a billionaire. And if it all went to shit, they would pick up their designer bags and abandon her without so much as blinking. A company, just like a relationship, should be based on loyalty. But the fact was that she had given more of herself to Julienne—and prioritizing her personal life had caused her to loosen her hold on Revenge.

She glanced at the desk and jumped. She had ten missed calls from Kerstin—she must have set her mobile to silent. With butterflies in her stomach, she called back.

"I've found out who's behind the purchases," Kerstin said right away.

Faye swallowed.

"Yes?" she said as calmly as she could.

"Henrik Bergendahl."

"But that can't be . . ."

Faye closed her eyes and sagged against the backrest. Jack's former business partner. Shouldn't she have seen this coming? Even though Henrik was now more successful than ever, he had been in a bad place for a while. But she hadn't given him a thought.

"And that's not all," Kerstin continued. "I've just found out that Irene Ahrnell has sold her holding to him."

FJÄLLBACKA—THEN

I hurried home from school. Dad was going to Dingle to get the car repaired and wouldn't be home until late. That meant a few rare hours of freedom.

Mom had promised me that we would sew. Grandma had told me that Mom had long dreamed of becoming a dressmaker. Even when she had been little she had made amazing fashion creations for her Barbie dolls. Now she only had time to sew household necessities, but she had begun to teach me.

I wasn't really all that interested in learning to sew. But when we sat side by side in front of Mom's Husqvarna sewing machine that Dad had let her buy after much pleading, it was as if we were in our own little bubble. I would watch in fascination as she threaded the machine with practiced and competent hands, showed me which buttons ensured straight stitching, which ones created zigzags, which seams to use where, and how to tie off the thread when you were done. I loved every minute of it.

Today, she had promised to help me make a pair of harem trousers. I had smuggled in some shiny purple fabric from the sewing shop, and I was picturing how beautiful they would be when they were done.

When I entered the house it was completely silent. I called out cautiously, not entirely certain that Dad wasn't at home. But no one replied.

I looked around the hall. Mom's coat was hanging on the hook. And her shoes were neatly stowed on the pine shoe rack. Something within me shifted anxiously.

"Mom, are you at home?"

Still no answer. It would be another hour or so before Sebastian got home. Mom and I were supposed to have a long time to ourselves—a rare gift—and I knew that she wouldn't miss it for the world. She loved our brief stints at the sewing machine. Perhaps she'd gone for a nap?

I carefully climbed the stairs to Mom and Dad's bedroom. The steps creaked but no one seemed to hear. I turned right and saw that the bedroom door was shut, which made me feel relieved. She had probably just lay down for a bit.

I gently opened the door. Yes. She was in bed. Her face was turned away from me. I crept into the room quietly—as quietly as I could—still not sure whether I should leave her to sleep or wake her. I knew she would be disappointed if we missed our time with the sewing machine.

When I reached her side of the bed, at first I merely frowned. Mom's eyelids were fluttering, as if she were falling asleep. Then something on the floor caught my attention. A white bottle. The lid was lying beside it. I bent down and picked up the bottle. Sleeping tablets.

Panic struck. I shook Mom but she didn't react.

My thoughts raced but at the same time a clarity and calm descended on me. I knew just what I had to do.

I leaned her over the side of the bed, her face pointing down, and I pushed my fingers into her mouth, farther and farther down into her throat. At first nothing happened. Then she suddenly began sobbing against my fingers and eventually I felt warm vomit gushing over my hand and onto the floor.

Tiny, tiny pieces of the tablets were in the midst of the mess, mixed with spaghetti from lunch. I continued to keep my fingers in her throat until there was nothing left to come up except bile. Then I pressed her head against my breast.

While her dismal sobs echoed between the walls, I cradled my mother in my arms as if she were a child. I had never hated my father more than in that moment. And I knew two things. That I would never be able to tell her what Sebastian had done. And that I had to get us away from them at any cost.

"Is there a law in this universe that says everything has to go to hell at once?"

Kerstin poured a cup of tea for Faye. Broms was full of patrons breakfasting. The noise and her own frustration were giving Faye a headache.

"I think you're referring to Murphy's law," Kerstin said. "But yes, I have noticed during the course of my life—which has been somewhat longer than yours—that things have a tendency to clump together. Happiness clumps together. Grief clumps together. Accidents clump together."

"Then we're definitely seeing some clumping right now," Faye muttered while sipping her tea with a grimace. "Who drinks stuff like this of their own free will? I need a strong coffee."

She stopped a passing waitress and hissed:

"A cappuccino, please."

"Have some food." Kerstin nodded at the table. They had ordered sourdough, boiled eggs, yogurt and muesli, and fruit salad.

Faye shook her head.

"I'm not hungry."

Kerstin ate in silence while Faye waved irritably at the waitress, who still hadn't brought the cappuccino. She had barely slept a wink all night.

"Don't take your frustration out on the staff," Kerstin said.

"I'll do as I please."

Faye finally made eye contact with the waitress, who quickly rushed off toward the kitchen.

The sun was shining outside the window. People were hurrying about, focused on their own things, and for a moment Faye wondered whether they—just like her—were living lives in which they were being torn between hope and despair.

"You need to talk about it instead of yelling at people," said Kerstin. "Irene went behind your back despite her promises. She sold to Henrik—Jack's old partner."

Faye thumped her fist on the table. She wasn't angry at Kerstin or the staff. She was just angry.

"I'm getting chia pudding," she said, standing up.

She wasn't really hungry, just as she had told Kerstin, but she needed some time alone to gather her thoughts. She stood in the long line and got angrier with every passing minute. When she eventually got to the front she ordered a chia pudding with everything on it: blueberries, cranberries, and coconut flakes.

When she sat back down at the table, Kerstin looked at her without saying anything. Faye not only polished off the chia pudding, but everything else too, taking huge bites. Once the food was inside her stomach in one big mass, she caught her breath and leaned back. Only then did she realize that she had finally received her cappuccino.

"First things first," she said. "I can't understand why Irene sold. She must barely have finished digesting the food she ate at our lunch before she did it. I've always considered her loyal and honest. I don't get it."

"There must be something more in it," said Kerstin. "But that'll have to wait. Right now we can only contend with the fact that she has actually sold."

"And to Henrik," said Faye despondently, knocking back the cappuccino.

She raised the cup toward the waitress.

"You'll end up with a stomachache," Kerstin said dryly.

"I can't end up with more of a stomachache than the one I've already got. I've made so many mistakes, Kerstin. That's what gives me a stomachache. I underestimated Henrik's hatred of me. I underestimated Revenge's vulnerability. And I overestimated the loyalty of our shareholders."

"Both you and I made mistakes in that case. I didn't see this coming either."

"True. But to be perfectly honest, that doesn't make it any easier to take."

Faye was uneasy within her own skin and she stood up. Behind her, the waitress set down a new cappuccino on the table, but Faye just carried on—away from everything.

Her phone buzzed in her hand and she looked at it. The number wasn't saved in her contacts, but she still recognized it. It was Yvonne Ingvarsson.

"Yes, what do you want?" Faye said abruptly.

The woman on the other end took a deep breath. Faye thought that she almost sounded expectant.

"I'm afraid I have to notify you that there was an escape from a prison transport earlier today. One of the prisoners who escaped was your ex-husband, Jack."

PART TWO

PART TWO

Aftonbladet can now reveal that one of the two escaped prisoners is the convicted murderer and former financier Jack Adelheim. He was found guilty two years ago of the murder of his daughter. Prior to his conviction, he was the CEO of the scandal-hit investment company Compare, which he founded. He was previously married to businesswoman Faye Adelheim.

The police still have no trace of Jack Adelheim and the second prisoner who disappeared from a prison transport. The Swedish Prison and Probation Service remains reticent about how the escape took place.

"We have identified shortcomings in our procedures—that much I can say. But we want to investigate this fully before I offer any comment," says Malm, press spokesperson for the service.

Aftonbladet, 10 June

Faye was reclining on her terrace with her feet on the table. She slipped her fingers into the inside pocket of her Chanel bag and took out the photograph that she kept there. It was a picture that she had taken herself of her mother and Julienne on a beach in Sicily. The sea behind them was like a mirror, and Julienne, with her long blond hair tangled and damp, was curled up in her grandmother's arms. It was the only existing photo of the two of them together. Faye didn't dare take or keep photos of Italy. Instead, she had to keep their memories in her heart.

She gazed at the photo for a while before replacing it in her bag. She had to find somewhere better for it. Somewhere more secure. Her entire body ached with longing for Julienne—it was so strong that for a moment it even outweighed the worry she had been feeling around the clock since she had heard the news.

Jack had been on the run for five days. Yet despite

the authorities' reassurances to both Faye and journalists that they had assigned significant resources to the search, they hadn't caught him.

The panic of the first few days had begun to dissipate. The police called her daily to check that she was okay and it seemed improbable—not to mention insane—that Jack would turn up here. Even if he did turn up at the apartment or the office, she was certain she could handle it. What kept her awake at night was his insistence throughout the trial that Julienne was alive, that Faye had hidden her somewhere.

She had done everything she could to ensure that Julienne and Ingrid were safe in Italy. Apart from the photo that Faye kept in her bag, she'd eliminated all traces of their continued existence. Though she knew she was taking a huge risk in carrying the photo with her, she needed to look at it sometimes and remind herself about what mattered and why she was doing what she was doing.

Her train of thought was interrupted by the ringtone on her mobile. She felt a wave of warmth when David's name appeared on the display. He was due to come over in an hour or so and she wandered over to the wine rack to uncork a bottle to let it breathe.

"Hi baby, I miss you," she said.

There was silence for a moment and she realized that something was up. For an instant, she thought she might hear Jack's voice. Hear him say that David was dead.

"I'm going to struggle to make it tonight," David said. His voice was tense, almost a whisper. "Johanna is kicking up an almighty fuss. She's shouting and screaming. The girls are very upset. And scared."

Faye sighed and made an effort not to get annoyed. It wasn't his fault.

"I'm guessing it didn't go so well, telling her you'd met someone . . ."

"I didn't even have time to. Some acquaintance saw us together in town. It's mayhem here."

"So what does she want? You've already decided to get divorced. Surely it's none of her business if you're seeing someone?"

"I wish things were that simple. She thinks it's too soon and she's angry that she heard it from someone else. What picture we show to the outside world is something that really matters to Johanna. And we haven't told anyone else that we're getting divorced."

"But can't you come anyway? Surely it won't help for you to stay there and mess around trying to appease her?"

David sighed.

"She insists that I take the girls to riding camp tomorrow. She says they feel forgotten, that I think about sex more than I think about them."

"She's the one who's been stopping you from seeing them."

"I know," he said curtly, pausing for breath. "Sorry. The kids are my weak point and she knows that. I don't want them to end up getting caught in the middle. I hope you understand."

Faye sighed. She had to look at the situation rationally. Appease Johanna. At least for the time being. And David was sleeping in the guest room, so any attempts by Johanna to proposition him would be fruitless.

"It's okay. I miss you, but I understand. Kids always come first and that's how it has to be."

"Thanks," said David, and she heard the relief in his voice. "Thank you for making the hard stuff easier."

"See you tomorrow."

"Can't wait. I promise to make it up to you."

After the call, Faye sat there with her phone in her hand. Despite having reassured David that it was all fine and that she would be okay, she couldn't help feeling lonely and abandoned.

For the first time since they'd met, she felt disappointed in him, even though she knew that was unfair. David couldn't help that he'd had kids with a woman who'd turned out to be something other than he had first thought—no more so than Faye could be blamed for Jack. What kind of man—or human being—would he be if he didn't try to do what was best for his daughters? On the contrary, his love for them said a lot about the kind of person he was—someone Faye wanted to get to know far better.

Faye reached for the phone and messaged Kerstin, asking if she wanted to come over and have a bite to eat. She realized she was starving and didn't want to eat alone. Kerstin arrived within five minutes: one of the many benefits of living next door.

"I brought some cold cuts and cheese," she said. "I went past the market earlier today."

"Kerstin, you're an angel."

Faye poured a glass of Amarone and handed it to Kerstin, who sat down on the sofa.

"What's happened?"

"I don't want to talk about it," said Faye, filling her own glass.

The conversation with David was weighing on her mind and she needed to gather her thoughts.

"Are you up to talking about Revenge, then?" said Kerstin, reaching for a slice of prosciutto. "We can't afford not to."

"I guess so," said Faye. "We need to figure out who our allies are now. We won't be able to solve this on our own."

"You know who I think you should contact."

"And you know that I think you're crazy for even having that thought, let alone suggesting it . . ."

"Maybe we need a little craziness right now."

Faye nodded slowly. Despite it being summer, she had lit the fire in the living room and it was crackling merrily. She held her glass up toward the fire and contemplated the red wine glittering like rubies against a background of flames. She reached for some Taleggio. She finished chewing it before replying, buying herself time to think.

No matter how much she hated the idea, she knew Kerstin was right. They needed Ylva Lehndorf on board. But could she bear to let Ylva back into her life?

Before she had stolen Faye's husband, Ylva had been a rising star in publishing—an industry she had revolutionized in the space of just a few years. As a matter of fact, it had been Faye who had convinced Jack to hire Ylva—she'd had her eye on her ever since she'd been at the Stockholm School of Economics. That was why the betrayal when she had found them in bed together had been a double whammy. But now she couldn't help looking at the situation through fresh eyes. God only knew what Jack had told Ylva to turn her against Faye. Wasn't Ylva also one of Jack's victims? Like Faye, she had been infatuated and manipulated. Tamed and caged. And he had exploited her love—he had made her stop working, turned her into a suppressed little housewife. But the fact remained: Ylva Lehndorf was one of the most brilliant economists in Sweden and right now she had a red end-of-year sale sticker stuck to her forehead.

"Okay, I know what you think about Ylva. Perhaps that's the right way to go."

She took a sip of her wine before continuing. "I've been thinking about someone else who could help us."

"Oh?" said Kerstin, leaning in. "Who?"

"Alice Bergendahl."

"Alice? The bored, soon-to-be-divorced house-wife from Lidingö?" Kerstin laughed.

"Yes, exactly. Her."

During Faye's marriage to Jack, Alice had seemed like the personification of an unachievable ideal. She was the perfect housewife. Beautiful, loyal, and understanding. Sexy without being vulgar. She looked like a seductive pixie with tastefully done silicone implants and legs so long you could sail a ferry under them.

That was why Faye's surprise had been all the greater when she had been plunged into Alice and Henrik's divorce, courtesy of the gossip rags. Previously Alice wouldn't even go to the bathroom without consulting her husband, and then pausing en route to check whether he wanted sucking off before or after dinner. It had come as a shock when she suddenly turned up in the evening tabloids and celebrity magazines with an armada of divorce lawyers at her side. The protracted divorce had been the talk of the town and the hottest topic in Stockholm society for a couple of months.

Faye was curious about what had precipitated the

transformation of the previously accommodating Alice. But she already knew that there had been a rebellious streak in her, given that Alice was one of the women to have invested in Revenge without her husband's knowledge.

"Nothing creates unity like a common enemy," said Faye. "Although I can't understand why Henrik is doing this. He's done well for himself. He's landed on his feet, and more than clawed back whatever he might have lost."

Kerstin put a hand on Faye's shoulder. She squeezed it gently.

"It means nothing to a man like Henrik that he's made a success of himself again," she said. "You dragged him into a scandal; you harmed his reputation. For men like Jack and Henrik, that means you wounded their pride—their manhood. That's why he hates you. That's why he wants to take Revenge from you."

Faye nodded.

"You're probably right," she said. "But I think you're underestimating Alice. If there's anyone who knows his weak points, it'll be her."

"Alice. And Ylva," said Kerstin thoughtfully, reclining on the sofa. "That's probably not such a bad combination, you know."

Faye took another sip of wine. Maybe they were on to something. She looked at Kerstin.

"I need to speak to Irene too. I have to find out why she betrayed me."

Alice and Henrik Bergendahl's splendid mansion was at the very tip of Lidingö and had its own private sandy beach. A jetty ran out into the water and beside it there was a large motorboat bobbing up and down, glittering in the sun.

"I'm glad you called," said Alice. "I've actually missed you."

They were sitting in a lounge suite on the enormous terrace just six feet from the shoreline. On the table in front of them, Alice had set down four or five bottles from Henrik's wine cellar. She was wearing a simple red dress and her long blond hair was in a chignon.

When Alice had first opened the door and seen Faye, she had looked shocked. Her embrace had been stiff, but once they had sat down outside, the conversation had begun to flow more easily. Now it almost felt as if she were talking to an old friend.

"It's pretty lonely some evenings," Alice continued.

"Where are Henrik and the kids?"

"We've got an apartment on Danderydsgatan too—he's had rooms decorated for them there."

Alice leaned forward, read the label on one of the bottles, nodded, and then reached for the corkscrew.

"We find ourselves in new times," said Faye.

"Better times. Well . . . Sorry. Of course I didn't mean that." It took a split second for Faye to realize that Alice was talking about Julienne's death. "I'm really sorry about what happened, and I think about her every day."

"Thank you," Faye said softly, accepting the glass that Alice held out to her. "Let's talk about something else. Why don't you tell me what happened with Henrik? The uncensored version, if you don't mind."

Alice took a sip and then nodded slowly.

"Well, as you know, I was **fine** with the fact that Henrik was notoriously unfaithful to me," she began. "So long as he kept it tidy—on the side—and it didn't affect me or the kids, I considered it a price I was willing to pay. Successful men are unfaithful. That's what I thought. Sometimes I told myself it was the very key to their success. You know, the hunger. For money, power, and, well . . . women. I suppose I wasn't entirely innocent toward the end either, as you know."

Her well-shaped lips bent into a knowing smile and Faye remembered the hot young guy with the tattoos who Alice had been seeing once a week, while telling Henrik she was attending Pilates classes.

But then there was a hint of sorrow in Alice's eyes.

"In August last year we hired a new au pair. She was the daughter of one of Henrik's childhood friends, one of his biggest financiers and clients. She was seventeen, in her senior year, and needed cash for a trip to Rhodes with her friends. You know the type. She rode a moped. Tossed her hair and was always chewing gum. Probably had Hello Kitty pants from H&M. The thought never even crossed my mind."

Alice shook her head.

"What happened?"

"I came home one afternoon after she had picked up the kids. I parked, got out of the car, and could hear the kids rampaging around the garden. I came around the corner and discovered they were on their own. The bathroom is downstairs and the window was open. From inside I could hear . . . well, you know . . ."

Alice moistened her lips, drained the final drops from her glass, and pushed it away. Faye felt for her. She had walked in and found Jack with someone else, so she knew that nothing in life could prepare someone for that kind of shock. She remembered being frozen to the spot and then storming into the room in tears. Jack had announced he wanted a divorce, and Faye had begged him to stay—while Ylva Lehndorf and Jack were still naked in bed. She had promised to forget. Get her act together. If only he didn't leave her.

She shivered at the memories welling up.

"I thought I'd be angry, crushed. But instead I realized I had to act. Immediately. I got out my phone and filmed them through the crack in the window."

"That video . . ."

". . . is worth a couple of hundred million kronor to the right blackmailer." Alice laughed. "And I took a couple of stills just to be sure. Zoomed in good and proper. Faye, you have no idea. I'm getting half of everything. If I don't, then Sweden is going to see rather more of financier Henrik Bergendahl than they would like. And I'm very doubtful that Sten Stolpe will want to carry on doing business with Henrik after seeing him taking the apple of his eye from behind."

She shrugged slightly.

Faye leaned forward.

"Why are you still here in the house, given what happened with Henrik and the au pair?"

"Because it's the house of my dreams. I've always been happy here. I'm not going to let him take that away from me. But I don't use the bathroom. Once the divorce goes through, I'm going to have it converted into a walk-in closet."

It was a still, light evening. A fish splashed down in the water and Alice turned toward the noise, stroking her own arm in a slow movement. She suddenly looked infinitely sad.

Faye cleared her throat gently.

"Is everything okay, Alice?"

"I don't know."

"Do you miss Henrik?"

Alice laughed and stared at her.

"Are you crazy? I miss the kids when they're not with me. But building your life around a man, waiting for him to come home, only seeing yourself in his reflection, by his side . . . being more a member of the household staff than his partner. No, I don't miss that. It's just that the days without the kids are lonely. The only people I spend any time with are my divorce lawyers."

"I hope they're good-looking at least. Fuckable."

"Considering what I'm paying them, they should look like Greek gods. Alas. The chubby, bald look seems to be du jour in legal circles."

"Oh, that's a pity. But here's to you," said Faye with a laugh. "You need to find a man. I'm sure we can sort you out."

"Yes, after all these years with Henrik's micropenis, it's about time I was reminded of what it feels like when it's actually in there," Alice said. "Cheers."

Faye laughed so hard she nearly spurted wine

through her nose. This new Alice was one she could be friends with.

They brought their wineglasses together, and Faye echoed her loudly. Both Henrik and Jack had always admonished them for saying cheers in that way.

"Vulgar," the two of them said together in put-on voices and then collapsed in laughter again.

They did it again just for the hell of it. Faye took a swig. It was an exquisite wine.

"You have to fill your days with something, Alice. Otherwise you'll go under. No disrespect to your divorce lawyers, but you need something to fight for. Everyone does."

Alice nodded slowly. Her gaze swept thoughtfully across the water.

"I met Henrik when I was young and let him deal with everything to do with money. I've spent my entire working life as a well-paid, beautiful housemaid. We're being honest with each other, right? Well, the thing I'm good at is throwing parties, smiling at my husband's guests and making them feel comfortable. That was my area of expertise for all those years. Who would hire me?"

Faye shook her head. She sympathized with Alice. And in practical terms, the description had been accurate. But Alice had left out the most important bit.

"You're a social genius, Alice. You know what

makes the men in power tick because you've had them all around here as guests. And you know how women work. The rich ones who can pay their own way. That's not the kind of knowledge you pick up at university. It's actually worth a great deal."

"To whom?"

"To me. And Revenge."

Alice stared at her for a moment and then burst into peals of laughter.

"Honestly, Faye, I know you've had a glass of wine, but what on earth do you need me for? I appreciate the gesture, but you don't need to do me any favors just because you feel sorry for me. I'm worthless, but I'll manage." She made a sweeping gesture with her wineglass. "Besides, you've got Kerstin—there's no one who can compete with super-efficient Kerstin."

Typical women, Faye thought to herself. Selling themselves short, unable to see their own worth. That was how we were raised. It's what the world taught us. And the world is run by men who benefit from us wandering around in it seeing our worth only in relation to them.

She fixed her gaze on Alice.

"Don't say that about yourself—don't say you're worthless. If you repeat it too often, it'll stick and become the truth. And then the same will happen to your daughter. Kerstin is barely working part-time these days. She got involved with an orphanage in

India—and a rather attractive man called Bengt who's been introducing her to the delights of Mumbai—and now she goes out there as often as she can. I don't begrudge her that. She deserves a fresh chance. But I need someone. I need you."

She raised her glass to her mouth without letting Alice out of her gaze.

"Do you think I built Revenge by being nice? Handing out jobs as favors to my friends? No, I would never hire someone to be nice. I would never give a job to someone whose input didn't immediately generate cash. You haven't been to college—so what? Academic education isn't worth a damn in real life. You know that. You've talked to those men with the fancy diplomas from American colleges and known you were smarter than them. You don't understand figures, but you understand the world and the people operating in it. So quit feeling worthless. You're already committed any-way, because you were one of the initial investors in Revenge."

Alice looked at her with a raised eyebrow.

"Cut the crap, Faye. Why exactly are you here?"

She folded her arms and waited for an answer. Faye looked at her appreciatively. Alice really was as smart as she had hoped.

She took a deep breath. "Someone is trying to take Revenge away from me. I'm on the verge of losing everything I've built."

"Surely you've still got capital?" Alice said with a frown. "Since the sale?"

"Yes, I'll be fine financially. More than. But that's not the point. Revenge is me—and Revenge is Chris too."

Alice nodded. She sipped her wine and looked down toward the water. The tranquility was disturbed only by the call of a bird in a small copse of trees.

Faye let her words sink in. After a while, Alice turned back to her.

"Who's buying up the shares?"

"I didn't know at first. It was hidden in a tangle of buyers from Sweden and abroad. But eventually we managed to see through it all and find the person behind it."

"Henrik," said Alice.

Faye looked at her in surprise.

"Did you know?"

"No, no," said Alice, waving a hand. "If I had, then I would have warned you. But I'm not surprised. I don't think you realize how much he hates you. For a while, I thought about getting in touch to let you know how pissed off Henrik was, but you . . . you had other stuff on your plate. Besides, I couldn't see him acting on it. Henrik talks a big game, always has."

Faye gazed out of the window where the setting sun cast a golden glow over the water. The spectacular view was lost on her; she was too busy trying to decide how much she should reveal. In the end she decided to put all her cards on the table bar one. Alice didn't know that Julienne was alive. And it had to stay that way.

She poured more wine for herself and for Alice.

"He's very close to succeeding. I wasn't on my guard. At first I was . . . wrapped up in grief and anger. Then I let myself relax. Believed it was over."

Alice nodded and was silent for a moment. Then she raised her glass in a toast.

"I assume you're looking for a partner in crime. It would be fucking amazing to upset that arrogant bastard's plans."

Faye laughed and they clinked glasses merrily. Perhaps there was still some hope for the sisterhood, despite the betrayal of the investors.

Alice had invited her to sleep over, but Faye wanted to get back to the apartment and brainstorm ideas with Kerstin. However, when the taxi headed past Jungfrugatan she asked the driver to pull over. This was where Irene Ahrnell lived. Faye had been around to her place for a magnificent dinner after the Revenge launch and she recognized the building.

For a moment, Faye hesitated. She pictured the beautiful woman in her mind's eye. Always composed. Always dignified. How could she? Then she paid the driver and got out.

Faye pressed Irene's buzzer at the main door.

It rang for a long time and she thought perhaps Irene wasn't at home. She checked her watch: almost ten thirty. Perhaps it was too late to be dropping in on her. She was debating whether to press the buzzer again when quick footsteps behind her made her turn around. It was only a jogger in colorful running tights, but Faye's heart was racing. Since Jack's escape, she had tried to avoid being alone in the street at night, but stopping at Irene's had been an impulsive act. All at once, every small movement at the corner of her eye seemed threatening. She pressed the buzzer hard again. This time Irene answered.

"Hi, it's Faye. I know you probably don't want to talk to me . . . but can I come up?"

Faye held her breath. Kerstin had warned her not to have this discussion with Irene before they had dealt with the more pressing issues. But for Faye, speaking to Irene was pressing. Granted, her holding had already been sold, but she liked Irene. Trusted her. She couldn't understand how this had happened. And she needed to understand. Perhaps it was also the key to what was happening, even if Kerstin didn't think so.

"Irene?" said Faye. "Please?"

The door whirred, and, throwing a final glance over her shoulder, Faye hurried inside.

The elevator was old, cramped, and infinitely slow. When it reached the third floor and she drew aside the rattling black grille she saw Irene waiting for her at the door. She was wearing a gray lounge set, had no makeup on, and had a terry-cloth headband holding back her short hair. The shine on her face gave away that she had been in the middle of her skin-care ritual before bed.

"Come in," Irene said in a low voice.

It was clear from her closed face that she didn't want to talk to Faye, but she had let her in at any rate.

"Would you like a cup of tea?"

"Not really," said Faye with a grimace.

"I don't blame you."

Irene went into the kitchen, got out two wineglasses, and opened a bottle of Chablis from the fridge. Faye followed her into the spacious living room where they'd had their aperitifs before that dinner. Lofty ceiling, stucco.

They sat down on a sofa covered in a large Josef Frank print. Faye wondered how to begin, but Irene solved that problem for her.

"I . . . I was meaning to get in touch with you. I realize how this must look. And believe me, I haven't slept for almost a week. But . . ."

"But what?" said Faye, unable to stop her wounded emotions from creeping into her voice.

Irene delayed her answer. She turned her wineglass around in her hand, then put it down on the marble coffee table, stood up, and bought herself some time by turning on some lamps.

Faye didn't push her. She saw at once how haggard Irene was and all the anger drained from her. Something had happened and she owed it to Irene to give her the chance to explain herself.

Eventually, Irene sat down next to her on the sofa and picked up her wineglass. She settled in the corner, drew her legs up under her, and took a deep breath.

"It was the morning after the day of our lunch. A man was waiting for me outside the door on the street. He had an envelope for me that he asked me to look inside. And he said that once I'd looked inside the envelope I should expect a call. I took the envelope and he vanished before I had time to react. At first I laughed at it. It felt like something from some dumb spy movie. But then I got up to the apartment and I . . . I opened the envelope."

Irene took a mouthful of wine.

"What was inside?"

Irene didn't answer. She blinked a few times before finally meeting Faye's gaze.

"The envelope contained my secrets."

"Your secrets? I thought your life was an open book."

"That's what everyone thinks. I've managed to craft my own background, my own story that everyone believes. It's not hard, you know. Drop in the occasional anecdote. The odd planted story. A cohesive media narrative. No one asks any questions."

Faye nodded. She of all people knew that. If only Irene knew. The media's basic task—other than reporting—was to scrutinize critically. But no one in Sweden ever scrutinized a good story. And both Irene and Faye happened to be excellent at just that: good stories.

"I didn't grow up in Bromma. My parents weren't lawyers. My mom was the only parent I knew. An alcoholic bitch called Sonja. I hated her with all my guts. But I repeated her mistakes. Ended up in the wrong crowd. Drank too much. Took . . . other stuff too. Got pregnant. Couldn't, didn't want to, keep the kid. So I gave it up for adoption. I have no idea where it is today. Well, I had no idea. There were photos of her inside the envelope. She's grown up now."

Irene laughed when she realized what she had said.

"Of course she's grown up now. Stupid observation. She . . . she's around forty. A prosecutor, in Jönköping, of all places. Husband, two kids. Happy life—at least, judging by her Instagram handle, which I've been stalking like mad ever since."

"And you don't want to ruin her life . . ."

Irene met Faye's gaze. An ocean of pain could be read in it. Faye's anger vanished. She understood. Completely. You did what you had to. To protect your own.

"No, I don't want to ruin her life. So I sacrificed you. That's the hard truth, I can't hide it."

Irene had aged before Faye's very eyes. They

weren't close enough friends for Faye to put a hand on hers to comfort her, but she set down the glass and clasped her hands in her lap.

She spoke calmly to Irene—she wanted her to take in every word she said.

"I understand you. I completely understand you, and I would have done the same thing. And I'm guessing you're not the only one to have sold your shares who received an envelope like that. I have to confess I've been feeling hurt, upset, and confused. It's felt like a knife in the back. But now I understand what happened and I'll say it again: I would have done exactly what you did. You've given me an important piece of the puzzle. Thank you."

"It doesn't feel like there's much to thank me for," said Irene in a muffled voice.

"There is," said Faye, standing up. "Now I've got to go home. And it's time for you to go to bed."

Irene accompanied Faye to the door.

"I've asked around about Henrik's company since all this happened," she said.

Faye raised her eyebrows.

"Oh?"

"The way they treat women there," said Irene, making a face. "They're just eye candy, they never get to rise through the ranks, they don't listen to them. It's as if they haven't changed with the times."

Faye sighed. Hearing Irene say this was like a reminder of all her years with Jack.

"I'm not really surprised," she said.

Irene shook her head.

"Nor am I. But, Faye, I'm so relieved to have spoken to you," she said. "I've been feeling so awful."

Faye laid her hands on Irene's shoulders.

"First: there are no hard feelings on my side. And second: Are you using Revenge's creams, or are you cheating on us?"

Irene grinned.

"Cheating. I'm old school. I only use Nivea, like a grandma."

"Fucking Nivea," said Faye, giving her a hug.

As she went down in the tiny elevator, she could see Irene through the grille. They waved to each other. Faye leaned her head back against the mirror in the elevator. Irene had given her an answer but she wasn't sure that it helped her.

FJÄLLBACKA—THEN

I was probably the only person in Fjällbacka who didn't like sailing. The sea scared me. That was why I was surprised to hear myself say yes when Sebastian asked whether I wanted to come sailing with him, Tomas, and Roger.

Although Sebastian had visited me in the night again several times, he had been very friendly toward me some days. Like he used to be. When it was us against the world.

Maybe, I thought to myself, the outing was a way of apologizing. Setting things right. I wanted to see it like that. Wanted to forget. For things to be like they were before the door to my bedroom had opened that night.

The island we were bound for was called Yxön and it was uninhabited.

The sailboat was called **Marika** and it belonged to Roger's dad.

We assembled on the jetty at nine o'clock that morning. It was a Friday. Tomas and Roger arrived fifteen minutes later dragging a bag, a tent, and four crates of beer. We climbed aboard. Roger was big and taciturn. He answered only when spoken to, but he seemed like a gentle giant. Kind but stupid. He always stayed close to Tomas, as if watching over him like some kind of bodyguard.

Roger passed a beer to Sebastian, who opened it and took a couple of gulps. Sebastian had never drunk in front of me, but I didn't want to make him uncomfortable in front of his friends by pointing that out. So I remained silent. I sat down in the bow, pulled my legs up to my chest, and stared out to sea as we cast away.

I didn't dare look at Tomas. I felt his eyes on me and tried to pretend not to notice. There was something suave about him. It always felt as if he would be more at home in the big city. Perhaps it was because his parents were rich—at least by the standards of Fjällbacka—and his mom placed great emphasis on the right look; she spent a lot on his clothes. Today he was wearing beige shorts and a white polo shirt. Sitting close to me, he was the most beautiful thing I'd ever seen.

"Want one?" said Tomas, proffering a beer.

"Is there enough beer to go around?" said Sebastian.

The fact that he had been kinder of late didn't mean he was kind. He was standing there holding a cigarette in his hand. I was not used to seeing him smoke.

"No reason Matilda can't have a beer," said Tomas. "We've got loads with us."

I took the can. Smiled. But still didn't dare meet his gaze. Perhaps I would meet someone like Tomas when I moved to the city.

I had saved up some money working part-time in a patisserie. Every krona I earned was going toward leaving Fjällbacka.

The beer tasted bitter and I made an effort not to grimace. But after forcing myself to drink half a can, a warmth began to radiate from my stomach and I began to relax. The more I drank, the better the warm beer tasted.

"Thanks, by the way," I said suddenly, feeling a new boldness as I looked Tomas in the eyes for the first time.

"Thanks for what?" he said, grinning.

"You helped me the other week when I dropped my books."

"It was nothing. It was that dickhead Stefan who tripped you up, right?"

I nodded and Tomas passed me another beer.

"Don't worry about those inbred morons," he said, the shimmer of the sea in his eyes.

I was surprised that Sebastian didn't interrupt to say something self-important, but when I looked over at him I saw that he was lying on the seats with his eyes shut. He appeared to have fallen asleep. I was suddenly embarrassed. I could feel Tomas's eyes on me.

Hope fluttered in my breast.

The black Mercedes pulled over on Götgatan and Faye paid before getting out.

The sun was shining, making the rooftops of Södermalm and the distant Globen arena shimmer beautifully. A busker's electric guitar whined mournfully.

Faye made her way through the crowds to the Muggen café. She stopped a little way off and tried to see inside the dark venue. The interior décor comprised worn-out sofas and armchairs in an array of colors and fabrics. On the walls, there were old paintings in gilded frames without any discernible theme or intention behind them.

Just as she was about to cross the street, she caught sight of a face inside that she recognized. But it wasn't Ylva, it was the police officer Yvonne Ingvarsson. Her heart skipped a beat when she realized that the person the policewoman was speaking to was Ylva.

Faye quickly moved inside a stuffy convenience

store and sat down on a bar stool at the counter in the window. From here she had a view of the door of the Muggen café.

Yvonne's snooping was getting increasingly intrusive. Although Ylva had taken Jack away from her, Faye had won him back. She had secretly filmed them screwing and sent the footage to Ylva. Then she had crushed both Ylva and Jack. Ylva didn't know anything that could hurt Faye, but her animosity posed a genuine risk. Right now, it was even more important to win her over to Faye's side.

After five minutes, Yvonne left the café. Faye stood and waited a moment before crossing the street and opening the door to Muggen.

Ylva was standing behind an old-fashioned cash register that was clearly there for decorative purposes rather than functionality, since a small sign informed patrons that the café was cashless. Her hair was up in a chignon and a tight black T-shirt was stretched across her boobs. Two people were in front of Faye in the line, and Ylva processed them quickly and efficiently.

Finally, it was Faye's turn. Ylva gasped when she caught sight of her.

"A coffee and a cheese and ham sandwich, please."

Ylva nodded and prepared Faye's order.

"That'll be . . ." Ylva coughed. "That'll be eighty-nine kronor."

Faye tapped her Amex Black on the card reader.

"I assumed you'd show up sooner or later."

"We've got a mutual problem," said Faye.

Ylva nodded, but her eyes wandered to the people standing behind Faye.

"I've got to take orders from the people who are waiting, but take a seat and I'll come over when I get a gap."

Faye nodded, took her coffee and sandwich, and went to a seat at a table for two by the window.

She looked at her phone. David had messaged. Every time she saw his name on the display her heart leaped for joy.

With a smile, she opened the message and read it.

I couldn't help myself when I saw this. It's so you. And I took a chance on you liking it.

Faye pulled up the picture he had sent. And gasped. David had managed to identify the single photographic work in the whole world that she wanted the most. It was a photo of Faye Dunaway, in the pool at the Beverly Hills Hotel, taken by Terry O'Neill, the morning after she had won an Oscar. How could he have known? How could he know her so well after such a short period of time? Faye couldn't help cracking a big smile.

She put away her phone and helped herself to a napkin, which she doodled on with a fountain pen. Then she got her laptop out of her bag, put it on top of the napkin, and opened her inbox. She didn't look up from her emails until Ylva sat down on the chair opposite her.

Ylva brushed the crumbs off her top and then smoothed it out. She didn't quite meet Faye's gaze.

"Has Jack been in contact with you?" Faye asked.

Ylva shook her head vigorously.

"No. And I don't think he will. Why would he? I didn't mean a thing to him."

She said it so straightforwardly, as if it were obvious that Jack had never loved her. Faye didn't want to think about what her life with him had been.

"He hasn't been in touch from prison, either?"

"No. I don't think he's at all interested—not in me, not in Nora."

Faye looked through the window. She rarely thought about the fact that Julienne had a little sister who was now almost two.

"How are you getting on?"

"Surely you can see for yourself?" said Ylva, holding out her hands. "I lost everything after Jack. No one would hire me, and how was I supposed to do my old job when I also had a baby to look after? But I'm getting by. We're getting by."

Faye took a sip of coffee. She was convinced that Ylva was right. She would manage. She was a survivor.

"Are you afraid?" Ylva asked.

Faye nodded slowly.

"Yes, I am. Jack killed our daughter. And he hates me. For testifying against him and for moving on. Becoming successful. For having everything that he had."

Ylva looked over toward the register, but there was no customer waiting for assistance.

"I'm sorry," she said. "For everything. For what we did to you. For me being stupid and naïve and going along with everything he said. And I'm so, so sorry about what happened to Julienne. Now that I've got Nora, I can't even begin to imagine . . ."

Her voice broke and Faye realized that she felt sympathy for the woman in front of her. They had both been tricked by Jack. They had both paid the price. The past was water under the bridge.

"Are you happy serving people coffee?" Faye asked.

Ylva fidgeted on her chair.

"It's my job—no better or worse than anything else."

"You've got a work ethic and you're conscientious," said Faye. "I'm pretty sure that your bosses have never had a better employee. You're a perfectionist, and you should know that I respect you."

She picked up the computer, pulled out the napkin with the doodles, and pushed it across the table. Ylva bent forward and examined the napkin suspiciously.

"What's this?" she said curtly.

"A contract of employment."

"Oh come on," said Ylva, her face turning red. "You won, Faye. You don't have to come here and rub it in my face. I get it. I lost and I shouldn't have done what I did."

Faye put her hand on the laptop and slowly closed it.

"In my inbox, I've got almost one hundred and fifty emails from people who want to invest in Revenge ahead of our expansion in the USA. Mostly men. I need someone who can do finance— properly—to go through the proposals and check out the investors. I want to know who I'm getting into bed with."

"Why me?"

"Because you're the best woman for the job. And because I believe I can match the wage they pay you in this joint, thus bagging myself one of Sweden's best economists for a song."

Ylva looked dumbfounded.

"But . . . I took your husband."

"Yes, I forgot to thank you for that," said Faye, smiling briefly. "I then stole him back, even though it was only to con him out of his company. The way I see it, it's one all."

"I just don't get what I have to offer."

"This is how it is. This is information that I don't want getting out, but I'm going to take a chance and trust you."

"You can," said Ylva gravely, and Faye believed her.

"Revenge is well on the way to being bought out. It began secretly, but it's now out in the open."

"Bought out? But who—"

"Henrik Bergendahl."

"Jack's former partner?"

"Yes."

Ylva nodded. Processing the information she had been given.

"He must hate you."

"Yes, even more than he hates Alice."

"Alice?"

Faye waved her hand dismissively.

"It's a long story. They're in the middle of a divorce, and a dirty one at that. Henrik fucked the au pair."

"Who hasn't Henrik fucked?" Ylva muttered.

The bell above the door rang but the person seemed to change their mind and left again.

"The problem is that Henrik has capital. Lots of capital. Enough to be able to afford a takeover. And I don't think this is some sudden impulse—I think he's been planning it for a long time."

"Isn't there something you can do? Have you checked all your agreements? Spoken to the shareholders? There's nothing improper that's happened that you can leverage?"

Faye smiled with satisfaction.

"That's exactly why I'm here," she said. "I need someone who can ask exactly those questions, think like this, and help me find answers. And then some."

Ylva shook her head.

"I still can't wrap my head around the fact that you're offering me a job."

The bell rang again. This time a young woman stepped in and headed for the counter. Ylva got up.

Faye also got to her feet, gathered her things, and handed over a business card.

"Get in touch if you're interested. But there's one condition you need to fulfill before the job's yours. I need you to draft a plan to help me stop the people who want to take over my company. Consider it an admission exam."

She picked up the napkin and pressed it into Ylva's hand.

"This is fully valid. As soon as you sign, you'll become Revenge's finance director. Providing you can give me the information I need. And contact me if you hear from Jack. We both have to keep one eye looking over our shoulders. He's dangerous."

She raised her hand in a wave, turned on her heel, and left the café.

She knew deep down that she was dreaming, yet Faye was unable to extricate herself from the dream. It had been happening a lot of late. Not always the same dream. But the feeling was always the same. And it was always unpleasantly realistic.

She'd come home from the maternity ward with Julienne. Still in her bubble. Still completely absorbed by the little being who had completely possessed her from the moment she opened her eyes for the first time.

She was worn out, tender, exhausted. Since they had come home, she had done the nights with Julienne alone, and she hadn't slept more than an hour or two at a time.

Nevertheless, Jack thought it was a good idea to ask her to host a big business dinner for key investors. As always, she did what Jack wanted.

She prepared for the dinner for days while trying to meet Julienne's needs at the same time. She wanted to be beautiful at the dinner, but nothing in her wardrobe fit her new-mom body. Her tummy was soft and bulging, her boobs were huge and filled with milk. Eventually, sweating, she managed to squeeze into a kaftanesque garment she had bought for one of their trips to the sun. Underneath the kaftan, she was wearing pregnancy leggings with elastic at the waist and a pregnancy bra with inserts to soak up leaking milk.

When Jack caught sight of her, he inspected her from head to toe with a look of disgust.

The guests arrived and Faye and Jack received them in the hall. The men had small, half-starved women with them. Size o clothing and cheek fillers to make sure they didn't look hollow-faced and haggard. Jack's gaze moved from them to her, and she could tell she wasn't living up to the ideal he wanted to present.

Halfway through the starter, Julienne woke up. Faye got up to go and see to her, but Jack's hand on her arm made her sit back down again. She looked at him, pleading, but his gaze was stern.

Faye smiled stiffly at their guests while her daughter screamed in the nursery. Some of the women looked at her sympathetically, while the men chuckled and made comments like: "It's good to let them air their lungs a bit."

Eventually, Jack gave in to Julienne. He brought her out in his arms. Her face was swollen from sobbing and her pajamas were wet with tears. Jack's face was stiff with anger, as if Faye had made Julienne cry. Without saying a word, he passed her over to Faye, and she gratefully pressed Julienne's little body to hers. Jack's fury vibrated against her. The men's laughter echoed between the walls of their beautiful dining room, unaffected. But the women's apologetic, sympathetic gazes were burned indelibly onto her soul.

What had she done? How had she ended up here?

Faye sat up in bed, gasping. It was just a dream. But Jack's gaze was still burning within her. She slowly lay back down, her pulse pounding in her ears. Jack was always there. She would never get him out of her dreams. He was always present. A part of her life for eternity.

Faye put her mobile back in her bag and looked at the range of wristwatches the fawning salesman was showing off. The police had just called for the daily check that everything was all right with her.

The watch that caught her attention was a Patek Philippe and it cost three hundred and fifty thousand kronor. Faye was aware that it was madness to buy it for a man she had known for only a matter of weeks. But it felt so right. She smiled at the thought of the Faye Dunaway print, now hanging on her living room wall, and nodded at the salesman in reply to his question about whether she'd made a decision.

"I'll take this one," she said, pointing at the watch. She handed over her Amex Black.

The salesman clapped his hands.

"An excellent choice," he exclaimed.

The situation with David's wife, Johanna, had begun to get under her skin. She couldn't help but notice how badly it was affecting David, even if he was trying to be stoic. Johanna was apparently incapable of accepting that he had moved on and was trying to keep him in her life at any cost. She still refused to sign divorce papers, despite David having agreed to give her half of everything—even though they had a prenup and he didn't have to give her a penny of his fortune. Faye admired him for that.

Faye said no when asked whether the watch was to be engraved. While she was signing the sheaf of papers the man had pushed across the counter to her, the mobile in her bag began to vibrate. She didn't recognize the number and at first she wasn't going to answer. What if it was Jack?

Then she got angry at herself—she couldn't let fear gain the upper hand. When she answered, it turned out to be a reporter from **Aftonbladet**. Faye sighed. She changed numbers regularly to stay one step ahead of the press, but somehow they always managed to reach her. The reporter introduced himself as Peter Sjöberg. Faye vaguely recollected his face from his online bylines. He was one of the hacks who had written column inch after column inch about Alice and Henrik's divorce.

"I'm obviously calling about your ex-husband's spectacular escape," the journalist said cheerfully, as if calling with a survey about which strawberries tasted best.

Faye frowned. She knew she shouldn't speak to him, but she couldn't help but be curious about the call. Reporters usually had information they couldn't publish for ethical reasons, but that didn't prevent them from sharing it in phone calls.

"Has he contacted you?" Peter Sjöberg asked searchingly.

"No," Faye said truthfully.

"Are you scared? Given your . . . history?"

"I don't want to answer that."

"Okay. I understand."

There was a brief silence on the line—she could hear someone whispering something in the background.

"Was there anything else?" she asked.

"Not really. Well, yes. Do you know the name . . ."

The reporter's voice was drowned out by the obsequious wristwatch salesman babbling on. He hadn't noticed she was in the middle of a phone call since she was using a headset. Faye pointed to her ear and the man held up his hands apologetically.

"Sorry, what did you say?"

"Well, I was just asking whether the name Gösta Berg was familiar to you?"

It was like a knife to her stomach. She went absolutely cold. She met her own gaze in the mirror behind the counter. She saw the terror in it.

"Why do you ask?" she managed to say, supporting herself against the counter.

"That's the name of the man Jack escaped with. I mostly wanted to ask you whether they knew each other. But I assume it was just coincidence—the opportunity presented itself and off they went together."

Faye ended the call, her hands trembling.

She handled the remainder of the purchase process for the watch mechanically. Sweat had broken out on her neck. When she had finished the transaction, she staggered out onto Biblioteksgatan and pushed her sunglasses onto her nose. She walked as quickly as her weak legs would carry her, resolving to go straight home and call her mother in Italy. How would she react when she found out that her husband had escaped from prison where he had been serving a life sentence for her murder?

Before Faye stepped off the street and through her door, she looked around anxiously. All of a sudden, it felt as if she were being watched from all directions. She quickly slipped inside and shut the door behind her, hard.

She squeezed into the elevator and leaned forward to examine her face in the mirror. She took a deep breath. Her pulse was no longer racing. Her heart was beating quite calmly in her rib cage. The elevator came to a halt on the fifth floor with a judder. Faye pulled the grille to one side and stepped out. The next moment she realized that she was not alone.

FJÄLLBACKA—THEN

I didn't understand what would happen as I sat there curled up in the bow of **Marika** with my arms around my shins, staring out to sea. Sebastian had woken and was sitting up. The boys were smoking. Drinking beer. Sometimes they looked toward me, eyeing me as they talked. I wondered what they were saying.

Tomas came over and passed me an open can of Pripps Blå. It was half-empty and lukewarm.

"Thanks."

I took a big gulp while holding my breath to avoid the smell.

"You keep it," he said when I held out the can. "There's plenty more."

He left me on my own after that. I opened a book I'd brought with me—**Moby-Dick**, since we were at sea. I also had **Robinson Crusoe** in my bag. It was an old copy that had once belonged to my grandfather. I drank warm, stale beer and read my book.

After an hour or so, the boys shouted that we had arrived. I raised my gaze and saw Yxön. A rocky, forested green oasis in the midst of all this blue. We moored beside some rocks, lowered the rubber dinghy, loaded it up with our backpacks and provisions. Roger lit a cigarette while rowing.

I put my hand to my breast and felt the necklace hanging there. I ran my fingers over the silver tears that felt so fragile even though they were pretty robust, according to Mom. The island grew larger before my eyes and I shuddered as a cold shiver ran down my spine.

Faye stared at the woman standing outside her front door. She had been on the verge of crying out in surprise. She took a deep breath as Ylva Lehndorf raised a hand in greeting.

"Sorry, did I scare you?"

"A little." Faye juggled with her keys. She stuck them in the lock and opened the door and security grille. "Come in."

Her body was trembling as she kicked off her shoes. Once Ylva had stepped into the apartment, Faye quickly locked the front door.

"What a beautiful home," Ylva said in a low voice.

"Thank you, I'm happy here. Come in. I've had a really shitty day, so despite the early hour, I thought I'd have a glass of wine. Do you want one?"

Ylva nodded with a wry smile.

"Good," said Faye, leading her into the kitchen.

She got out a bottle of Chardonnay, two wine-glasses, and a corkscrew. Good God, she was going to be an alcoholic by the time this was all over. Her wine consumption was getting beyond all reasonable measures, but right now she needed either wine or Valium to survive. And at that particular moment, she definitely preferred a well-chilled Chardonnay. She would have to juice-cleanse when it was all over, or check herself into the La Prairie Spa in Switzerland for a week of major detox. She opened the freezer and took out a bag of ice, which she poured into a metal bucket and passed to Ylva.

"Let's sit on the terrace."

Faye poured the wine and they sat in silence, staring out across the rooftops of Östermalm while sipping their drinks.

"Aren't you wondering why I'm here?" Ylva asked tentatively.

"No," said Faye, without dropping her eyes from the view. "I assume you're here because you've realized that my offer is too good to refuse."

Ylva nodded.

"If you still want to hire me, then I gratefully accept the job as finance director of Revenge. And I've got the plan you asked for."

Faye felt a tingle of expectation, but first she had something even more pressing to raise with Ylva. Something that overshadowed everything else.

"Has Jack still not been in touch with you?" she asked.

Ylva shook her head quickly.

"And you?"

"No."

Faye's mobile phone rang loudly, sounding across the terrace, and made both of them jump. They smiled at each other shamefacedly. Faye assumed it was another journalist and put her iPhone upside down. When a text arrived to say someone had left a message, she called her voicemail.

"Hello, Faye, my name is Johanna Schiller and I'm married to David. I'd like you to call me as soon as possible on this number. We need to talk."

The voice sounded tense, almost neurotic, Faye thought to herself. Ylva stared at her quizzically.

"Is everything all right?" she asked cautiously.

Faye considered her answer carefully. It ought to be okay to tell her about the affair with David—after all, he was divorced . . . or would have been if Johanna hadn't strung out the process. She wasn't proud of being the other woman, but Ylva of all people ought to understand.

She summarized the events of recent weeks and Ylva listened with an intent expression.

"Do you have a guilty conscience?" she asked when Faye had finished her account.

Faye thought about this for a while as she drank her wine.

"I care about him a lot, and he feels the same way. We're two adults. Obviously it would have been preferable if the divorce was finalized, but she refuses to let go. Are David and I meant to stay away from each other? No, I don't have a guilty conscience."

Faye reached for the bottle and refilled their glasses.

"What are you going to do? Are you going to call back?"

Ylva nodded at the phone.

"No. It's not up to me to solve this. That's for David. I don't know exactly how much he's told her. Unfortunately, she found out about us before he had time to say anything, but I didn't think she knew it was me in particular that he had been seeing. Either way, what good would talking to her do? It might just make things worse."

She looked at Ylva with curiosity.

"Did you have a guilty conscience?"

Ylva took a swallow of wine. Faye admired her calm—the self-confidence she radiated. Faye's tone had been neutral, but she really wanted to know. She suppressed the memory of Ylva and Jack's naked bodies in her bedroom. It was surreal to be sitting with the same woman talking about the moment that had—perhaps more than any other—changed Faye's life.

"Yes and no," Ylva said thoughtfully. "I mean, at times Jack made you out to be a monster, at times a doormat. And I was in love. Fuck me, I was so in love. And before I knew it, he had changed me in the same way he changed you. I didn't even notice it. It was as if I were a toy—a hollow tin soldier with a single purpose: to make the little boy inside Jack Adelheim happy."

Faye nodded slowly.

A police helicopter passed over their heads, going south.

She got up and went to the balustrade. Ylva joined her.

"I don't think he ever really stopped loving you, Faye. Not even during the most, uh, passionate points in our affair. Not when we moved in together, not when I fell pregnant with Nora. That was something that was always in the back of my mind, and it bothered me constantly. I was just a substitute. For you. I think all the women he was with were a sort of attempt to find you. What you had. You were the prototype for Jack's concept of love. That's the ironic thing in all this mess."

Faye had been holding her breath while Ylva spoke, and now she cleared her throat. Her chest had tightened. She didn't know why what Ylva had said affected her so strongly. Perhaps it was because she had already understood it but never dared to express it—not to herself or to anyone else. Now it had been confirmed to her for the first time by another person. And the other person wasn't just anybody—it was the one person on earth who best knew Jack, second only to Faye.

The dream returned to her again. About Jack. Him mocking her. Her weight, her weakness. But also the way he could smile at her and make her feel loved. In the dream, she still missed him, and that was the worst thing of all. She hated herself for that. But right now she couldn't afford to think about it.

They sat down again and Faye turned to Ylva.

"Tell me your thinking. Is there anything to be done, or is it all too late?"

Ylva put her feet up on the balustrade. She cracked her neck gently—an unpleasant sound that made Faye shiver.

"Sorry, family habit," Ylva said and laughed.

She took her legs down and looked at Faye.

"I've got some ideas. Nothing totally concrete as yet, but I need to know more first. There are still some pieces of the puzzle missing. But I've got one major advantage. I've worked with Henrik. I know how he operates. And as you know, it wasn't Henrik who was the brain behind Compare."

Faye snorted loudly and resoundingly. Ylva grinned.

"Yes, now I know that it was actually you. I didn't know that then. At the time, I thought it was Jack. It was clearly not Henrik. The fact that he's managed to get back on his feet—and then some—is nothing less than a miracle in my eyes. But there are lots of successful companies and fortunes that are built by people who aren't all that gifted. Networking and luck and timing can take you a long way . . ."

"Oh yes," said Faye, sipping her wine as she listened with interest to what Ylva had to say.

She realized she was starting to like her. And that everyone deserved a second chance. Well, maybe not everyone. But Ylva most certainly did.

"What I know about Henrik, among other things, is that he's sloppy. He's got no eye for detail, which means he's got no eye for the bigger picture. He misses stuff. Jack flew off the handle at him for that, often. We had to do a lot of damage limitation around Henrik because of all the balls he kept dropping. Don't get me wrong, Henrik isn't a dummy, that's not what I'm saying. We shouldn't make the mistake of underestimating him. And he's got no scruples when it comes to achieving his goals. That makes him a dangerous adversary. But if there's anywhere we can find a weak spot it's his carelessness. I've skimmed the contracts for Revenge, but I'd like to take twenty-four hours to go through them line by line. And I'd like to check a few details with my uncle, who is a contract lawyer. One of the best. The bits I can't make out he should be able to help me with."

"Kerstin and I have read the contracts too and I've had lawyers review them. What are you going to find that we missed?"

"That remains to be seen," said Ylva.

She had stood up and was pacing back and forth on the terrace as she spoke.

"There will be something in this entire affair that Henrik has overlooked. There are a thousand things—a thousand clauses that might throw a wrench in the works for him if he hasn't thought of them. Or we'll just have to . . ."

"What?" said Faye smiling slyly.

Ylva had come to life while she was talking. The grayness was gone, the fine veneer of depression had been vanquished, her eyes were sparkling, and her entire body was speaking.

"What do you have in mind?" Faye repeated.

Ylva stopped. She leaned against the balustrade. The wind caught her hair and swept it around her head. She smiled. A big grin.

"I was thinking that otherwise we'll have to make certain that Henrik has missed something . . ."

Faye smiled back at her like a Cheshire cat. For the first time in ages, she felt as if she could relax. She took a deep breath. And then slowly exhaled. She realized she had forgiven Ylva. It was time to turn over a new leaf.

It was dark inside the restaurant, but when David smiled at her, she could still see the twinkle in his eyes. Far too many days had passed since they had last seen each other. Faye's problems with Revenge and his problems with Johanna were getting in their way.

"You have to tell me more about the American expansion," said David. "We've barely had time to discuss it."

He took a piece of beef tataki with his chopsticks and proffered it to her.

"But first you have to taste this—it really melts in your mouth."

Faye savored the tender meat as it practically disappeared without her having to chew it.

"God, that's delicious. Here, for you."

She picked up a small lobster taco from the metal rack beside her plate and carefully placed it into his mouth.

"The USA has been in the cards for Revenge

from the very beginning," she said. "But I wanted to take it step by step. First Sweden, then Norway, then Europe. And then finally America once we had enough to bring to the table to give us a chance. I'm fully aware of how difficult it is for a foreign company to break through over there. The obstacles are hefty, we're competing with huge, well-established companies, and this industry is one of the most competitive out there. But that was what appealed to me from the very beginning. The challenge. So this is just an extension of that."

She wiped her mouth.

"By the way, I'm going to Amsterdam this weekend with Ylva and Alice."

"Oh? I got the impression the three of you barely know each other?"

"This is a great chance to change that—and you said you had a lot on with the girls over the weekend."

"I have," said David. "And I think you're right to do it."

He set down his chopsticks.

"I have to admit I'm incredibly impressed by what you've done, everything you've built up."

Faye blushed. She'd heard it a lot, but it meant infinitely more when it came from David.

She shrugged.

"I can't overlook the boost that Revenge got when Chris left me her company in her will. I'll be forever grateful to her for that, and I'll do everything I can to look after what she gave me."

"I know you are. And that you will keep doing that," said David with warmth.

They were interrupted by the arrival of new plates at the table.

"Dear God. I thought you were kidding when you told me you eat like a lumberjack!"

"Fat people are harder to kidnap," said Faye with a smile, picking up a piece of sashimi with her chopsticks.

David looked at her gravely.

"I love you whatever size you are."

Faye stopped with her chopsticks in midair. She stared at him.

"What did you say?"

David cocked his head to one side.

"You heard what I said."

"Say it again."

Faye melted under the gaze of his blue eyes as he smiled in a way that she had never seen before.

"I love you, Faye."

FJÄLLBACKA—THEN

When we went ashore, Tomas said there was a little cabin in the woods. We found it in a clearing after a short stroll. Outside, there was a fire circle and Sebastian began to set a fire. He seemed happier, more self-confident here with his friends than he did at home. He held his head higher and his actions seemed more decisive.

I too felt different. Lighter. I was wrapping myself up in the feeling of finally being included and accepted. As it was lunchtime, we grilled some hot dogs and ate them with great pleasure. The boys drank more beer while I stuck to Coca-Cola.

Tomas came to sit next to me. I could feel the warmth from his body and had to fight the impulse to move closer.

"Do you remember that disgusting dough they grilled with the hot dogs on school trips when we were little?" he said.

"God, yes. The one they mixed together from flour, salt, and water?"

"What did they call it? Troll dough?"

"Isn't troll dough the one you play with?"

"Maybe it was the same thing."

"Eww!"

I laughed. I could feel the laugh reaching all the way down to my diaphragm.

"Didn't you like the beer?" Tomas asked, pointing at my Coke.

"Sure, but I was starting to feel a bit dizzy," I said, feeling embarrassed. I hid the Coke can behind my back.

It tipped over and I leaped off the ground.

Tomas jumped up as well, looking around for something to dry the wet patch on my skirt with, but he couldn't find any paper. He picked up a lump of gray moss and began to rub it against the fabric, but the only result was that the stain was now wet and dirty.

"You're not the best at domestic stuff, huh?" I giggled, and Tomas shrugged sheepishly.

"Is it that obvious?" he said.

The glimmer was back in his eyes.

Roger and Sebastian were watching us narrowly. They were talking in low voices, their heads close together. A shiver ran down my spine, but I figured it was because of the wind.

When we had finished eating, we went over to the cabin. There was a big rusty key in the lock. I turned it and we stepped inside. There wasn't much to see.

"Not exactly a luxury retreat," said Tomas, and Sebastian thumped him on the back.

"It's free. What were you expecting? Just because you sleep between silk sheets . . ."

"Hey, watch it," said Tomas, throwing a punch into the air. Sebastian danced away from it with ease.

I looked around as my eyes began to adjust to the darkness. Outside, the sun was shining brightly, but inside the cabin it was pitch-black. Heavy wooden boards covered the windows. The only furnishing was a bed in one corner with a filthy mattress on it. An empty jam jar rattled as Roger kicked it. I jumped, my heart beating faster than a hummingbird's, but I quickly calmed down.

I wondered who had lived here. The cabin looked like it was at least a hundred years old. Had someone been able to live here? Year-round? Probably. I knew that lots of families had lived out on the islands—perhaps this little cabin had been full of children.

Sometimes I had fantasized about living on one of the windswept islands myself. With no company except for the gulls, hollyhocks, honeysuckle, and crabs scuttling into the crevices between the rocks.

I ran my hand along the wooden walls, following the lines of the wood deeper into the cabin. There were two rooms. I went into the innermost one, but the smell of mold was so strong that I immediately stepped out of it again.

"Hello?" I called out. No answer. The boys had gone outside. I went over to the closed door and pushed the handle. A shiver ran down my spine again as I realized the door was locked.

After being picked up by a chauffeur at the airport, Faye, Alice, and Ylva spent the afternoon cooling off in the hotel's rooftop pool. The heat wave that had hit Sweden was nothing compared with the dry, hot air in Amsterdam. They lay on their sun loungers fanning themselves, drinking margaritas, and discussing how to pass their evening. Faye was still thoughtful. She had notified her police liaison officer that she was going to Amsterdam for the weekend. There was still no news about Jack.

"You still haven't told us what we're doing here this weekend, Ylva. Right now isn't exactly the best time to be away."

"We're here for plan B. A safety net. A lifeboat, as it were."

"I don't give a shit why we're here," said Alice, sipping her margarita. "We're lying on the roof of a building in Amsterdam. With a pool. And we're drinking strong margaritas. Who needs a reason?"

"Today, we chill out," said Ylva, pulling her

sunglasses down over her eyes and turning her face toward the sun. "Tomorrow, I'll explain why we're here. And it doesn't matter how much booze you pour down my neck, I won't say a word until then. So make the most of today."

"Hear, hear," said Alice, taking a swig of her cocktail. "But if the plan is just to chill out and have fun today: Has either of you been to an Amsterdam coffee shop?"

"Do you mean one of those places they sell cannabis?"

Faye still couldn't quite let go of her thoughts about whatever it was Ylva wanted them to do here. But she had insisted and said it was a matter of insurance. In her desperation, Faye had had to be satisfied with that. She didn't have much choice right now other than to trust the small team she had gathered around her.

Alice smiled. "Exactly."

"Have you smoked before, then?" Faye said skeptically.

"Everyone did in Djursholm," said Alice. "It's not that I was some gangster. Just a teenager like any other."

"I don't know . . ." Ylva said hesitantly. "We need to be alert tomorrow too."

"Don't be such a scaredy cat." Alice waved the hand not holding her margarita dismissively. "Come on, Ylva, how often have you let yourself have some fun in the last few years? How often have you hired a babysitter?"

"I'm so grateful that your au pair was able . . ."

"That's not what I meant. Faye—you're in, right?"

Faye sipped her drink and waggled her toes in the sun.

"I don't know whether I—"

"Dear God, we're three stunning women in Amsterdam. What did you have in mind for us to do? Sit in our rooms and watch TV? No, I suggest we hang out here for an hour or two, get a bit of a tan and do some daytime drinking, then head out for some nightclubbing this evening—and on the way there we stop at a coffee shop. Okay?"

Ylva and Faye both muttered something that sounded affirmative, but Ylva looked just as nervous as Faye felt. Alice didn't waste time, waving over one of the servers and asking him for recommendations for nearby coffee shops. He said the best ones were in the red-light district and suggested they make sure to drink plenty of water. Partly for the heat, but also because newbie hash smokers risked dehydration.

"It's cool. I've smoked a lot of ganja. I'm like the Bob Marley of Djursholm," Alice said and giggled.

Despite missing David, Faye was pleased she had gotten away. A trip with two funny, smart women in a buzzing city like Amsterdam was just what she needed.

She began to warm to Alice's plan. She had to dare to live a little. And forget about the problems in her life.

When the server brought them fresh margaritas, she downed what was left of her old one and accepted the new glass. They were in the eye of the storm. A little relaxation from the chaos and anxiety of what was going on back home. As Alice put it: she needed this.

Five hours later, they were in a coffee shop and had eaten almost a whole space cookie each without anything happening. They couldn't feel anything. They were disappointed, hot, and bored. And since alcohol wasn't served in coffee shops, they were drinking their third round of dire cappuccinos. The inebriation from the afternoon by the pool was beginning to wear off and Alice grabbed hold of a girl who worked there—for the third time—to ask how long they would have to wait.

The girl, who had dreadlocks and a body covered in tattoos, repeated what she had said on the previous two occasions.

"Wait a little longer."

When she had disappeared, Alice shook her head.

"No, I'm not going to fucking wait," she said, stuffing her face with the rest of the cookie.

Two minutes later, Faye could feel her fingertips

pricking. She blinked a few times, and then looked searchingly at Ylva, who was staring at her hand with her mouth wide open. The world shook. It was like being lowered into an aquarium with fish swimming around in disco balls.

She fluttered her eyelids and looked at Alice.

Alice's lips were moving, but Faye couldn't work out whether she had lost her own hearing or whether Alice had lost the power of speech. She looked around. Everything was ebbing and flowing, swaying. She tried to speak but the moment she opened her mouth, she became uncertain about whether she had already said what she wanted to say. She thought about it until she realized she had forgotten what she wanted to say in the first place.

Ylva was giggling, forming her fingers into different shapes that she claimed were animals and holding them up.

"It's a monkey—can you tell, Faye? A monkey."

She suddenly stood up and Faye stretched out a hand toward her.

"You should probably stay here," she tried to say, but her tongue wouldn't obey her and Alice burst into a torrent of laughter.

Alice placed a hand on Faye's.

"Sorry."

"For what?"

"For being such a bitch before. For everything."

They fell into each other's arms.

"It doesn't matter."

"I'm so glad you've found that David guy," Alice slurred.

She stroked Faye's forearm with her fingertips.

"Me too."

Faye had never felt better. The initial fear had gone. Everything was wonderful, warm, and friendly. She smiled and waved to a pair of Asian tourists.

Alice spouted a long tirade of words, and Faye was able to make out only the occasional one.

"Faye?"

Alice tapped her on the shoulder.

"Faye?"

She took her eyes off the tourists.

"Where's Ylva?" asked Alice.

"I'm Ylva. And I'm Alice. I'm falling and falling and this is wonderland. You're a tiny rabbit!"

Her mouth was dry as sandpaper. Faye reached for the water.

Alice's head was moving in circles, as if she was vibing to a song, but no matter how much Faye tried she couldn't hear anything.

"I think we need to find Ylva."

Alice stood up, supporting herself against the table.

"Ylva!" she called out. "Ylva!"

Faye got to her feet. She was on the verge of falling over, but was caught by Alice. For a moment, they almost tumbled to the floor, but Alice managed to keep them upright.

"We'll find her. Let's head off on an expedition to find our friend."

"Let's do it."

They slowly went down the steps and staggered unsteadily toward a door. It turned out to be a back door and they emerged into a deserted, narrow alley. Ylva was lying on the ground on her back next to some bins. Faye had a shock when she saw her eyes—she could only see the whites and Ylva appeared to be having physical spasms.

Her dizziness was gone at once. Faye was sharp and completely clearheaded as she threw herself to her knees beside Ylva and tried to bring her to life, without success.

Faye could feel the panic rising.

"Ylva!" she screamed. "Ylva, wake up!"

Behind her she heard Alice calling out.

"Call an ambulance! She's dying! Please call an ambulance!"

Faye put Ylva in the recovery position and stroked her sweaty brow while Alice rushed back inside the coffee shop to fetch a member of the staff.

"Ylva, don't die. Please, Ylva, don't die."

Faye grabbed hold of her small hand with its bitten nails and held it firmly. Memories of sitting beside Chris in the hospital in the final hours came back to haunt her. Why had they come here?

Why had they had to try space cookies? In truth,
Faye hated drugs, hated not being in control. Now
the adventure had cost them Ylva's life. Why couldn't
she have made do with not knowing? So goddamn
fucking stupid. The guilt was suffocating her.

"There they are." Behind her, Faye heard Alice's
voice. Tense. Almost a falsetto. "Help her. You've
got to help her. She's dying!"

Faye turned her head. A burly man was saunter-
ing toward them.

"Hurry up," Faye screeched desperately.

Jesus, they were slow! He didn't seem to be taking it seriously—he didn't look at all worried.

He stopped beside Faye and bent forward.

"Don't worry, ladies, this happens all the time.
Her blood sugar level is low. I'll give you some
sugar for her. Then get her in a cab back to your
hotel and give her some food and water."

Ylva suddenly opened her eyes and Faye sobbed
with relief.

"Are you sure?" said Alice, flinging her arms
around the astonished man.

"I'm sure, ladies. This happens about ten times
every day," he said, laughing.

Then he produced a paper packet of sugar from
his shorts pocket, bit off the top, and asked Ylva to
stick out her tongue, which she did drowsily. Her
body was still shuddering with peculiar spasms,
and she was murmuring incomprehensibly.

"Good girl," he said, patting her on the head.

Faye was on the verge of tears she was so relieved. They hadn't killed Ylva.

Half an hour later, they were sitting on Faye's bed—red-eyed but otherwise fine—after having ordered practically every single dish on the room service menu. There was a knock on the door, and Alice got off the bed to answer it. Two members of the hotel staff dressed in white rolled in cart after cart filled with food. Hamburgers, pasta, big chunks of meat, fish, fried chicken, french fries. Large jugs of ice water.

The celebratory meal was served in the lounge area. The men wished the ladies a pleasant meal with a smirk—they probably knew what the dinner was for—and then they disappeared.

Faye, Alice, and Ylva threw themselves at the food, shoveling it onto their plates before settling back onto the bed to eat it. Faye had never eaten more delicious or desperately needed food. They drank glass after glass of water.

When they were done, they stretched out—sated and contented—on the big bed with their hands on their tummies.

"I have to take off my trousers," Alice murmured. "Otherwise I'm going to hurl."

"Good idea," said Faye.

They followed Alice's example and kicked off their trousers so that they were all lying there in their underwear.

"You scared us back in that alley," said Faye.

"What happened?" Alice asked.

Ylva shook her head slowly.

"I'm not really sure. I remember standing and talking to someone, but then I collapsed and couldn't get up. I lay there for a while like a beetle on its back, trying to get to my feet, but then I gave up. The next thing I remember is you two bending over me."

They switched on the TV and zapped lazily between channels.

Ylva drifted off first, then Alice's eyelids began to flutter. Eventually, both of them were snoring away on either side of Faye. She got out of bed, took her mobile out of her bag, and went onto the balcony. The night air was cooler. She enjoyed the gusts of cool air on her bare legs. Below her, the traffic was moving sluggishly. She sat down at the table and saw that she had missed a call from David. She was immediately concerned and called him back.

"Hi, darling, I was at a loose end earlier and started thinking about Revenge and the American expansion," he said, and Faye could almost see his smile in front of her. "I got completely caught up in it—you really do inspire me, you know. I've got quite a lot of capital that needs investing, so I've put together a proposal that I'd like you to look at. If you want to, that is?"

Faye's own smile grew even wider.

"Of course."

"You don't think I'm sticking my nose in, then?"

"Of course I don't. How did it go with the girls and Johanna?"

"She wants to try again, but I've explained that it's you I want to be with."

"How did she take it?"

"Not especially well, but why don't we talk about that later? I don't want to ruin your weekend with Alice and Ylva."

"I miss you," said Faye.

"And I miss you."

When they had ended their call, Faye saw that she had a text message from Kerstin. She opened it and her good mood was gone at once. Yvonne Ingvarsson had been to the apartment looking for her. She slowly put down the phone. She had to do something about that Yvonne. She was playing with fire and one of them was going to get burned soon. Faye had no intention of it being her.

"Dear God, how could I let myself be talked into doing this?" said Ylva, putting her hands to her head.

"Surely you're not still hungover," Alice said airily, waving at the server to bring her a new drink.

More patrons were beginning to fill the hotel bar and the rising hubbub made Ylva massage her temples.

"I was lying in an alley yesterday. In Amsterdam. After eating a hash cookie in a coffee shop. I think I've **earned** the right to be slightly hungover today."

"Well, I can't feel a thing," Alice said cheerily, smiling at the server as he brought her a fresh cosmopolitan.

"I'm thrilled for your sake," Ylva muttered. "Beyond thrilled."

Faye looked at her with a frown.

"You're the one who says we've got work to do here," she said. "Alice and I still don't know what this is about. Are you going to be up to it?"

"Give me a couple of hours, an Alka-Seltzer,

and some acetaminophen and I'll be right back on track. So, yes, it's still on. And, yes, I'm going to explain. I just need to get this . . . throbbing headache out of my head."

"You don't need fucking acetaminophen—you need the hair of the dog," Alice said dryly, gesturing to the server once again.

He came over briskly, bowing slightly.

"A Long Island iced tea. And a tequila shot. For her," Alice said in English, pointing to Ylva.

She groaned.

"You'll be the death of me, Alice."

"Sweetie, I'm a Lidingö housewife. I know how to get rid of a hangover."

The cocktails arrived, and with a desperate but hopeful look at Alice, Ylva took both glasses.

"I'm trusting you right now."

"You can always trust me," Alice said magnanimously.

Faye looked amused as Ylva downed her tequila shot in one go with a grimace.

"Bottoms up. But now I really want to know why you dragged us all the way to Amsterdam. Right in the middle of a monumental crisis."

"The Swedish Patent and Registration Office," Ylva said.

Alice, who had just taken a big mouthful of her cosmopolitan, coughed her drink onto the table.

"The Swedish Patent and Registration Office?" she said, wiping her mouth.

Faye was also staring at Ylva, who reached for her Long Island iced tea. She was actually gaining a bit of color.

"They're having a conference here this weekend. At this hotel. The big party's tonight . . ."

"And?" Alice said with irritation.

"Yes—I'm not sure I'm with you either," Faye said, holding out her hands.

"Revenge. Rights. Patents. Plan B?" Ylva attempted.

Faye shook her head.

"Nope. Still not with you. Alice?"

Alice shook her head too and then winked at a man at the next table.

"Alice, focus and I'll explain," said Ylva.

Faye noticed that Ylva was enjoying being one step ahead. She was welcome to this one.

"But seriously, Ylva . . . what are we supposed to do about the fact that the Patent and Registration Office is here?"

Ylva gave a wry smile. She looked around, lowered her voice, and explained her plan in short. Alice laughed out loud.

"That's genius, Ylva! You're amazing."

"You too, Alice. And you're going to be an important resource tonight."

Faye raised her eyebrows.

"Do you have any idea what you're unleashing here, Ylva?"

"I'm counting on the fact that I do," Ylva said with a grin.

An hour later, the three of them were all tipsy and Ylva pointed at the bar.

"There. Kent, Börje, and Eyvind."

She looked at Faye and Alice.

"You know what you have to do?"

"You've explained that most clearly," Faye said, downing a Hot Shot.

"We're hot, we're funny, we're smart," said Ylva, still keeping her eye on the men at the bar. "It'll be like taking candy from a baby. We'll just have to hope they don't recognize you, Faye."

"They work at the Patent and Registration Office. I hardly think they'll know who Faye is," Alice said thickly, and Ylva hushed her.

"They're not the only ones who are here. The whole department is. But they're not due to eat dinner for another two hours. We've got time."

Alice stood up, swaying slightly.

"Time to pull ourselves together," said Ylva, steadying her.

Alice took a deep red lipstick from her handbag and applied it liberally to her lips.

"**Mes dames,**" Ylva said, making an ushering gesture toward the bar.

Alice strode up to Kent, Börje, and Eyvind on her long legs.

"Did I hear you speaking Swedish?"

The men looked at Alice in delight and were even more delighted when Ylva and Faye joined them.

Three drinks later—on the Patent Office's tab—
the six of them were on their way up to Faye's big
suite for a cocktail aperitif.

Ylva had picked out Kent, while Faye was charming Börje and Eyvind was close at Alice's side with
puppy dog eyes.

When they reached the room, Ylva had prepared
a drinks table with every form of alcohol and mixer
anyone could ever ask for.

The men exchanged small yelps of delight.

"Bloody hell, what a place! Börje, we haven't got
rooms like this!"

"Jesus Christ, Kent, this is what I call a hotel
room! This must be one of those soooouuuuites!"

"**Suite,**" Alice said, throwing herself onto the sofa
and pulling Eyvind alongside her. "Faye, darling.
Won't you mix me and this sweetie a G&T each?"

Faye stifled a smile. Alice was eating poor Eyvind
for breakfast.

She made a drink each for Alice and Eyvind and
then turned her attention to Börje and Kent. Börje
was looking at his watch anxiously.

"Isn't dinner in an hour?"

"Don't worry," Kent said quickly, happily accepting an enormous drink from Ylva. "We'll have a
quick drink here with the ladies, and we'll be down
in time for when it starts. It's fashionable to be late,
anyway!"

Eyvind mumbled in agreement, his eyes firmly

fixed on Alice's neckline. She put an arm around him and smoothed back the hair at his temple.

Ylva and Faye exchanged a look. They had mixed the drinks using little but spirits. Given how much the men had drunk down in the bar, they wouldn't notice how strong the drinks were.

Faye discreetly checked that she had her mobile phone close at hand and she saw Ylva do the same.

Before long, both Börje and Kent had nodded off on the sofa. Alice leaned closer to Eyvind and licked his ear. Faye took out her mobile phone. She took care to ensure that Alice looked good in the photo. She was always meticulous about things like that.

FJÄLLBACKA—THEN

I hammered and shouted, but they ignored me. Their voices penetrated the wooden walls, as did the smell of grilled hot dogs. They were in a good mood. Laughing loudly. I sank to the floor with my back to the door. I pictured Tomas's face before me—the friendly smile, the sparkling eyes. Had I understood any of it?

What was Sebastian thinking? Had this been his idea? Why had he wanted to bring me? Had this been the plan from the beginning, or had I done something wrong?

Time passed. Although I had no watch, I thought at least two or three hours had elapsed. I stood up and tried again. Pounded on the door.

"Please, let me out," I pleaded. "I'm thirsty."

They didn't answer.

"Sebastian? I want to come out. I want to go home."

The conversation outside continued. They laughed. I assumed it was at me for sounding pathetic. I **felt** pathetic and stupid. Light shone through the crack at the bottom of the door—it was still daytime.

I was like a dog. A mad, repressed dog. A lovesick, stupid mongrel. A little kindness and I had rolled onto my back and dropped all suspicion. Tomas's sparkling eyes and deep smile lines had made me abandon everything I knew. The knowledge that no one could be trusted.

The rage inside me slowly began to awaken. Above all, I was angry at myself for being so naïve. I pounded my fists against the door again. I could feel small splinters digging into the skin of my hands. I welcomed the pain. I hit even harder. Roared until my throat ached. Eventually, I sank down with my back to the door again.

More time passed, I lost track of how long.

They were talking in lower voices now. Their voices were hoarse, whispering. There was something unnerving about that.

I got up again and pressed my ear to the door, trying to hear what they were saying. Now the panic began to hit me. What was I going to do if they left me here? I would die of thirst. No one would find me. The panic increased and I pounded on the door again.

To my surprise, it sounded as if they were heading for the cabin. I stepped back and stood there with my arms hanging by my sides. The key turned in the lock. Sebastian stepped inside.

Roger and Tomas came behind him.

None of them said anything—they simply stared at me with their dead, inebriated eyes. I took another step back, pressed myself against the wall, and tried to make myself small.

But there was nowhere to escape to.

Someone had tried to get into the apartment at Östermalmstorg. The marks showed clearly in white, like huge scars on the dark wood of the front door. Faye put down her cabin bag, bent forward, and examined them. Her heart was pounding violently in her breast. Her father? No, more likely Jack. He must have been here and tried to get in, clearly without success. It was like a warning—a message that he was after her. Faye quickly glanced over her shoulder, put her keys in the lock, turned them, opened the black security grille, stepped into the hallway, and locked the door behind her.

She leaned against the wall, closed her eyes, and tried to gather her thoughts. It was better that he was after her rather than Julienne.

Indeed, the fact that Jack had showed up could be seen as advantageous. He had shown his hand and demonstrated that he had no intention of staying away.

Faye rooted in her handbag for her phone, dialed the number for her liaison officer with the police, and explained what had happened. Ten minutes later, two uniformed officers arrived. They inspected the door, took notes, and asked a series of questions that Faye answered to the best of her abilities.

"You have to find him," she said when they had finished asking their questions. "He's going to hurt me. He's already killed my daughter."

The policeman looked at her calmly.

"We know the background. We haven't got the resources to protect you twenty-four/seven, but we'll make sure we do everything we can to catch him. Now we know he's in Stockholm. And you've got your liaison to check in with daily."

"How am I supposed to go to my office and carry on living my life when he's stalking me?"

"Do you have anywhere else you can stay for the time being? Until we catch him?"

A sound from the doorway made Faye turn around. When she caught sight of David, she rushed to him and flung her arms around him.

"I saw the door. Has Jack been here?" he asked, pulling her into an embrace.

Faye nodded, tears forming in her eyes as she smelled his familiar scent. David turned to the policeman.

"What can you do about it?"

"Not much. As I just explained to Ms. Adelheim,

we can't protect her around the clock. Maybe you should check into a hotel instead?"

The policemen departed, leaving them alone. For the first time since Faye had met him, David seemed really worked up. He paced back and forth by the kitchen island with a glass of apple juice in his hand.

"He can't be allowed to ruin things for you—to shut you down like this. I know a man with a security company. We can sort out some bodyguards. You have to be allowed to keep working as usual without having to look over your shoulder. That fucking idiot. Who does he think he is?"

"I can't have bodyguards, David."

"I'll pay. He can't stop you from living. He's done that enough. Jesus, I hate guys like him."

Faye had a warm feeling inside at the thought of his concern.

"It's not about the money. If I have to have protection, then he's managed to scare me. Cow me. And who knows how long this will last? He might stay hidden for months. If we're lucky, he'll be caught soon. At least now the police know he's in Stockholm."

David stopped in front of her.

"I know you've only just gotten home, but I'd like us to go away—just for a couple of days. Until things calm down a bit."

Faye caressed his cheek. Yes, she really did want to go away with him.

"What do you think of Madrid?" she asked. "I have to go anyway, for a meeting. We could fly out early, celebrate Midsummer there?"

He took her hands and drew her to him.

"As it happens, I'm one of those guys who loves Midsummer. Schnapps, herring, Västerbotten cheese, maypoles. But for you, my love, I'm happy to sacrifice it all. **Yo amo Madrid.**"

Faye took David's hand as they strolled along Strandvägen. She remembered the evening they had broken into the boat and made love for the first time. In many ways, her relationship with David was the most straightforward, most natural one she had ever had.

With Jack, she had often been uncertain and had adapted to please him. She had always been at war with her own internal instincts over the fear of losing him. When she spent time with David, she never even had to consider forgoing anything. He showed clearly and wholeheartedly that he wanted her the way she was. Perhaps it was age? Perhaps it was just that she and David were a better match than she and Jack had been?

"What are you thinking about?" he asked, looking at her in amusement. "You're smiling . . ."

"Us, as it happens."

"We're good together," he said. "I like it when you think about us."

The sun was shining, and the heat had arrived with gusto.

They passed the pier at Nybrokajen where the Djurgården ferries waited to fill up with tourists, while to the right Berzelii Park opened up before them. People were half reclining on the grass in the shade, eating their lunch.

When they reached the Grand Hôtel on Blasieholmen, Faye stayed in the lobby while David took the elevator up to his room.

It was cool and felt pleasant. Faye closed her eyes, enjoying the murmuring voices echoing between the stone walls.

She was looking forward to the trip to Madrid—it was their first trip together. She had one business meeting, but other than that, she was going to ensure that she and David had a wonderful time together.

Her mobile vibrated in her handbag and she took it out.

"Henrik was just in the office," said Kerstin.

"At Revenge? You're kidding!"

"Afraid not. I wasn't there, but Sandra in PR called."

"Revenge isn't his yet, he has no right . . . What did Sandra say he was doing there?"

Faye was so worked up that she stood from her armchair.

"He went around introducing himself to the

staff. Inspected the office. According to Sandra, he acted like he owned the place. He asked everyone to send in their CVs so that he could, as he put it, 'determine who will be assets for the company.'"

"The cheeky bastard. Irene told me how he treats women in his current company—the few that he even hires—chauvinistic shit that he is."

Faye almost collided with a white-haired lady in a chinchilla fur coat and several strings of pearls.

"Sorry."

"Excuse me?" said Kerstin.

"No, no. I wasn't talking to you. But what does he think he's playing at? There was no point in that except to wind me up. Which he's succeeded in doing."

"What are you going to do?"

"I'm going to remain calm, not do anything hotheaded, and stick to Ylva's plan."

"It went well in Amsterdam, in other words?"

Faye recollected a couple of key moments from the trip to Amsterdam, but decided it was best Kerstin knew as little as possible about what had happened there.

"It was above expectations."

"Well, then. Let's ignore Henrik for now and do what we have to do."

"Yes. We'll ignore him," Faye said, ending the call. But she could feel herself grinding her teeth.

An agitated voice made her turn around. A

woman with long, dark hair was remonstrating with the receptionists. Faye recognized her right away. Naturally, she had googled her and spotted her penchant for Chanel dresses. It was Johanna Schiller, David's wife. Faye got out her phone, put it to her ear, and crouched as she hurried for the exit. If Johanna caught sight of her, she would probably cause a scene. She must be here to find David. As Faye exited through the revolving door, she heard Johanna continuing her argument with the receptionists:

"What do you mean, you can't give me a key? It's my husband staying here. David Schiller. I'm Johanna Schiller. Surely I can have a key to my own husband's room?"

Faye clenched her fists in frustration and anger as she quickly continued on her way down the steps and toward the water. Everything Johanna was doing was so low. She couldn't leave David alone. Not even here. And she was using their two daughters to blackmail him. It was so selfish.

Faye ended up standing on the quayside. One way or another she was going to deal with the conflict, but not now. It was just as well David handled this stuff himself. She found an empty bench and sat down. She still hadn't told David that Johanna had tried to get hold of her. She didn't quite know why she was hesitating. When they were together, she mostly wanted to pretend Johanna didn't exist.

She didn't want to talk about her. If David wanted to talk about her then she didn't stop him. But she preferred it if Johanna didn't force her way into their bubble.

She still had her mobile phone in her hand, and now it rang. It was Ylva.

"Hi, Ylva, recovered from the weekend yet?"

Faye could hear right away that something was up. Ylva was gulping as she spoke, sobbing.

"He's been here. Jack has been here."

FJÄLLBACKA—THEN

Tomas and Roger tried to carry me to the bed, but I kicked, screamed, and bit so much that they dropped me on the floor. Instead, they grabbed hold of my feet and dragged me along behind them. My gaze roamed over Sebastian's relentless face as they dragged me. For some reason, it made me go quiet—at least for a bit. There were three of them. I didn't stand a chance. I realized that. They laid me on the bed, then tore off my trousers and underwear.

"No," I pleaded. "I don't want to."

But I didn't struggle. That would only make it worse. It was as if my whole body had gone numb and would no longer obey me.

Their eyes were dark, and they showed no emotion when I begged them to stop. Roger held my arms tightly. Tomas pulled out his cock and parted my legs forcefully. There was still a sparkle in his eyes. But it was a gleam of a different kind.

He penetrated me.

It stung. It hurt so much.

He thrust. Faster and faster. I gritted my teeth. Closed my eyes. His body smelled of beer and smoky fat. It took only a minute or so before I felt the convulsions in Tomas's body and the hot stickiness as he spurted his seed into me.

Then it was Roger's turn.

He smelled of cigarette smoke. He was more violent. I noticed that he liked seeing my fear as he violently pushed into me. I gasped. He didn't drop his gaze from my face. Constantly staring at me, wanting to see how I reacted. I felt helpless. Powerless. I turned my head so at least they couldn't see my face. That retained a shred of my self-esteem—or so I imagined.

Sebastian lit a cigarette and leaned against the wall, watching. I hated him. But most of all I hated myself for being a sappy teenager who'd been happy when my big brother had asked me if I wanted to come with them. When Sebastian spotted me watching him, he turned around and looked out of the window. Then and there, I realized how similar he was to Dad. I'd never seen that before.

I remembered when I was five years old. I hadn't noticed that Mom and Dad fought. I hadn't heard the cries. In the middle of a dream, I'd woken up, picked up my teddy, and, half awake, half asleep, I'd wandered into Mom and Dad's bedroom. I did that sometimes—curled up on Mom's side while she put her arms around me protectively, her back turned to Dad.

I was already at the foot of their bed when I realized they weren't asleep. At first it looked like they were wrestling. Dad was holding Mom's arms. Mom was naked. I'd never seen Mom naked before. I didn't understand what was happening. But I did see that Mom was crying.

Now, as I saw Sebastian standing at the window, he had that same expression on his face that Dad had had then.

The neighbors' agitated voices and a TV show were audible through the walls of the gray block of apartments in a suburb somewhere on the outskirts of Stockholm. Ylva was sitting on a chair in the kitchen, with her head buried in her hands.

Her body was shaking. She was crying silently. Faye stroked her back, trying to comfort her.

The police had left a little earlier. They had apologized for what had happened, created a police report, and promised to do everything in their power to find Jack. Jack had given Ylva the number for his mobile and said that she would know when it was time to get in touch. He had added that it was a burner and that he switched the phone on only occasionally each day. **So there's no point in the police trying to trace me,** he'd said before leaving Ylva.

"But he didn't do anything," Ylva said, brushing away her tears. "He just gave me the mobile number and then beat it. He didn't even want to see Nora. I think he . . . he just did this to bring you out into the open."

Faye shuddered.

She heard a child's cry from the bedroom. Amazingly enough, Nora had slept through both Jack forcing the front door and the visit from the police. But now she had woken up.

"I'll take her," Faye said softly.

Ylva didn't reply.

Faye got up. Next to a neatly made single bed there was a small extendable bed. She approached Nora carefully. She had seen her before only on TV and in the papers. Jack's daughter.

Faye would have loved to have more kids with him, but when she had gotten pregnant again Jack had said he didn't want any more children after Julienne. In hindsight, Faye realized it was because he had already met Ylva.

Jack had forced Faye into an abortion. She remembered the hours of nausea at the hospital with Chris at her side, since Jack hadn't even bothered to show up. Had he been with Ylva or someone else that time?

It didn't matter now.

Nora was lying on her back, looking up at Faye with big blue eyes. There was no doubt about it— she was Jack's daughter. And Julienne's half sister, come to that. She was a copy of her father. Faye stared at her as if bewitched before bending down, holding out her arms, and picking her up. She held the child close to her breast.

"There there, there there," she hushed.

Nora quieted down. Allowed herself to be embraced. The intensity of her crying reduced as Faye made her way back through the apartment to the kitchen.

Faye ended up standing in front of Ylva with Nora in her arms. Ylva couldn't stay here, she knew. Jack might turn up at any moment and actually manage to get in. Another screech rang out from the apartment next door. Down in the car park, someone was revving up a moped.

"This is what we're going to do," said Faye. "You can borrow whatever you need from me to buy an apartment in the middle of town. And you'll pay it back when you can."

Ylva looked up, glanced from her daughter to Faye, and then opened her mouth to protest. Faye interrupted her.

"This isn't up for discussion—it's strictly a business decision on my part. If you live here your work will be poorer, and you'll always be worrying that Jack might come back. And since your duties involve assessing new investors in Revenge, that affects me too. You've already shown me what you're made of. You've given me what I need and you've been loyal."

Ylva smiled feebly.

"Thanks."

"Until you find a new place, I don't think Alice

would mind you and this little lady moving in with her. She's pretty lonely in her big house out on Lidingö in the weeks when she hasn't got the kids. And Jack won't find you there."

Ylva wiped away the last of the tears.

"That sounds good," she said. "That means I can carry on going through the investors in peace and quiet."

Faye winced. She still hadn't said anything to the others about David wanting to invest in Revenge's American expansion. Ylva had warned her against mixing business and her personal life again, so they would probably end up at loggerheads about her considering David as a potential investor. David's proposal would be reviewed just as thoroughly as all the others and on the same terms—that was important to Faye. He had turned up last, so he'd be assessed last. If they got that far. There was a lot to deal with first.

"Pack a bag with your essentials and we'll take a cab to Alice's. I'll call her now," Faye said, sitting down at the table with Nora on her knee.

She was longing to be in Madrid. She would regroup and return to Stockholm with a plan to destroy Jack. And stop Henrik's attempt to steal Revenge from her.

PART THREE

Residents at a property in Östermalm raised the alarm on Tuesday night when they heard screams and shouts from an apartment. "It sounds like someone's being killed," a woman said when she called in.

When uniformed officers arrived on the scene, there was no one there. A police spokesperson declined to issue any further comment on the incident.

Aftonbladet, 26 June

David's mobile rang. Once again, it said **Johanna** on the display and he sighed, turned it over on the table, and tried to look unconcerned.

Faye smiled at him and David returned her smile.

They were in a tapas restaurant beside a beautiful cobbled square, not far from the Puerta del Sol.

The sun had set but the evening was still scorching hot. The dulcet tones of street buskers echoed between the whitewashed façades. Faye was wearing a thin white dress, while David was wearing a pale blue linen shirt and thin cotton trousers.

A plate of garlic-fried gambas had arrived and was sitting between them, while to Faye's right there was a bottle of Chardonnay at rest, tempting her in its silver ice bucket.

"Do you want to talk about it?" Faye asked, nodding at the phone.

David shook his head.

"Not really. I don't want to talk about anything that isn't to do with us."

"Then we won't."

"We'll just have to confront all that stuff when we get home. Can't we just be in the here and now, you and I, in Europe's most beautiful city?"

Faye raised her glass.

"You're right."

"I'm so incredibly in love with you—do you know that?" said David.

Despite Johanna's persistent attempts to ruin their trip, they'd had two amazing days in Madrid. Faye fell more in love with David with every minute she spent in his company. He was considerate and kind. Held the door open, pulled out her chair, insisted on paying for everything, bought her flowers and chocolate. Yet he was also modern in his views on equality in a completely straightforward way, and he could grasp that women were treated as second-class citizens in comparison to men. In the boardroom, in the street, in educational institutions. He was interested in what she had to say and asked follow-up questions. Not out of a sense of obligation, but because he was genuinely interested in her thoughts and opinions. His eyes sparkled when she spoke. He made her feel appreciated and loved in a way that Faye had never felt before.

Faye realized that she was smiling and David was looking at her quizzically, but she merely shook her head and waved it away. It was impossible to put her emotions into words.

"Excuse me."

David stood up to go to the men's room. The restaurant's toilets were in one of the buildings lining the square. Faye followed him with her eyes. His mobile phone was still on the table. For a moment, she considered picking it up, going through his conversations with Johanna, trying to understand what she wanted. Seeing how he addressed her. She had made a note of his PIN on one occasion when he had entered it in front of her. But she left the phone where it was. She wanted to show she trusted him.

Going through David's private correspondence would be an intrusion into his personal life. And even if he never found out, **she** would know what had happened. Instead, she turned her attention to the patrons scattered around her. Faye had noticed that many couples barely spoke to each other. Instead, they sat there scrolling on their mobiles, their eyes dead. It was a waste of time—a waste of life. Beneath a big tree, there were some children playing, chasing each other with laughter. Faye smiled sadly. She wished Julienne could have been here to meet David. He could be the father she had missed since Jack had abandoned them.

The realization hit her like a slap in the face. She realized that she could see a future in which she one day had children with David.

Her train of thought was interrupted by his voice.

"Faye . . ."

He sat down opposite her. All of a sudden, he looked anxious, and the worry put a knot in her stomach. Something was wrong, she could see that on his face. She gripped the edge of the table, readying herself for what was about to come.

"Faye, I've been thinking . . ."

She swallowed. No matter what he said, she would try to behave with dignity. Not show weakness.

"I've been thinking about how we thrive together," David continued. "Well, I can only speak for myself. I love being with you. And I hope you love being with me."

He looked at her questioningly, with an expression of vulnerability that he rarely displayed. Faye reached across the table in relief and took his hand.

"I love being with you," she said.

David's azure eyes seemed to shine more brightly than ever. He squeezed her hand.

"I know it's early days, but I can't stand being apart from you. I'd like it if we started looking for somewhere together—a home that we can create for ourselves. A new beginning. I hope you don't think I'm getting ahead of myself."

He looked away in embarrassment.

The waiter arrived with more dishes that he set down in front of them: pimientos de Padrón, tortillas, jamón, croquetas, and albóndigas.

Faye heard herself laugh. A laugh that rose up

into the velvety dark Spanish night, among the cobblestones and brick walls. Somewhere a little way off, probably at one of the many other restaurants nearby, someone began to play a violin, a heartfelt, melodious sound that slowly wound its way through the narrow streets.

"I'd really like to share a home with you, David. Can't you move into the apartment that I'm renting for the time being? Until we can get something of our own. I've already been asked whether I want to extend my contract, and you've given me a reason to spend more time in Sweden."

"Sure?"

David squeezed her hand again.

"It can be a tryout," she said, smiling at him. "You can move in as soon as I'm on track with the American expansion."

David pulled a small package from his trouser pocket, beautifully wrapped with a white ribbon around it.

"Don't worry," he said with a wry smile. "It's not a ring."

He winked.

"Not yet, anyway."

Faye cupped the package in her hands, trying to guess what was inside it, but of course it was impossible. Slowly, she removed the bow and lifted the lid. Inside was a beautiful, ornate silver locket on a chain.

She lifted it out carefully.

"I love it. It's wonderful."

"You happened to mention that Kate Gabor photographed you and your . . . your family on some occasion before it all happened. So I got in touch with her, explained who I was and why I wanted her help. Open the locket, Faye."

Faye looked at the silver locket. With trembling fingers, she opened it gently. She saw her favorite photo of her and Julienne. The love between them was so powerful—she was stroking her daughter's hair with such tenderness. Faye stared at the portrait. And then at David. She blinked away the tears.

The violinist was now playing "Kalinka." The darkness of the night enveloped them and Faye realized she was happier than she had been for a long time. Then she remembered what she had with her. For David. She wiped away the tears and took the box containing the Patek Philippe wristwatch. She'd been waiting for the right moment to give it to him. As she watched him unwrap it, she put the locket around her neck and stroked it lovingly.

Maybe, just maybe, she was ready for a new family.

Neither Faye nor David wanted the evening to end, so when they had finally eaten every single tapas dish and paid the bill, they strolled through the streets of Madrid, hand in hand. The city felt enchanted. More alive than anywhere else that Faye could remember. There were musicians on every street corner playing their beautiful, lingering melodies. Children played football or were absorbed in noisy games. Loved drunk couples were sitting on park benches. Young people were smoking weed and drinking wine on the grass.

Everything was bathed in the deep golden hue cast by the streetlights.

David and Faye didn't say much—words felt superfluous and inadequate—but occasionally they would stop and look at each other, smiling happily.

Eventually, David suggested they have a nightcap. So they sat down at a rickety table outside, side by side, facing the street, and ordered a bottle of wine.

Faye looked at David.

Her heart was beating so hard in her breast.

"When I'm with you, I don't feel bad about any-thing," she said. "Instead, I want to tell you about my weaknesses, the things I'm ashamed of, to get them out into the open. Apart from Chris, I've never felt like that with anyone."

"It's the same for me. I think it's because we both know the other doesn't have any ulterior motives. The weaknesses and failures are never going to be used as weapons against us."

A waiter in a white shirt, black waistcoat, and bow tie opened the bottle of wine and let Faye try it. She nodded and he poured them a glass each before setting the bottle in an ice bucket, bowing, and disappearing.

Faye wanted to tell David everything about her life, while at the same time she knew she couldn't do that. But one day, she would have to tell him about Julienne, otherwise a life together would be impossible. There were a lot of things you could sweep under the carpet, but a daughter wasn't one of them.

"Around a week before we met for the first time, I was in Rome," she said. "I was wandering around on my own. I found a party. There was a young couple there. We talked for a while and I went home with them."

David raised his eyebrows, bringing his glass to

his lips. A moped whizzed past at high speed. The street smelled of gasoline. Somewhere, a dog was barking.

"It was fascinating to be so close to two people who were so in love, and somehow, to become part of their love. It was the most intimate thing I've experienced. Making love with another woman's man while she watched. Do you understand?"

David looked at her seriously.

"I think so."

A couple passed them, hand in hand. They were wearing workout clothes.

"It was so clear they were doing it for each other's sake. That I was an instrument of their pleasure. A way to give each other pleasure. It was a new and special feeling. Almost an out-of-body experience."

Faye sighed. The watch glittered on David's wrist and he kept glancing at it in delight. But for some reason she felt sad. Although she knew she ought to be happy, the melancholy was powerful.

"We women are raised to be so afraid that someone is going to steal our man—our partner—so we limit ourselves. We remain constantly vigilant for any sign of betrayal. I'm never going to live like that again. I was betrayed by Jack, but I'm going to trust you. That's my choice. Otherwise I'm committing violence on my own life. Limiting it. I hope you never let me down, but that's on you—not me."

He fumbled for her hand, concealing it in his own. "I'm not going to let you down, Faye."

The glow from the candle was reflected in the watch on his wrist. Faye squeezed his hand tightly. She wanted him as a safe harbor in which to rest—a refuge where she didn't have to think about everything else she was grappling with. But if she was serious about letting him into her life, he had to know more about what was going on.

She took a deep breath. It was time.

"Someone is trying to buy out Revenge. And that someone is alarmingly close to succeeding."

FJÄLLBACKA—THEN

I had left my shoes somewhere in the cabin. When the boys finally let me out, I just wanted to get away from there. So I stumbled out into the dusk and across the rocks barefoot.

Roger, Tomas, and Sebastian dragged the luggage—now significantly easier to handle since the heaviest thing, the beer crate, was almost empty. I walked at the back of the column. Ahead of me, their broad, tanned backs jogged along. At the beginning, the plan had been to go home earlier, while it was still light. But they had insisted on staying a bit longer. And given that I was locked in the cabin, it didn't much matter what I thought about it.

Over the past forty-eight hours, they had come in to see me whenever it pleased them—always all of them together. Never one by one. After the third time, I stopped protesting—I just lay there and let them do what they wanted.

My body ached. It was bloodied and stank of

cum, sweat, and beer. It was a constant battle not to throw up.

"It was more fun when she put up a fight," Roger had said when I parted my legs for him.

They never spoke directly to me. Not when they were raping me. Not before or after either. Instead, they talked to each other about me as if I were a loyal, long-serving pet.

I barely felt any joy when they let me out and said it was time to go home.

They had already packed. All I had to do was plod along behind them.

The dinghy was tied up where we had left it and they loaded the stuff aboard. The atmosphere was different now. Surly. Inflammable. I kept quiet so as not to further irritate them. To avoid drawing their ire.

After having breathed the rotten stench of the cabin for two days, tasting the sea air was like new life.

I looked toward the rocks and trees from my position at the back of the dinghy. I thought to myself how different they looked now compared with when I had arrived. It wasn't just the light, it was also that I—the observer—was a different person.

We climbed aboard the sailboat and Tomas started the engine. He gestured for me to go over to him. I got up and slowly went to him, wrapped in a blanket I had found.

I waited patiently with my arms around my body.

There was a cold wind.

"You don't tell anyone about this. Ever. Got it?"

I didn't answer.

Tomas let go of the wheel, grabbed my arm, and looked me in the eye.

"Got it? You're just a stupid whore. If you tell anyone I'll throttle you."

Then he smiled and the sparkle was back.

"And why would you tell? You liked it—I could see that."

Tomas put his arm around me and I let him. Even though his touch disgusted me. It seemed like an eternity since I'd felt his eyes on me while I'd been in the bow. An eternity since I'd allowed myself to feel any kind of hope.

"She won't squeal," said Sebastian. "I promise to make sure she doesn't squeal. After all, it was me who trained her up."

I stared toward the horizon and put my hand to my breast, but stiffened as I stood there with Tomas's arm around me. The necklace that Mom had given me was gone. The beautiful charm with its silver tears was back in the cabin. I turned my head. Yxön was no longer visible.

The necklace was gone forever.

"Can I come by sometimes?" Tomas said. "You'll share with me, right, Sebastian?"

Tomas squeezed my shoulder. Then he licked my cheek. Slowly. Wetly.

"Of course I can come around, can't I, Matilda? After all, you like me."

I nodded slowly. I felt his beery breath and the pain in my upper arm, which he was still squeezing with his hand, and something happened inside me. For the first time in my life, I realized that sometimes it was necessary to kill.

"I heard that you've made a new acquisition in Rome . . ."

"Good news travels fast," said Faye, flashing a broad grin at Jaime da Rosa, the owner and CEO of a Spanish beauty company.

They weren't the biggest in Spain, but just like Giovanni's company in Italy, they were a key to several of the manufacturing, distribution, and logistics gaps that Revenge needed to fill before they could take the American market by storm. They had indulged in a bit of small talk and dined on some divinely delicious tapas, but now—over a cup of espresso—it was time to get down to business.

"Bad news travels fast too."

Jaime had a heavy Spanish accent, but his English syntax was perfect and his vocabulary extensive, so they had no difficulties understanding each other. Faye had learned Italian to a high level, so she could understand most of the conversation if it was in Spanish, but she would struggle to make herself understood as well as she needed to. Hence they were speaking English.

"What do you mean?" she said, waiting while she took a piece of chocolate from the plate in front of her.

"I have good friends in Sweden. There are rumors about Revenge. About a buyout."

The square of chocolate seemed to grow in her mouth. Faye had been worrying about this moment. So far, she had managed to keep the press from writing anything, and she guessed that Henrik didn't want a leak as of yet either—preferring to drop the bomb in grandiose style in the media once it was a fait accompli. But Stockholm was a small city, and the business world in Stockholm was even smaller—she wasn't surprised that the rumors had begun to reach other shores.

How she dealt with this conversation would be decisive. If she didn't continue working toward the American expansion in which she had invested so much time, energy, and hope, she might as well throw in the towel. If she did that, she didn't even deserve Revenge.

"There are always rumors, Jaime. You know that as well as I do. I'm guessing it's the same here in Spain. In Madrid. If I started asking around, how many rumors do you think I'd hear about you and your company? A handsome man like you . . . There must have been stories about you over the years? How many lovers have the gossip rags pinned on you, Jaime?"

She smiled at him, straightened her neck, and let her eyes flash as brightly as her diamond rings. He laughed loudly, flattered.

"Yes, you're right. There have been a lot of claims that haven't been true."

He leaned in and winked at her.

"But I'm afraid a great deal of it has been true . . ."

"I'd already figured as much. You're a bad boy, Jaime," Faye said with a giggle, while inwardly sighing.

Men. Sometimes she wondered how they had ever managed to preserve the patriarchy throughout human history.

"It's good to hear that it's just evil tongues wagging," said Jaime. "We're looking forward to completing our deal. From what I understand, there are just a handful of minor details left to iron out. My lawyers say we can sign the contract within a week."

"That's what I've heard from my lawyers too."

Jaime drained his espresso, propped his elbows on the table, and eyed Faye from beneath his mop of hair. She knew what was coming. There were so many meetings with so many men where she danced this dance. They all wanted the same thing. First business. Then pussy. As if it were part of the deal.

Faye smiled broadly. Over the last few years she had mastered the art of dealing with situations like this.

"I thought . . ." Jaime lowered his voice and looked her in the eye. "If you didn't have any plans this evening, I might show you some of my favorite hideaways. I know all the best restaurants and the top chefs are my personal friends. And I've got a little apartment here in the city. I work such long days that sometimes it's too late to go home to my beautiful villa in the mountains. Perhaps we can round off the evening there with coffee and . . . ?"

He waved at the server and asked for the bill.

Faye groaned loudly in her head. None of them were ever even original. Coffee and . . . in their little shagpad.

"That would be really wonderful," she said. "But I've got my dearest friend with me for the weekend, and her daughter too. She's five years old and, while she might be a bit lively, she's super cute. Of course I can't leave them at the hotel on their own, so maybe . . . ?"

Faye smiled sweetly when she saw the panic spreading on Jaime's face.

"Argh, I just remembered that I promised my wife I'd be home for dinner this evening. I'm so very sorry. But I'd be happy to recommend some restaurants to you. Child-friendly ones . . ."

"Oh, what a pity, but I'd be most grateful for those recommendations. So sweet of you."

Jaime hastily placed cash on the table, stood up, and nodded. He proffered his hand.

"Be in touch next week."

"Yes," said Faye, shaking his hand.

She watched him for a long time as he headed toward his office.

Laughing softly, she checked the time, picked up her bag, and strolled back toward the hotel. The shop she had found on Google while she was still in Sweden was on the way to the hotel. David was going to get another surprise.

David was in the middle of a business call when she arrived back in the room with two large bags in her hands. His face lit up. He gestured to her that he would be finished in five minutes and she blew him a kiss in reply. That meant she had time to prepare the surprise.

Outside on the big terrace, she whistled as she extracted everything she had bought. In front of her, Madrid's rooftops spread out into the distance, and she pushed away all her worries and all her thoughts about anything other than being here in a city she loved with a man she loved. She, the woman who had thought she'd never again trust a man. David seemed to be wrapping up his call, and Faye hurried to finish. When he emerged onto the terrace, she turned toward him and gestured at the table with her hands.

"Tadaaa!"

"What on earth is all this?" David said, wide-eyed.

"Since I took you away from Midsummer, I thought I'd bring Midsummer to you. I googled before we arrived and found a shop nearby that sells Swedish stuff. So here's some herring, knäckebröd, Västerbotten cheese, schnapps, sour cream, chives . . . well, everything you can think of. The only thing I wasn't able to arrange was a maypole, but I suppose we'll have to make do. And look! I've made wreaths!"

She grinned and produced two wreaths that she had quickly assembled with the help of a florist. She placed one on her head and one on David's. He looked kooky but kind of sexy—an irresistible combination. He put his arms around her and kissed her.

"You crazy thing. But as per tradition, I propose we start by dancing around the maypole."

"What are we waiting for?" said Faye, dragging him toward the bed and humming the melody to **"Små grodorna."**

David had suggested that they go to the VIP lounge, but Faye had insisted on settling down in a small café close to the Real Madrid store so that they could people-watch other travelers.

Faye loved airports. Barajas in Madrid was no exception. People from all corners of the globe passed by in a steady stream. Every now and then, she caught a word in a language she didn't recognize. Parents telling off their kids, carrying them, encouraging them, shouting at them. There was an air of expectation. People were going to see their loved ones again or finally take a couple of days' vacation after months of toil.

Perhaps her love of airports was because she hadn't flown until she had been in her twenties.

Yvonne Ingvarsson's number flashed on her display and Faye hastily rejected the call.

When Faye had spoken to Kerstin that morning, she had said that Yvonne had stopped by again—on Midsummer's Eve, of all days. Faye sighed. She had reached the end of her tether worrying about the policewoman's investigations, which seemed to be taking place entirely on her own initiative. She had no idea how Yvonne had figured out her past identity, but no one else from the police had contacted her about anything whatsoever to do with Julienne since Jack's trial. Yvonne clearly hadn't shared what she'd discovered with any of her colleagues. She was just a petty woman trying to take down someone she was jealous of, and Faye couldn't worry about her anymore.

As soon as she got home, Faye was going to deal with her. For good. She and David were going to move in together, Jack and Gösta would be apprehended before long—she was sure of it—and she was going to get Henrik's mucky paws off Revenge somehow.

David was working with intense concentration at his laptop. Occasionally, he took business calls on his phone—always pacing back and forth and making huge gestures as he talked. She loved to see him work. Seeing his focus and his obvious passion for what he did. Sometimes he would pose a quick-fire question without giving any context. He'd ask what she thought about the business potential of using DNA technology in health. Or what impact she thought Brexit would have on the euro. Sometimes she was able to answer, sometimes not. He impressed her on a daily basis with his knowledge, his expertise, his dedication. He was well grounded in a way that Jack never had been.

Eventually, he shut his laptop and turned to her.

"What are you thinking about?" he asked. "The buyout?"

"No, no, I'm not thinking about that right now. I'm thinking about . . . nothing."

He picked up a croissant. He took a bite and crumbs fell into his lap. Faye smiled. She was once again struck by how amazing it was that they had found each other.

"Have you had a chance to glance over my finance proposal, my darling?" David asked, wiping his mouth.

She shook her head.

"Not yet."

"Okay, I was just curious about what you made of it."

"Ylva is going to review all the investors. We should be done soon. I don't want them to think that I'm giving you any VIP treatment—that wouldn't look good. You know how it is. And apropos of what I told you yesterday, I've got a pressing situation I have to deal with first."

David nodded.

"Of course. That's true. And you've got your priorities completely right. I was just curious what you thought."

He averted his gaze, but Faye could see that he

was hurt. What did it matter if Ylva went through David's proposal a little sooner than the others? He was doing everything for her. Why should she stick to these kinds of principles when she could make the man who meant so much to her happy? She trusted him, after all. And even if Revenge's future looked uncertain right now, there was no harm in thinking ahead.

Faye put her hand on his thigh.

"I'll ask Ylva to expedite your proposal."

"There's no need," said David. "You're right—we probably shouldn't mix things up. And you've got more important things to deal with right now."

Faye leaned forward and forced him to look her in the eye.

"You're a brilliant businessman and I'm nothing but thrilled that you want to help me with Revenge. For me, it helps to do business with people I already know from the start are loyal and on the same page as me. Especially now. I've never needed loyalty as much as I do now."

David smiled and the furrow on his brow smoothed out. Had he been afraid of being rejected? By her? Maybe, she thought to herself, there was a degree of masculine ego in David that she hadn't noticed before. Or had ignored. On the other hand, he was a businessman. A winner. Every setback—in business or in life—was a defeat.

"Sure?" he asked, now as unconcerned as he had

been a couple of minutes earlier. He caressed her hand lovingly.

"Absolutely sure."

His grip became firmer and he guided her hand higher up his thigh toward his groin. She felt his penis against the palm of her hand. She cupped it.

"Do you want me to take care of that?" she asked.

He nodded.

They ambled around the airport for a while, hunting for somewhere secluded. They found a handicapped bathroom, looked around, and sneaked in, giggling.

As soon as they had locked the door, David took command.

"On your knees," he said, pointing in front of him.

He unzipped his fly. She took him in her mouth.

"Look me in the eye," he said, and she nodded and opened wide and sucked.

The floor was hard. Her knees hurt, but Faye liked that. When David came in her mouth, she swallowed while looking up at him.

Yvonne Ingvarsson's hair was standing on end and her bloodshot eyes were staring with hostility at Faye. The sound of children shouting in the apartment next door was audible through an open window. There was a dog barking down in the courtyard.

Faye took pleasure in the police officer's surprised expression. She waited for Yvonne to speak, but when the policewoman said nothing she decided to take the first step.

"May I come in?"

"What are you doing here? How dare you show up at my home!"

Faye didn't answer. They continued to size each other up in silence until Yvonne stepped aside. The hallway was dark, with stacks of newspapers, cartons, and bottles stashed against the walls. There was a smell of cigarette smoke and grime. Faye stepped across the mess and set off down the narrow corridor without taking off her shoes. Yvonne stood immobile, her arms at her sides. Judging by her expression, she was seething at the deliberate lack of courtesy, but Faye ignored her.

She passed a small bedroom and a bathroom before reaching the darkened living room. The blinds were down. The TV was flickering silently. Faye tried a light switch with no luck, so she went to the window and opened the blinds. Light streamed in and revealed the chaos.

The walls were adorned with pictures of Greece. Turquoise seas and white buildings gleaming in the sun. A framed **Mamma Mia!** poster had pride of place in the room—just above the sofa.

Faye's heart was pounding—she knew that the next few seconds would make or break everything.

She had to get Yvonne to stop her snooping. She couldn't be allowed to ruin everything. Faye couldn't risk it—not now.

"What are you doing here?" Yvonne asked her again.

"Does it feel strange?" Faye flashed her a brief but icy smile. "You've visited me several times, so now I'm returning the favor."

"There's a difference. I'm a police officer and I'm investigating a crime. It's my job."

Her voice was flat.

"No. You're not investigating a crime. My ex-husband was convicted of the crime that you apparently believe I committed. What's more, you're off on some sort of one-woman crusade. There's no investigation. The only place there is one is inside your head. No one else thinks there's anything to investigate. You're all on your own, aren't you?"

Yvonne didn't reply.

"I'll take that as a yes."

Yvonne swallowed. Her lips trembled. She was a completely different person here—in her own home—compared with when she had sought Faye out. The surprise seemed to have made her unsure of herself.

"You're, what? Fifty-five?"

"Fifty-nine," Yvonne replied.

Silence again. Faye began to get frustrated. Although Yvonne seemed more accommodating, she wasn't getting through to her. Not properly. Her attitude was apparently to wait and see.

"What are your dreams?"

Yvonne shifted her weight to her other foot but remained silent.

"You've worked for many long years. Bad pay. Awful hours. No one thanking you for trying to keep Stockholm safe. No family. After your shifts, you come here to this rathole and watch TV. You like Greece. You've got six years left until retirement if they don't fire you before that since you're an awkward weirdo, and then you'll slowly waste away."

Faye smacked her lips thoughtfully. "I like awkward weirdos," she said to herself.

She glanced at the pictures on the walls and stopped at the **Mamma Mia!** movie poster again. Pale sand. Turquoise water. A jetty. A yacht in the distance. Happy, smiling people. And suddenly she knew how she could influence Yvonne Ingvarsson. Everyone had their price. And she had just realized what Yvonne's was.

FJÄLLBACKA—THEN

The wind picked up. I was sitting in the bow, staring into the twilight, clinging to the rail so that I didn't fall in. If I fell, I would die. The currents would take me and pull me down. My body would probably never be found. It would be an end to the nightmare and the fear. The thought was appealing. But other than the grief I knew it would cause Mom, I also knew I could never do it. The world could be grim and dark, but it could also be bright and beautiful. Like Mom. She was the light. We had to get away.

There were happy people everywhere. In the papers, on TV, on the radio. I saw their faces, heard their laughter, their stories. The novels I read were filled with them. Some of our neighbors in Fjällbacka seemed happy, even though they lived next door to hell. Our darkness didn't seem to spill over the garden boundaries. But who knew? I saw only the outside. Just like they saw us only from the outside, through their kitchen windows or the same old chats across the hedge about the lawn.

I'd had the misfortune to be born into the wrong family. A family that was broken from the beginning. I would have to break free, correct, repair. Mom didn't have the strength. It was up to me.

Roger and Tomas wouldn't keep quiet. They thought I was going to blab. But I knew they would be the ones who bragged about what had happened. Everything I'd kept silent about. Everything that had gone on behind closed doors in our home. The family's secrets. Everything would emerge. That couldn't be allowed to happen. Mom wouldn't survive it. They were her secrets too.

I pictured the moment when Sebastian had stood by the window. After the rape. During the rape. How his face had looked like Dad's. It would continue. It would all continue. Suddenly, it was clear to me and I knew I had to act.

Sebastian? I felt nothing but hatred toward him, but Mom loved him. I would spare him for her sake. Try to, anyway. I couldn't make any promises. Not any longer. But the others . . . They were going to die.

Faye whipped out her mobile and dialed the number for her British lawyer, George Westwood. Her heart was pounding as the phone rang. The stakes were high.

Yvonne watched her with a frown.

The lawyer picked up on the fourth ring and Faye greeted him briefly before getting straight to the point.

"I want to buy a house in Greece. On an island. Think **Mamma Mia!** When it's all sorted, I want the contract signed over into the name of a friend of mine."

Yvonne's eyes opened wide and her mouth gaped, but she shut it again. Faye recognized that she had her and relaxed.

"I want you to do this as soon as possible—it's a very dear friend of mine, George."

"Of course."

Yvonne began to pace back and forth across the living room floor. It looked as if she was wrestling with herself, but Faye had seen her look and sensed the changed mood. She understood she had already won.

"And just to make sure you understand quite how dear this friend is to me, I'd like you to transfer three million kronor to an account associated with the transaction. For unforeseen expenses."

Yvonne stopped and stared at Faye. The hostility in her gaze was gone. Now she just looked downright shocked.

"From the account in the Caymans?" George asked. Despite the rather peculiar conversation, he sounded calm and collected. Almost amused.

"Yes, that'll be fine. I'll send the details later. Thanks, George. Let me know when it's done."

Faye stood up and put the phone back in her bag.

"Did you just try to bribe me?" said Yvonne.

"No, all I did was buy a house in Greece for someone I think deserves a break in life. Consider it a thank-you for your long and faithful service from a grateful citizen."

Yvonne stared at her. Faye smiled. She understood people like Yvonne. She was petty and jealous of Faye, and had become hell-bent on destroying her. But now that Faye had offered her the chance for a new life, Faye knew that Yvonne's sense of self-preservation would win out. What Faye was offering was far more than she could ever expect from taking Faye down.

One crisis averted. Now she had to deal with the crisis at Revenge.

When Faye got home, Kerstin was waiting for her in the apartment. Although they had keys for each other's places, they rarely made use of the opportunity to let themselves in except to check up on the apartments when the other was away.

She had spoken to David about the fact that she would be sharing their home for only half the year, but he didn't understand why she had to spend so much time in Italy. She had offered him the same reasons she'd given to the press—that she needed another base too, a home and a country where not everything reminded her of Julienne. He hadn't completely bought that and had tried to persuade her that now she could make her base in Sweden with him, with new memories. She knew that in the not-too-distant future she would be forced to tell him the whole truth. Then he would understand. But for some reason she was dragging her heels. She trusted him—it wasn't that—but she was afraid of how he would see her once he found out who she really was.

"Hello! What are you doing here?"

Kerstin had opened a bottle of wine and set out two glasses. She patted the space on the sofa beside her.

"I've got a flight to Mumbai booked tomorrow, but I just wanted to check whether I should postpone. There's a lot going on right now and I'm worried about you. It feels like I'm abandoning you just when you need me most."

Faye sat down and held out her glass so that Kerstin could pour the wine. It was true that Faye had a lot of things on her mind. She had decided in the end not to worry her mother with the news of Gösta's escape, and for a moment she wondered whether she should confide in Kerstin. But there was nothing that Kerstin could do, and she had already burdened her friend enough. She took a sip and then let out a long sigh.

"There is a lot going on, Kerstin, but it's nothing I can't handle. You've done all you can—you've brought us to this point. Now it's Ylva's and Alice's turn to take over. Ylva's going to look after the register of shareholders while you're in India. And David has given me the energy to carry on. He's becoming so much more important to me."

Kerstin raised her eyebrows.

"You've gotten very close in a short space of time. How much do you really know about him? More than I found out?"

Faye placed a hand on Kerstin's.

"I know you've had bad experiences with men. Well, one man. And God knows I have too. But this feels right. I feel safe with him."

"Mmm." Kerstin looked skeptical and sipped her wine slowly, without meeting Faye's gaze.

Faye shook her head and changed the subject. They talked about Julienne and about that slime-ball Jaime. Before long, they were laughing like they always did—but they didn't quite manage to re-create that feeling of closeness.

Ylva and Faye were in Faye's office. Stockholm was visible through the window in all its splendor. The sky outside was veiled in a thin layer of cloud, but the sun broke through occasionally, revealing the spots the window cleaners had missed.

"Do you feel safe at Alice's?" Faye asked.

"Yes. And I think Alice is grateful for the company, like you said."

"Good. We've got to stick together. Have you heard anything from Jack?"

Ylva shuddered, just as she did whenever Jack was mentioned.

"No, nothing," she said.

"Hopefully they'll arrest him any day now."

Ylva nodded. She turned her laptop around so that Faye could see her presentation.

"I've done everything I can to stop the buyout. But far too many people are selling their shares. We're very close to a takeover. We may have to put Amsterdam into operation."

Faye shook her head with concern.

"I don't know, Ylva. I really don't know. With Jack in prison and Revenge taking off, I thought the battle was over, I could finally sit back and enjoy life. But now it feels like a game of whack-a-mole down at Gröna Lund, with enemies constantly popping up from different holes. Each time I whack one, a new one appears. I don't know how much more fight I've got left in me. Is it even worth it?"

She pushed the laptop away.

"I've got enough money to get by. Putting it mildly. I don't really need to work again. I could spend more time on other things, apart from business. Like David. Who knows where that might go? And Amsterdam . . . Amsterdam is a risk. It might blow up in our faces."

Ylva looked at her and pursed her lips.

"I barely recognize you when you talk like that. There are things we can do. You could buy up shares yourself. You've got the capital. You can fight. You seem to have given up in advance. This isn't the Faye I've come to know. Are you really going to let Henrik win?"

She sighed.

"I'll follow your instructions. You're the boss." Ylva shrugged. "But I have to say I think you'll regret it if you don't act more forcefully."

Faye didn't reply. She was drawing figures on the

desk with the tip of her finger. Her mobile buzzed. A text from David. Faye couldn't contain her smile.

Ylva leaned toward her.

"You look happy."

Faye nodded.

"I've never been happier with a man. I think I'm in love—I'm acting like a teenager. We both are."

"Good. You of all people deserve it. I hope I get to meet him soon."

"We'll arrange it. He's got a lot going on, what with his soon-to-be ex-wife."

Faye squirmed a little. What she was about to ask Ylva made her uneasy. Especially after the discussion they'd just had. She knew her former rival well enough to know that she would think it was unprofessional to let her feelings for a person give him an edge in the process. On the other hand, Revenge was Faye's company. Ylva was an employee. Faye could do as she pleased. All the same, doubt was gnawing away at her.

Asking for something like this was exposing herself, showing a crack. She looked across the office, through the glass doors she had insisted on when they had renovated, so that the staff could always see her when she was there. As CEO and chairman, she had personally recruited many of the staff. She had invested time and money in them—she wanted to see them develop and gain wind beneath their wings. She couldn't let them down.

Fuck it, Faye thought to herself.

"Speaking of David, he wants to become one of our investors," she said in as neutral a voice as she could.

Ylva nodded unsmilingly, not looking at Faye.

"That's nice." Her voice was cautious.

"I'd like you to go through his proposal and finances as soon as possible."

"So I should prioritize him?"

Faye nodded.

"Okay. No problem. Like I said, you're the boss."

There was silence for a while. Faye leaned back in her chair and contemplated Ylva, who was determinedly staring down at her laptop.

She took a deep breath. "You think I'll bring David on board regardless of how good his proposal is?"

Ylva looked up.

"No, you're way too professional to do that. I admire you and I think you know what's best for Revenge. I've only been here for a few weeks. Does it really matter what I think?"

"Yes, it matters to me."

Ylva sighed and folded the screen of her laptop down. She ran a hand across her brow.

"You've been seeing each other for, what? A month? You're in love. You're moving in together. That's wonderful. But getting him involved in Revenge? I don't know, but I think it's paving the way for trouble. Don't make the same mistakes you've made previously. What's more, you don't seem all that worried about making sure there's a company left to invest in. So, to be honest, your question is pretty much rhetorical. Tomorrow you might not even be at the helm any longer."

Faye felt her irritation rising.

"He's going to be a passive investor. He's got a lot of money and he happens to believe that Revenge will take the USA by storm. He **believes** in me. And he's the best man I've ever met. He's not like other people."

Ylva raised the palms of her hands toward Faye.

"As I said, do what you like."

"But?"

"No but."

"Well, there's something."

Faye was pissed off. With herself for getting angry and being unable to stop herself from asking for Ylva's opinion. And with Ylva for sticking her nose in, even though it had been Faye who had insisted she speak up.

"I can't say that I know Johanna Schiller," said Ylva. "But I have been to several dinners with her. She seems a pretty decent person. Not at all crazy and aggressive like you describe her. Perhaps you should hear her side of the story too. At least if you and David are moving in together."

Faye snorted and shook her head. She leaned toward Ylva, who calmly met her eye.

"People change. Once upon a time, Jack was a

pretty decent person too. But both you and I are painfully aware that he changed. Johanna Schiller is fighting tooth and nail to keep David in her life. She's even using his daughters against him—making sudden changes to plans and taking them abroad. Refusing to sign divorce papers."

"How do you know that?"

"How . . ."

Faye stopped herself.

Ylva, for whom she had done so much, despite everything that had happened, despite all the betrayal, was sitting there accusing David of lying. She took a deep breath to calm herself down and steady her voice.

"Because he's told me. Because I can see how this situation is close to destroying him. She's trying to crush him using their children."

Ylva held out her arms.

"You're probably right," she said in a low voice.

Faye continued to stare at Ylva, who looked down at the table. She didn't feel as though she was done, but she regretted it before the next words even came out.

"I of all people know. The fact is, it's not completely dissimilar to the way you tried to break me by becoming Julienne's best friend. Because that's what you did, right? Played moms and dads with Jack while I'd lost everything. To crush me."

"That's not fair," Ylva said in a low voice. "And you know it."

Faye's hands were shaking.

"From here on, keep your opinions on my private life to yourself. Focus on your job. And update me if there's any movement on the shares."

She grabbed her handbag and stood up so quickly that her chair fell over onto the floor. She threw a final, icy stare at Ylva before turning on her heel and leaving. She slammed the door hard behind her. The staff looked up before quickly returning their gazes to their screens.

Faye drove aimlessly along the narrow streets on Lidingö. Picturesque suburbs, trees, and small cafés all drifted past outside the window. It was all perfect. Intentionally designed and impersonal.

She could never live here.

Faye regretted her outburst at Ylva. After all, she was the one who'd asked for the woman's opinion. Demanded it. Put her friend in an impossible position. But Ylva had gone too far. Accusing David of lying. Why would he do that? Faye had seen for herself how crushed he had been after every conversation with Johanna. How she was doing everything to ruin his life. Had it been a mistake to hire Ylva at Revenge after all? Had Faye misread her? Perhaps she was jealous? What if she still secretly blamed Faye for her own misfortunes, for the separation from Jack, for being forced out of the industry?

Faye had picked her up out of the gutter despite the scars that Ylva had inflicted on her soul, scars that were still there. Like an invisible patchwork of lost dreams. And now, when Faye had finally begun to heal and finally found love, Ylva couldn't let her enjoy it. Ylva didn't appreciate how good things were for her. Thanks to Faye, she was staying with Alice. Thanks to Faye, she had a good job. And most important of all: she could have her daughter with her. Not like Faye, who was forced to be apart from Julienne. She missed her so much she was going to pieces.

Faye passed the Lidingö shopping precinct and narrowly avoided running over a ginger cat hurrying across the street. She pulled out her phone and called David. She needed to hear his voice. The phone rang but he didn't pick up.

"Fuck."

When it went to voicemail, she threw the mobile phone onto the passenger seat in frustration. She took a deep breath and drove onto the Lidingö Bridge.

She accelerated, zigzagging through the traffic. The speedometer was at one hundred and twenty kilometers per hour. She took delight in the speed. Instead of taking the new tunnel into the city, she turned off and headed toward Gärdet. She soon eased her foot off the accelerator and slowly passed the spot where—almost twenty years ago—she had kissed Jack for the first time. A quick, fleeting kiss. Then he'd turned on his heel and left. Left her behind. That kiss, that night—they had changed her life. Given her Julienne.

Her throat tightened. Tears stung behind her eyelids.

"Pull yourself together," she muttered.

She carried on, heading toward Djurgården. She felt calmer now.

Faye pulled off onto a small track through the woods, not far from the Kaknäs Tower. She switched off the engine. Savored the tranquility. Then she reached for her mobile. She thought for a while, then made up a name, stole a couple of pictures from an American woman's Facebook page, and created a fake Instagram account.

She followed a dozen strangers at random from the new account and then she entered Johanna Schiller's name into the search field. Her profile was set to private. 1,489 followers. "Petra Karlsson" was hopefully going to be follower 1,490.

FJÄLLBACKA—THEN

The islets and skerries that we glided past were dark and shapeless shadows in the twilight. This was Tjurpannan, a region made up of marshes, rocky shorelines, and heath. The unsheltered location made the waters around here treacherous.

Mariners had feared Tjurpannan since the dawn of time. The absence of any outer archipelago meant it was completely exposed to the elements.

Tomas had emerged from the cabin and rubbed his eyes sleepily. He exchanged a few words with Roger, and I assumed they were talking about me. Perhaps they were worried I was going to talk when we got back. Sebastian was nowhere to be seen. If they decided to throw me overboard, would he protest? No, I knew my brother. He was afraid of a thrashing—all he respected were strength and fear.

The dinghy was at the stern. I went back to it. The wind tore and tugged at my clothing. There were bubbles whirling to the surface, created by the blades of the engine. The oars were lying inside the boat.

Roger and Tomas watched me suspiciously as I went over to it and sat down not far from them.

"Be careful," said Tomas. "It's blowing pretty hard and you know what they say about Tjurpannan."

"No," I said, despite knowing full well what they said. What was more, I was surprised at his sudden consideration for me.

"If you fall in here they will never find you. It's the currents, you know."

He turned to Roger, took the last beer from the crate, and opened it.

I slowly and imperceptibly began to reach out my hand for one of the oars. A trough in the waves made the boat lurch. I braced myself against the rail. After a couple of seconds, I made another attempt.

Farther out to sea, there was an illuminated freighter passing by, looking like a prostrate skyscraper.

I felt the coarse surface of the wood under my fingers and drew the oar toward me. I placed it gently at my feet and glanced across at Tomas and Roger. They were standing hunched over the sea chart, examining it with looks of concern.

I took a deep breath. The first raindrops fell, moistening my brow. I opened my mouth, stuck out my tongue, and closed my eyes. Gathering strength.

I stood up, still holding the rail. The next moment, I filled my lungs with oxygen and then I screamed like I'd never screamed before. Perhaps it was the fear I'd felt in the last few days when I'd been locked in the cabin finally being aired. Tomas and Roger pitched toward me.

I pointed dumbly into the water.

"There," I gasped, before taking another gulp of air and screaming again.

They pushed past me and peered into the water and at that moment I took a step back and gripped the oar. I raised it. Swung it at the two of them. I knew I had to hit them both at the same time. As the oar came careering toward them, Tomas turned around. But he didn't have time to react or do anything to protect himself. The oar hit them at chest height and flung them over the rail. Just before I heard the splash from the water, I heard a cry.

I let go of the oar and stumbled forward to watch them disappear and die.

Tomas had somehow managed to catch hold of the rail and was holding on desperately. His gaze was filled with horror as our eyes met. I contemplated him silently.

"Please, help me," he begged.

His hand was cramping and his knuckles were turning white. He tried to grab hold with the other hand to heave himself up. Quietly, I leaned forward. I opened my mouth, put my teeth on his finger, and bit down.

He roared with pain.

I sunk my teeth in, biting all the way down to the bone, and eventually he let go. He fell, screaming. Hit the surface. Then he disappeared beneath it and there was silence.

David called just as Faye had parked the car in the underground garage and was heading upstairs in the elevator. He explained he was going to be late. Hassle from Johanna. Again. She was demanding money from him, otherwise she was threatening to call around to his colleagues in the world of finance to slander him.

"The other day, she said she was going to report me to the police for assault. I'm only putting up with this for the girls' sake. But I can't wait until this is over—when it's just you and me."

"Me too."

David sounded so resigned. If only Ylva had heard this call, she would probably have reconsidered her attitude—and then some.

Sure, she'd been to dinner with Johanna a couple of times. But people showed off their best sides in social settings—they'd rather donate a kidney than show a crack in the perfect façade. Humans were herd animals whose worst nightmare was

exclusion from the community. Of course someone like Johanna Schiller could show her warm,
human side for a couple of hours. And there was
nothing to say that she had always been the way
that David now described her as being. People
changed, as she kept saying. She, of all people,
knew that.

When Jack had left Faye, she had also descended
into a spiral of madness. She had completely forgotten who she was. And why.

She said goodbye to David—he promised he
would be there at nine—just as the elevator stopped
on her floor. She opened the door quickly, looked
left and right to make sure that Jack or her father
wasn't waiting for her, and then rapidly unlocked
the door and security grille.

The apartment was empty and desolate. Beautiful
without feeling like a home. A home needed life,
other people, a story.

Faye put down her bag, opened the sliding doors
onto the terrace to let in some air, and settled
down on one of the white sofas in the living
room. She missed Julienne and her mother so
much. She pulled out a folder of Revenge papers
with outlines for the American products she needed
to approve, but she skimmed the documents without enthusiasm. Sighed. Put them down on the
coffee table.

She couldn't do it. Not tonight. Why should she

spend loads of time on the American expansion when she was going to lose her company anyway?

She reached for her mobile and sent a text to Alice.

I have to get out tonight.
Meet me by Strandbryggan and I'll make sure David comes there.

At Strandbryggan, the party was already in full flow. A DJ was playing Avicii, a yacht adorned with the restaurant's logo was just casting off, and on deck there were two dozen happy twenty-somethings bouncing up and down.

"I feel old," Faye muttered as they stood in line.

"Not me. Quite the reverse, as it happens. I'm sucking up their youth," said Alice. "By the way, this is the first time we've seen each other since you and David decided to move in together. Congratulations."

They hugged and Faye took in Alice's warm scent of vanilla.

Alice was more beautiful than ever. She was wearing a short white dress along with some stratospheric heels that were catching the eye of all the young guys. Faye couldn't help but smile. A couple of years ago she would have been annoyed and jealous of the attention.

Alice smiled at two guys with face tattoos. The

unique thing about her was that she fit in wherever she went. Men of all classes, all backgrounds, all ages, were dazzled by her.

Bringing her on board Revenge had been a stroke of genius, Faye thought to herself with satisfaction.

The maître d', a young guy with glossy brown hair and wearing a white polo shirt and shorts, gave Faye a look of recognition.

"To be honest, we're full tonight, but what wouldn't I do for two such incredible beauties," he said, waving them over to a table.

Alice chortled happily, while Faye rolled her eyes.

"Pompous ass," she muttered.

He stopped at the table, drew out their chairs to let them sit down, and then gestured to a waiter.

"Get the ladies something to drink while they decide what they're eating."

Before long, they each had a glass of bubbly.

"How was the trip to Madrid?" Alice asked.

Faye smiled.

"That good?" Alice remarked, raising her glass.

They let their glasses meet with a chime and both burst out laughing at the same time, putting on affected voices.

"Vulgar!"

They laughed again and took a few generous mouthfuls.

"Where's David?" Alice asked. "I'd like to meet him and ask what he did to net you."

"He'll be here a bit later. You'll get to meet him."

"Finally."

The annoyance that Faye had felt for the last couple of hours had immediately lifted in Alice's company. Life felt uncomplicated. Fun. Exciting.

They ordered parmesan-crusted prawns on sourdough and a bottle of white wine, then they settled back. A boat with wide-eyed tourists passed by slowly, the waves from the boat making the wooden jetty they were sitting on bob pleasantly.

Her thoughts about David and Johanna slid away. Alice told her that Henrik had initiated a campaign to win her back. He had promised to change, go to couples' therapy, and work less.

Alice clenched her fists in irritation while rattling off all the promises.

"What do you feel like doing about it?" Faye asked.

"Nothing. A woman can put up with so much, but eventually her tolerance runs out. And life is more fun now. I loved just being a mom, focusing on my home, the kids, because it was a pleasant and sheltered life. But I'm never going to be dependent on a man again. Nor am I ever going to be an extra in my own life again. And I'm certainly not going to accept the combination of a tiny dick and some dodgy technique."

Faye snorted with laughter. Then she said: "Alice, there's something I have to ask . . ."

"Just a sec," said Alice, raising a finger. "I need the ladies'. The booze is going straight through me."

Alice pushed her chair out and stood up.

Faye watched Alice go and heard a beep from her mobile in her handbag. An Instagram notification. Johanna Schiller had accepted her follower request. Just as she was about to go to her profile, Faye saw David step onto the jetty and look around. She put away her phone, half stood, and waved.

David kissed Faye before sitting down next to her. When Alice returned a minute or so later, she and David hit it off almost immediately. Faye noticed that he was affected by her presence, just like all men.

Alice tossed her head back and laughed at something that David had said. He leaned across the table and gesticulated. Alice laughed even more.

They clearly had chemistry. Was it too strong? Faye felt David's hand on her thigh, and heard their laughter as if through a fog. How well did she actually know David? Should she have taken her conversation with Ylva more seriously? Maybe she should meet Johanna and hear what she had to say?

"Faye?"

The conversation had ground to a halt. She looked from one to the other and back again in confusion.

"What do you think about it? Wouldn't it be wonderful?"

Alice twinkled at her.

"Sorry, I must have had one too many. What do I think about what?"

David looked at her in concern.

"Are you sure you're okay?"

She waved away his worry.

"Just a little dizzy, but I've only got myself to blame. And the wine."

She dutifully threw herself into the conversation, albeit with her thoughts still elsewhere, and she put her hand on top of his.

The fact you were with someone didn't mean you stopped being attracted to other people. Obviously David thought Alice was attractive. He hadn't turned into an asexual robot simply because he and Faye were moving in together. Just as Faye did all the time, he too was allowed to find other people sexy, fantasize about them, be turned on by the thought of them, see a woman and want her.

There was something healthy about it. Regardless of what got into your head. Because the knowledge that your partner was attractive kept you on your toes. Ensured that you invested in the relationship. In yourself. If she wasn't afraid of losing David, would Faye be as attracted to him? People's driving forces when they were looking for a mate were roughly the same. That was why some individuals were deemed more appealing than others.

But if Faye had known she was the only one that David could have, would she have wanted him?

Wasn't it just that very knowledge—that Faye had no other options—that had allowed Jack to deceive Faye over and over again? She had had nowhere to go. Couldn't opt out of him. She had been stuck in her cage. Financially. Emotionally. In her world, Jack had been a god. But in Jack's world, Faye had been a toy that he knew no one could take away from him.

Prohibit and suppress someone's thoughts, and they only ended up echoing louder, pummeling with more strength to get out. They went from a figment of the imagination to reality. If David was fantasizing about sleeping with Alice, where was the harm in that? Why leave him wondering? Why not say, "Hey, you two go home together and I'll see you tomorrow"?

In theory that might have worked. Faye reckoned she had learned enough about emotions and sex in the last couple of years to avoid getting jealous. To understand that a screw was a screw. But she also realized at the same time that she wanted to join in.

The realization hit her with full force: She wanted Alice too. Not as a partner, not to share her life with, but just in the moment. She wanted to consume Alice, her body, her soul. Be reflected in her beauty. Because Alice was attractive. Because she was a goddess.

Unattainable.

She glanced toward Alice. Then she shifted her gaze to David.

She squeezed David's hand tighter.

She felt the idea take root in her body. Tingle. Grow stronger.

"Don't you think it's a bit loud?" she said. "Why don't we go back to the apartment?"

The logs in the fireplace glowed orange and red, and the hue they cast made Alice's and Faye's dancing bodies look like flickering shadows on the white walls. The terrace door was open and ABBA's "Dancing Queen" was seeking its way out and marrying with the light summer night.

They raised their fists toward the ceiling and then formed their hands into microphones, yodeling along with the chorus.

David was sitting in an armchair sipping a whiskey. He had loosened the top buttons on his shirt. His eyes were cloudy and inebriated. A smile was playing on his lips. Faye loved to see his smile—it turned her on and made her wet.

"Dance with us," she called out, waving at him to join them.

She felt her power when he stood up and came toward them. He was with them on their terms—hers and Alice's. They had invited him, not the other way around. They were in charge of the tempo, the rhythm. They were leading the dance.

Faye realized at that moment that she'd never seen David dance, but he let loose, took a couple of dance steps to one side, and then shimmied back to them.

"I haven't been this drunk since I graduated from high school," he said.

"Me neither. And I've definitely never danced this much," Alice hooted.

The combination of dance and booze had made Faye lose all the tension and worry that she had been carrying around inside. All that mattered was right here and right now, in this room. Two people who meant a lot to her on a bright summer's night in Stockholm.

The rest could wait. The world could wait.

The ABBA song faded away, to be replaced by First Aid Kit's "Fireworks."

They leaned back, reached into the air with their hands, and sang along.

Alice's blond hair was down, her body moving rhythmically, sensually, without her even thinking about it—although she was probably aware of how beautiful she was. A moment later, Faye pulled Alice to her and kissed her.

Her lips were soft and moist. Her tongue tasted of mint and alcohol. They were pressed against each other, and when Alice nuzzled Faye's lower lip, it ran through her like an electric shock.

Faye turned her head. David had returned to the armchair and seemed to be bewitched as he watched them without saying a word. She could feel Alice's hard nipples through her dress against her own. They held each other while looking teasingly at David.

She could tell that Alice was in. There was something in their kisses that had gone from playful to hungry in a way that couldn't be misinterpreted.

She and Alice moved toward David and stopped right in front of him. Faye stepped behind Alice and slowly pulled the straps of her dress outward and down over her upper arms. The dress slipped slowly off Alice's body and settled in a small heap at her feet, leaving her naked between David and Faye. David gaped, but didn't move. Instead, he sat completely still with the whiskey glass resting against his thigh, his gaze fixed on Alice.

"Do you like her?" Faye asked, stroking Alice's nipples.

Alice groaned and tilted her head back onto Faye's shoulder. Faye allowed her hands to slowly wander down. In between Alice's legs. She found her wetness and stroked her the same way she loved to stroke herself.

"Do you like her?" she asked again.

David nodded slowly. He had unbuttoned his trousers and pulled out his rock-hard cock and was slowly caressing it top to bottom with his right hand. Faye carried on stroking Alice for a while as David's hand moved up and down.

Alice took a step forward to David. She straddled him. She ground back and forth on his thigh in time to the music. She ignored his cock and forced his hands away from it. Instead, she began to rub against it, but without taking it. Faye went behind the armchair and unbuttoned David's shirt. She drew her fingers around his nipples in circles and gently pinched them. Then she began to stroke Alice's nipples. She leaned across David, and her and Alice's mouths met with wet tongues, while Alice continued to move up and down, grinding against his penis.

It was as if David were paralyzed—he was in their power.

"Touch her," Faye whispered, grabbing hold of his hand and placing it on one of Alice's breasts.

Faye stood up and undressed completely, pulled Alice toward her, kissed her, and then pressed Alice's head between her legs. Faye groaned and braced herself against the wall.

David looked questioningly at Faye and she nodded. He quickly tore off his own clothes and came to stand next to Faye, in front of Alice. Faye nodded in response to Alice's unspoken question. She wasn't jealous. She was the one who was sharing. David. Alice. Right here, right now, there was no one who owned anyone else.

Alice was on her knees, swapping between them to satisfy them both. Faye met David's gaze, smiled slightly, bit her lip, and took a firmer grasp on Alice's hair.

"Now it's our turn. You can watch. Come on."

Faye took Alice's hand and pulled her over to the sofas. Alice lay down on her back on one sofa, and Faye lay down on top of her in the reverse direction with Alice's tongue between her legs. She in turn began to slowly lick Alice. From the corner of her eye, she saw David sit down beside them, his hand moving up and down slowly.

Her eyes darkened with pleasure as Alice licked her. When she felt the orgasm begin to build inside her, she let it explode, and she cried out loud. She stopped licking Alice, rolled to one side on the huge sofa, and looked at David meaningfully.

"I want to see you with her," she said.

He got up and came over.

Alice got on all fours and presented her ass to David, who quickly penetrated her. Faye felt the excitement shooting through her body in waves as David thrust harder and harder. She began to stroke Alice's clitoris and she could feel his hard cock striking her hand. With her spare hand, she caressed his balls—they were hanging there loose and warm.

"Do you like that?" she asked him hoarsely, despite the answer being clearly written on his face.

After a while, Faye couldn't hold herself back—she wanted him. Her entire pussy was throbbing and hot with wetness and desire. She positioned herself next to Alice on all fours too, and he swapped to her. Inebriation meant she saw everything as if through a mist: the light, their naked bodies, the crackling fire.

Voices and panting.

It all felt dreamlike.

Her head was spinning.

Alice's mouth around her nipples. Alice's fingers stroking her as David thrust into her so that delicious pain spread throughout her body to every nerve ending.

She said things she had never before said, thought thoughts she had never before thought.

Afterward, all three of them flopped across the sofa. They laughed, breathing heavily. Tender, sweaty, sticky, excitement still lingering in their bodies, ready for more.

Some moments in life, you forget you're a person, and that in itself is the very essence of humanity, Faye thought to herself as she closed her eyes. Then she felt Alice's lips moving down her body. She loved Alice. She loved David.

FJÄLLBACKA—THEN

Tomas's and Roger's bodies had been swallowed by the foamy surface of the sea. One moment they had existed, now they were just memories. Fish food. The currents around here were countless and wild—I hoped their bodies would never be found.

I grabbed hold of the wheel and maintained the same course that Roger had set.

Sebastian came out of the cabin, where he had been sleeping off his bender. He looked around groggily.

"Where are Roger and Tomas?" he asked, looking surprised.

He came closer and peered at me.

"What's happened?" he said. "You've got blood all around your mouth."

I had deliberately not bothered to wash it off. I would need to scare Sebastian into silence.

He called out for Tomas and Roger. I watched him without expression.

"They fell into the water," I said quietly.

"What did you say?"

I fixed my eyes on him and he must have seen something new, something frightening in them. He reeled backward.

"I hit them with an oar and made them fall overboard," I said, nodding to the oar that was still lying in the very spot where I'd attacked them. "Roger went in straightaway. Tomas clung on, so I bit his hand until he let go. That's why there's blood around my mouth."

Sebastian's eyes opened wide and he took a step toward me.

"We both know that you won't dare do anything when you're on your own," I said calmly. "Those days are over."

He stopped a couple of feet away from me. I licked my lips, feeling the metallic taste of Tomas's blood.

"If you ever touch me again, I'll kill you, Sebastian. Do you understand? I'm no longer yours to do what you want with. And if you ever tell anyone what happened here, I'll say it was you who pushed them overboard and tell them everything that happened. I've got proof of your rapes."

The last bit was a lie.

Sebastian muttered something, but I ignored him.

"The only reason you're alive is that Mom loves you."

I tried to figure out whether I could feel anything

in relation to what I had done. I had killed two people. But I realized with satisfaction that I had simply done what I had to do. To survive. Perhaps it was at that moment that I became an adult.

Sebastian stared at me. But the anger that had been there so clearly was gone. He seemed resigned. Defeated.

"Now I'm going to tell you what to say when we arrive," I said. "You're going to tell the police they fell into the water. That we turned back to search for them but that the seas were too heavy. Do you understand? You will then repeat this story every single time anybody asks. For the rest of your life."

"Are you okay, sweetheart? No regrets about yesterday?"

David looked at her searchingly, stroking her hand with his fingers. Faye appreciated his concern. It would have been strange if it hadn't been there. But she was able to answer truthfully when she said: "No regrets. We're three adults with our own free will, and I love you and Alice. Well, in slightly different ways . . ." She laughed. "But still. It was great. It was love. It was respect."

"You're amazing," David said, and she could see in his eyes that he meant it.

"Oh, you're just saying that," she said. Transparent fishing.

"You do know that I think you're the most beautiful woman on earth, right? Or do I need to be even clearer about that?"

"I think you need to be even clearer," she said, bending forward to kiss him.

There was something about David that made her

thirst for his compliments. It was exquisite when he showered her with terms of endearment. And kisses. She had no doubts after the night before. David had made love to both of them, but throughout he had been clear that he loved her.

"By the way . . ." He sounded hesitant. "We were talking about meeting for lunch, but I have to go away today. To Frankfurt. Boring business stuff to attend to. I'd rather see you, but . . . work calls."

"Of course," Faye said, caressing his hand. "I of all people understand. I'll be away a fair bit too, and it would be really weird if I didn't get it when you had to go away."

"Sure?"

He looked at her from under his mop of hair, and she loved him for his consideration. In her youthful naïveté, she had thought Jack was her dream man. But David was something else. Above all, he wasn't Jack.

David raised her hand to his mouth and kissed it.

"There's no one like you, you know that? When I get home tonight, I want to take you out for dinner. Frantzén. Okay?"

Faye nodded and David kissed her in a way that took her breath away. Dear God, she loved this man.

Faye toweled her hair a little more when she reached the bedroom. She tied the sash on her dressing gown. If she wasn't going to get a cozy lunch with David today, then she wanted a little extra luxury this morning.

At that moment, her mobile lit up on the bed. A text from Ylva. Faye clicked on the message.

Come to the office. Henrik is here. He's been holding back more acquisitions that he's only just reported. He's got a majority.

Faye reeled. She almost dropped her mobile. It couldn't be true. How the hell had this happened?

She dressed quickly, did her makeup even more quickly, and leaped into a taxi. When she arrived at the office, no one would look her in the eye. Alice met her in reception and they exchanged brief smiles before the gravity of the situation descended on them.

"He's in your office," said Alice. "I'm not coming in there with you. For obvious reasons. But Ylva is up there, outside. She's waiting for you."

Faye nodded, firmly gripped her Chanel bag, and took a deep breath before taking the elevator to the top floor. Ylva met her as the elevator doors opened.

"Having the nerve to come here so soon after securing a majority," Faye said. "It's insane."

"Don't let him see how you're actually feeling," Ylva said. "I'm going to try and save what can be saved. And remember: there's always plan B."

"Okay," Faye said grimly, patting her on the shoulder.

Ylva nodded encouragingly and hurried into her office. From the corner of her eye, Faye saw her busy herself with the assortment of papers scattered across her desk.

Slowly, unhurriedly, deliberately under control, Faye sauntered toward her office, which was at the far end of the open-plan area. She could see Henrik through the window and she could see that he had seen her. She held her head high and forced herself to breathe calmly. She couldn't lose her temper. She couldn't afford to let emotion get in the way right now, even if part of her wanted nothing more than to go up to him and wipe that conceited smirk off his face with a well-aimed swipe of her heavy Chanel leather Boy bag. It had rivets on the outside.

Instead, she stepped into her airy office with calm and control.

"Hello, Henrik," she said, nodding to him. "You already seem to have made yourself at home."

He didn't nod back. Instead he grinned.

"The first thing I'm going to do is rip out all this and refurbish the place. Jesus Christ, who was your designer? The ice queen of Narnia? White, white, white. Sterile and cold. Just like you."

Faye sat down in one of the visitor's chairs, smoothed out her Dolce & Gabbana silk skirt, and clasped her hands in her lap.

"Yes, I must confess that it doesn't have the same cozy feeling you prefer. What are you going to go for? Bar in the corner? Football pennants on the walls and a big moose head that you claim is a hunting trophy from one of your trips but that you actually won in an auction at Bukowskis? You know, it might be tricky getting it up, given there's nothing but glass walls here, but maybe you could stick a giant suction cup on the back of it?"

She smirked and saw that it was driving Henrik mad. In the two years that had elapsed since she had last seen him, his hairline had receded dramatically.

"You know, it's not especially flattering when the light catches your head at that angle. But I know several people who've been very happy with what the Poseidon Clinic has done for them. They shave the hair off, pick a spot on your neck and harvest the follicles, and then implant them where it's gone thin. Really great results."

She raised two thumbs and Henrik grasped the edge of the desk. For a moment, he looked like he was going to explode. From her seat, Faye couldn't see into the open-plan office behind her, but she guessed that every single member of the staff was pretending to work while doing everything they could to see what was going on inside her office. Which would soon be Henrik's office, she thought to herself, suddenly feeling nauseated.

"I know what you're trying to do," Henrik said with a grimace. "You're trying to drive me up the wall, just like you did with Jack. You ruined his life, Faye. You took everything from him. And, yes, I've heard your lies about him and I don't believe a single word of them. Jack wasn't like that. Jack was . . . I know you're lying."

He spoke through gritted teeth and Faye swallowed. She controlled the urge to answer cuttingly that he had no way of judging what Jack was and was not capable of. Especially not in relation to his own daughter. But she guessed it was pointless. Henrik wasn't there to listen.

"You didn't just take everything from Jack. You took everything from me too."

"You seem to have managed all right anyway," Faye said acerbically, looking at his tailored Armani suit and his Patek Philippe Nautilus.

"No thanks to you," said Henrik.

Faye shrugged.

"You've always liked being a victim, Henrik. Even back at college. Everything was always someone else's fault."

"Do you think you're in a position to have this sort of attitude toward me, Faye?"

"Does it matter what sort of attitude I have? Does that change anything?"

Henrik smiled, reclined, and put his feet on the desk. All of a sudden, he looked at her in amusement.

"No. Nothing whatsoever, really. I'm doing what I planned to do. It's done. I'm the majority share-holder and I'm going to propose a new board of directors as soon as possible. Without you."

Faye held out her arms.

"Well, congratulations. You'll soon have Revenge in your hands. Take the office now, it's yours. But do you have any vision? Do you know anything about how to run a company like this?"

Henrik sat up in his seat.

"Faye, the problem with you is that you're an empty shell. You're just an exterior and there's noth-ing of any value underneath it. Jack knew that. I know that. Everyone around you notices it as soon as they get to know you. You can trick people for a bit, but sooner or later, they realize who you are. No one can love you, Faye."

He chuckled. His eyes were bright, and once again in her mind's eye she saw how the rivets on the bag would rip open his fiery red skin.

Instead, she stood up slowly. She sat down on the edge of the desk. He appeared to find that discom-fiting, and shrank back in his desk chair.

"I understand where this need to assert yourself comes from, Henrik. Alice has told me everything. But they can even perform operations for that these days. They can definitely add an inch. Maybe you should consider it. Because you can't use my company as a penis extender . . ."

She smiled scornfully at him, stood, picked up her Chanel bag, and swept out of her former office.

Behind her, she heard a crash. Henrik had thrown something right at the glass wall. She smiled: 1–0 to her. She had kept an even temper, he hadn't. She only hoped it wasn't a Pyrrhic victory.

The heat didn't dissipate. Faye left the office on Birger Jarlsgatan and strolled toward Stureplan to eat lunch alone. She needed to gather her thoughts, sort through them, after what had just happened. Revenge had been lost, but she hoped only temporarily. Ylva seemed to be putting all her faith in plan B.

Faye had always struggled to think when sitting still with nothing but empty walls to look at. She needed external stimuli—to see people, to hear them.

The tourist season was in full swing. Clusters of tourists were wandering around the city. She didn't blame them. Stockholm was beautiful—she loved the place. But she couldn't enjoy it in the same way she had when she had first arrived from Fjällbacka. Her eyes had grown accustomed and were no longer as keenly alert to its beauty.

Faye reached Stureplan and stood immobile for a while under the big concrete mushroom, wondering where to go.

The outdoor area at Sturehof was full. Granted, she had nothing against being seated indoors, but she would have preferred not to bump into anyone she knew. Not now, when the rumors of her loss of Revenge were probably spreading like wildfire. She walked toward Strandvägen, passing the luxury shops without looking in the windows, feeling how the walk was waking up her brain. The water in Nybroviken glittered in the sun. The quaysides were filled with people. She stopped at the crosswalk and waited for the light to change.

She felt empty. The brief euphoria she had felt in getting Henrik to lose his composure had gone. Instead, she felt nothing. She searched for her rage. The darkness. The turbid water. But all she found was emptiness in those depths. It surprised her. Took her off her guard. She always knew how to deal with rage, but she didn't know how to deal with nothing.

She was used to fighting. She had been fighting since childhood. She had crossed all the lines drawn by people, the justice system, logic. Laws and morals. She had crossed them all without blinking. But now she was lost. She didn't feel like herself, and she didn't know how to deal with a Faye who wasn't on fire.

Her phone buzzed in her pocket. It was probably Ylva calling. But Faye didn't feel up to it quite yet. Something that Henrik had said in their conversation was gnawing inside her. But she didn't know exactly what. It was there, just beyond reach in the murky water. Something he had said that she ought to have caught.

The light changed to green. As she crossed the street, she glanced toward one of the waiting cars. A taxi. Through the windshield, behind the driver, she saw two faces she recognized. David and Johanna. Faye averted her gaze and hurried across, reached the pavement on the far side, and came to a stop. The lights changed to green for the traffic and the taxi pulled away. Her heart was pounding in her breast.

Had he seen her?

Before Faye had left the office, she had sent a message to David asking whether he was able to fly home any earlier from his business trip. She wanted to tell him about the takeover, about Henrik, and ask his advice on how to proceed. She wanted to lean against him, bury her face in his shoulder, and hear his calming voice in her ear.

But he had replied that he couldn't, that he had some things to finish up and that he'd see her when he got home late in the evening. He hadn't said a word about Johanna. Had she missed something?

Faye pulled out her phone, her hands trembling, and quickly scrolled through their conversation. No, it said there clear as day that he wasn't coming back to Stockholm until late tonight. Perhaps it was an emergency? Perhaps one of the kids was seriously ill, or had hurt themselves, and he'd had to return home as a matter of urgency . . . Was that why he and Johanna were in the same taxi?

Faye saw Ylva's face appear before her and heard the words again.

How well do you know David?

Fuck Ylva. Fuck David. Fuck Henrik.

She clenched her fist so tightly her nails cut into the palm of her hand.

All sorts of things might have happened. She couldn't blow up right now—not until she had all the facts. She loved David. Everything was so straightforward with him. They wanted to enjoy life, together. To never hold each other back. Could that have made Faye completely blind? Was she going nuts?

She walked on as if in a trance and found an empty bench in Berzelii Park. She could see happy diners at Berns.

Her mobile phone buzzed. She got it out. She saw David's name as the sender. What a relief—now everything would be explained. Of course it was an emergency.

But when she opened the message and read it, it was like a knife to her gut.

Missing you and can't wait for tonight. So crappy having to be far away from you. Miss Stockholm, miss you.

Just like that. The words that she had read so often and always believed.

Around her, she saw people hurrying past, going places, together with others. She suddenly wished she were one of them. She suddenly wished she was not Faye.

With her hands shaking, she went on Instagram, searched for Johanna Schiller's profile, and looked at her posts. A man settled down next to her, cracked a beer can open, and took a swig.

"Nice day," he said.

"Is it?" Faye replied abruptly.

He chuckled.

She scrolled down through the photos. To the week when she and David had met. It took a while. Johanna was a frequent poster. On some days there were three or four different pictures. Some of them were of David. On a jetty, at the dinner table, in a restaurant, by the barbecue. Smiling, laughing, hugging his daughters, kissing Johanna on the cheek. Happy kids. Sunsets. Beautifully assembled dishes.

Faye's jaw dropped.

Dinner with my cuties.
My husband surprised us with homemade lasagna.
Barbecue hygge with the family.
Minibreak: the west coast is the best coast.

Each caption followed by at least six emojis.

Faye got out her laptop, opened it, went to her calendar, and compared dates. David hadn't mentioned going to the west coast. On the date in question, he had been on a business trip. And according to Johanna's Instagram account, they were not in the midst of a fractious divorce—on the contrary, they appeared to have an idyllic relationship. Of course, social media could tell lies and present an illusion that wasn't true, paint over the cracks, prettify. But this?

Her heart was pounding in her rib cage. Her stomach was in a knot. She remembered the later stages with Jack.

She pulled up David's number on her mobile. She had to talk to him, hear his voice, get an explanation. There had to be some mistake.

Faye got his voicemail.

She sent him a text asking him to call as soon as he could.

How blind had she been?

Why hadn't she returned Johanna's call or listened to Ylva? Or checked the Instagram account sooner? How could she have been blind and deaf? Again?

She got up from the bench. She knew where David's office was—or at least where he'd said it was. Did it even exist? She hurried through Berzelii Park, around the corner of Berns, and headed for Blasieholmen, where several of Stockholm's most reputable financial firms were based. Her phone rang, making her jump. She tugged it out, hoping it was David, but it wasn't. It was Ylva.

"Yes?" she said, answering irritably.

"I need to talk to you."

"I don't feel like talking about Revenge right now. Give me a couple of hours to digest it."

"Yes, well, about Revenge, we need to meet up and make a plan—see what we can do to avoid losing control of the company. But that's not what I wanted to talk to you about."

"Please, Ylva, this isn't a good time."

"It's about David. You'll want to see this. You may not believe me, but you asked me to go over his proposal, his finances, everything. That's what I've spent the last few days on. Everything is here. Paper doesn't lie. Paper doesn't pass judgment."

Faye stopped. She looked out across the water toward the elegant nineteenth-century façades. It was all so beautiful. How could it all be so beautiful when she was in the midst of a nightmare?

"Where are you?" she asked.

"I couldn't stay at the office after Henrik came by—who knows how long it will be before he chucks us out. So I came back to Alice's."

"I'll come there," said Faye.

"Are you okay?"

"I don't know," Faye whispered. "I don't know."

"Where are you?"

"Berzelii Park."

"Stay there. I'll pick you up."

Heaps of papers were scattered across the desk in Alice's study, which had been placed at Ylva's disposal when she had moved in. She pulled out a chair, firmly pushed Faye into it, and sat down next to her.

They hadn't said a word to each other in the taxi.

"Thanks," Faye mumbled.

Ylva looked her deep in the eyes.

"There's nothing to thank me for. You would have done the same for me. What's happened? Well, apart from the obvious—the massacre we witnessed this morning. But there's something else. Want to talk about it?"

Faye sighed. "Can you open that window? I need some air . . ."

Ylva nodded and went over to the window. Speaking slowly and hesitantly, Faye said: "I'm beginning to think you were right. I don't know . . . Jesus, I don't know anything any longer."

Ylva scrutinized her with a frown.

"What do you mean?"

Faye ran the nail of her middle finger along the desktop. She didn't know where to start. She was burning with shame.

She cleared her throat.

"All this time, David has been seeing Johanna as if nothing has happened. To be honest, I don't even know if he ever had any plans to get divorced from her. All those stories about him fighting for the two of us, that it was going to be us, I think it was all a lie. They went to Marstrand together when he told me he was at home all weekend fighting with her. They were on the rollercoasters at Liseberg in Gothenburg when he told me he was on a business trip to Tallinn."

Faye couldn't stop the tears.

"Please forgive me, Ylva. For the way I treated you when you tried to tell me. I know you had my best interests at heart—that you wanted to protect me."

Ylva shifted closer to Faye and put her head on her shoulder.

"None of us wants to hear that kind of thing about the person we think loves us," she said. "And I didn't know for certain. I had no idea. All I knew was that he was exaggerating to you how crazy Johanna was."

"I don't understand how I could be so blind. So stupid."

Faye was sobbing by now. Ylva stroked her hair, hushing her.

Eventually, Faye was able to wipe the tears from her face. With a sigh, she put a hand on the stack of papers in front of her.

"So what does this prove, then? I assume it's bad news."

Ylva cleared her throat. Faye could tell from her expression that she was worried about hurting her.

"Out with it!" she said. "I can take it."

"David Schiller is pretty much broke. You and Revenge are his last hope. And it's actually worse than that. It's all connected."

Then she began to explain.

FJÄLLBACKA—THEN

There was a phone booth in the harbor. While Sebastian tied up, I rushed over to it, grabbed the receiver, and dialed 90000 for the emergency services. Half an hour later, the jetty was crawling with people. Someone had tipped off the local paper and a reporter and photographer from **Bohusläningen** were prowling back and forth, waiting for an opportunity to talk to us.

They were circling me and Sebastian like sharks anticipating their prey, but the policemen asked them to wait until we'd had a chance to explain what had happened. I must have looked scared and so small. But inside I was proud. Sebastian was as pale as a corpse. I stayed close to him all the time. The police and the others probably thought I was sticking to him because I was afraid, but my only aim was to ensure that he stuck to the story I had given him.

"And you're saying they fell in?" one of the policemen asked.

Sebastian nodded.

"We turned the boat around and went back, but there wasn't a trace of them," he said in a low voice.

The police exchanged tired glances. There was no suspicion, just sorrow and resignation.

"You shouldn't have gone out in this weather," said the policeman, before he turned away.

"I'm sorry," I whispered. "But we were missing home. It was Tomas who wanted to."

Eventually, it was the reporter's turn. He wanted to talk to me rather than Sebastian. I probably looked more young and innocent, which would generate greater sympathy from readers. During the interview, the photographer took pictures of me.

"I refuse to believe they're dead. I hope they find them," I said, trying to look as unhappy as possible.

Faye walked slowly along Humlegårdsgatan, her sunglasses a screen between her and the surrounding world. It was surreal. The people, the laughter, the joy. How could they be so unaffected? Her world had just been smashed to smithereens and her future had been thrown away.

David and Henrik were working together. They had managed to conceal it well. But not so well that Ylva—with a little time, stubbornness, and diligence—hadn't been able to find the traces. And in one way, they had been clumsy. As Ylva had pointed out, Henrik's weakness was that he was careless. They already knew that he had planned to report several of the acquisitions at the same time, to try to spring his new majority on them and allow him to propose a new board as quickly as possible.

However, what Ylva had managed to figure out even before the new owner of the shares had been made official was that David was one of the investors backing Henrik. That too had been hidden in a slipshod fashion in a Maltese corporation, but following the revelations of recent years, Malta was no longer the safe haven it had once been for companies that wanted to engage in tax planning or hide something. Another mistake by Henrik.

But it didn't matter. His mistakes had simply allowed them to discover the connection between David and Henrik. It hadn't offered up anything that would help them prevent the loss of Revenge.

And now Faye realized what had been gnawing at her since the quarrel with Henrik at the office. He had intimated it there and then. He had said that no one could love her.

She didn't need to search for a motive behind the two men's actions. Henrik wanted to restore his wounded manhood. Which was ironic, given that you can't restore something you never had in the first place. And David? It was quite simple: money. And power. For him, she had merely been a way to achieve those two things. She saw that now. Several of the people who had sold to Henrik lately could only have been gotten at thanks to information that David had accessed on her laptop. She felt absolutely hemmed in on all sides.

Faye got out her mobile and sent a text to David.

Can you call me? There's something we need to talk about.

Everything had gone to shit. She had lost control of Revenge. And she had lost David—or, more specifically, the person she had thought he was. She had lost something that had never even existed, which it should have been impossible to grieve for. But for her, it had become real.

Her mobile vibrated in her hand.

Things have gotten messy in Frankfurt. Have to stay a few days. Missing you.

Faye swallowed and then swallowed again. And then she made up her mind. She was going to sell everything off and leave Sweden for good. Withdraw. Julienne was in Italy. It was there, by her side, keeping her safe, that she belonged. Following David's betrayal and the fact that Revenge would soon have slipped out of her grasp, there was no reason to carry on.

She would head up to the apartment, fetch her things, and go home to Julienne. She'd leave it to the lawyers to handle the sale of her shares in Revenge. She no longer had to worry about the American expansion. That would be up to Henrik before long. She would never set foot in Sweden again. She didn't really even want to go up to the apartment, but the photo of Julienne and her mother was in a plastic wallet behind the bathtub. It was proof that her mother and daughter were both alive. She couldn't leave Sweden without it.

David had left various items in the apartment, but Faye didn't even have the strength to chuck them into the fire.

And Ylva and Alice? Perhaps they would be disappointed in her, but if she stayed there was a risk they would be pulled down into the mire with her. They'd be much better off without her.

She keyed in the code and opened the door. She had to wait a while for the elevator.

Faye got in and pulled the grille shut. She saw each floor pass by. She readied herself. Just a couple of minutes, then she'd be in a taxi on the way to Arlanda.

The elevator came to a halt.

Faye went straight to the front door, her heels tapping briskly across the floor. She put the key in the lock and turned it. At that moment, she heard a scraping sound behind her and felt the cold steel against the back of her neck.

She turned around slowly. She knew it was Jack before she saw him. Like she always did.

PART FOUR

At least one person lost their life when a summer house outside the town of Köping was burned to the ground on Wednesday evening. By the time fire services arrived on the scene, the cabin was already engulfed in flames.

"These kinds of older cabins often have inadequate wiring in place. It's not unusual for short-circuits to lead to these sorts of accidents," said Anton Östberg from Västra Mälardalen emergency services.

The identity of the deceased remains unknown, and it is unclear whether there were other casualties.

"We have just begun an investigation, but there is much to suggest that this was a tragic accident," said Gun-Britt Sohlberg from Köping Police.

Aftonbladet, 27 June

The tip of the knife was now digging into Faye's ribs. Jack's mouth was curled into a triumphant and contemptuous smile.

"Open the door," he said. "Otherwise I'll stick the knife in your throat."

Faye's heart was pounding violently in her breast.

She did as he said and unlocked the door and the safety gate. Jack shoved her into the apartment and locked the door behind them. There was nowhere to escape.

He pushed her ahead of him and forced her down onto the sofa. Then he grabbed her handbag, rooted through it, and scattered the contents onto the coffee table.

"You tricked me, you tricked everyone. You've ruined my life. I know I didn't kill our daughter. I don't know how you did it, but she's alive. She must be. You've got my daughter somewhere."

Faye wasn't able to summon up an answer. She was paralyzed, almost numb about what was happening. Jack had appeared so suddenly, she still couldn't grasp that he was here.

"I'm going to find Julienne and prove that you framed me. When I'm done with you, the whole world is going to know what a deceitful whore you are."

Jack was talking fast and in a strained voice—he sounded almost manic. He kept pacing back and forth across the living room. His hair was greasy and his clothes dirty.

Gone was the elegance that had impressed Faye so much.

He grabbed her mobile phone and began to look through the photos. Faye waited calmly, knowing there were no traces of Julienne there.

"You can search everywhere," she said. "I'm not hiding anything from you."

When he didn't find anything, he cast the mobile away, rushed over to the sofa, and thrust his face close to hers.

"You had me convicted of the murder of my own daughter!" he shouted. "Everyone in Sweden, my family, my friends, everyone thinks I'm an animal. A child killer."

Saliva spattered her face.

"Do you know what they do to us in prison? I'm going to find her and prove what you did! I'll take everything away from you, just like you did to me!"

His reaction made Faye feel more confident, even

if she realized she was in mortal danger. Her words still touched Jack—she thought and hoped so, at any rate. As long as she could influence him, she could get out of this with her life intact.

Jack pushed her down into the sofa, raised the knife, and lowered it slowly toward her face. Faye pursed her lips and forced herself to look him in the eye.

"I ought to cut off your face," Jack hissed. "You've cost me everything."

Her heart was racing, but Faye didn't so much as flicker.

"I've missed you," she whispered.

Her voice sounded so believable that she actually wondered whether she was lying or not. For a moment, she thought she had him.

"Jack, it's me. Faye. You love me. I would never have done what I did if you hadn't left me, hadn't humiliated me."

Jack looked at her searchingly, almost tenderly.

The next moment he raised his left arm and slapped her face.

"You're not even called Faye. Your name is Matilda. And when I'm done with you here, I've promised your dad he can have the pleasure of killing you for what you did to him."

"What are you talking about?"

Faye rubbed her cheek, curling up and making herself small. Her chest felt tight.

"You know what I'm talking about. I was in the same prison as him. I know what happened in Fjällbacka. How you took everything away from him, just like you did to me. And then you ran off to Stockholm and thought you could start over."

"That's not true," Faye said, trying to rally her thoughts. "You're mistaken."

A new blow landed, this time on her stomach. She lost her breath and rolled to one side.

"Please, Jack," she panted. "I don't know who you're talking about—someone has fooled you. It's not the way you think it is."

Jack got up and paced back and forth again. Faye looked at him narrowly. Did he believe her?

"Do you think it was coincidence that Gösta and I managed to escape together? We found each other in prison. I promised that if I found a way to get out I would take him with me. Apparently he has a bone to pick with you too . . ."

Jack smirked.

"When we heard we were going to be transported at the same time, I realized it was a golden opportunity. One guard who needed a piss later and we were out."

Faye shut her eyes for a moment, then opened them, forcing herself to look at Jack.

"Leave here," she said. "You're only making it worse. I won't tell the police you were here. I can give you money so that you can leave the country and start over. I love you. I've always loved you. No man is like you, no one has ever been able to replace you."

Both of them jumped when her mobile began to ring. Jack picked it up from the floor and looked at it. It was a very familiar number.

"It's the police," said Faye. "They call me every day or so to check everything is all right."

Without any expression, Jack handed over the mobile.

"Answer it. Say everything is fine. If you try in any way to give me away, I'll stick this knife in your stomach," he said, poising the blade just below her breasts.

Faye pressed accept to answer the call and hit the speakerphone button. Jack crouched in front of her, knife at the ready.

"Hello?" she said.

"Hi, it's Oscar Veslander of the Stockholm Police," a voice said.

Faye held her breath.

"This is just our daily call to check that everything is okay."

Faye met Jack's gaze. She was unable to recognize the man she had shared her life with. Who was he?

"Yes," she said, Jack nodding. His hands moved down toward her groin. "Everything's fine."

Jack cut her top to shreds with one movement. Faye was shaking.

"Where are you?"

Faye gritted her teeth and pulled herself back to avoid the blade.

"Hello?"

She looked down at Jack, whose face didn't display even a flicker of emotion.

"I'm at home, just working," she said in a monotone.

"I'm afraid there's no news about your ex-husband, but I promise we're doing everything we can to find him."

"Good. Great. I know you're doing your best."

Her voice wavered.

If Faye hadn't been certain before, she was now: Jack was out of his mind. Completely unpredictable. He might very well decide to kill her. She had to get out of here.

"Have a nice day. And call us if you have any questions."

"Thanks. You too."

Faye ended the call and looked down at Jack.

He got up slowly, without lowering his gaze from her. Suddenly, without warning, he struck her again. She collapsed on the sofa. He wrenched her phone from her. She looked up at him.

"Jack, you have to disappear now. Escape. Otherwise the police will arrest you. I won't say anything. Not that you were here, not about what you did."

He didn't reply.

All that was audible was his heavy breathing. Jack sat down in front of her, pulled a lock of her hair to his nose, and drew in the scent.

"I've missed your scent. Despite everything you've done to me, I've still missed it. You're the love of my life. No one else meant anything—get it? Do you understand that I did what I did because I could?

Because the women were throwing themselves at me? I was weak. But it was only you who meant anything."

Faye shuddered. It sounded as if Jack was saying farewell.

"Are you going to kill me?"

"I don't know. I did make a promise to your father that he could be the one to kill you. But maybe I will instead."

Her pulse was beating so fast she was dizzy. Her eyes darkened.

"No, Jack. You're not a murderer. You don't have it in you. It's me. Faye."

She placed her hands on his cheeks and forced him to look at her.

"You've got another daughter, Jack. What'll happen to her if you're convicted for another murder? The police'll catch you sooner or later. And Julienne . . . you're right. She's alive. She's safe. If we forget about this, if you can forgive me, she'd be thrilled. She still talks about you. You're her hero, Jack. In spite of everything, you're her hero."

Faye swallowed and looked searchingly at Jack to see whether her words had had any impact. In years gone by she had been able to read his innermost thoughts the second he came into the room. But now his face gave nothing away. He had been transformed into a stranger.

"And I miss you." She let the tears flow. "Despite

everything you did, I love you and always have. But you hurt me. You humiliated me. You crushed me. All I wanted was to live with you and Julienne, but you tricked me, Jack. First you deprived me of work, the right to the thing I'd helped create. Then my own family. You replaced me."

Jack's teeth were grinding. His facial expression was beginning to soften. She rejoiced internally. Perhaps he might just leave?

"Julienne," said Jack. "Have you got a photo of her? I think about her every day. Every second."

Faye remembered the pictures she had found on Jack's computer. The awful, dreadful photos. Julienne's vacant stare. She didn't want to show him her one photo of her daughter. But what choice did she have? Her priority right now was to survive long enough to prevent him from getting anywhere near Julienne. Somehow she needed to persuade him to lower his guard . . .

She nodded slowly.

"We can call her. Just think how happy she'll be to see you."

Jack's eyes narrowed suspiciously. He shook his head and put her mobile on the table.

"No. No phones. No technology."

She took a deep breath.

"I've got a picture of her. Want to see it?"

"Where?"

"Move and I'll get it."

Jack got up slowly.

Once Faye was on her feet, he brandished the knife at her.

"If you try to trick me, I'll kill you right away. Don't you forget it."

"I know."

She went to the bathroom with him on her heels. Inside, she worked the bathtub away from the wall, stuck her arm down behind it, and retrieved the plastic wallet with the photograph of her mother and Julienne. She straightened up again and passed the wallet to Jack. He took it and examined the photo without saying a word. But the glint in his eye scared her. He was looking at the picture of Julienne as if she were his prey, as if he could do whatever he liked with her. He slipped it into his jacket pocket.

At that moment, Faye realized she had made a mistake. Jack had somehow tricked her. And now he was going to kill her. He raised the hand with the knife in it. Faye screamed and everything went black.

FJÄLLBACKA—THEN

Although they never found Roger's and Tomas's bodies, they held a ceremony for them.

I was there in the church and heard every single word about what fine upstanding boys they had been. Mourners were in tears in the pews. The priest struggled to keep his voice steady. Personally, I wanted to be sick when I remembered all the things they'd done to me and what I'd had to endure.

Their smiling portraits mocked me from the altar. I put my hand to my breast where the necklace that Mom had given me had once hung with reassuring weight. They had taken the last of my confidence away from me.

The only thing I could think about was how Roger and Tomas had held me down, forced themselves into me, and laughed at my pleas for them to stop. The way that Tomas's sparkling eyes had been transformed into something cold and hard.

I hated them for what they had done and I was so happy they were gone.

I didn't even feel sorry for their parents or Roger's grandmother. They had raised them and made them into what they had become. It was their fault too.

But the whole community celebrated their lives and grieved for them. And it widened the gulf between me and Fjällbacka—it just increased my resolve to leave and get away from the hypocrisy. The silence. The holding of tongues.

Faye opened her eyes. She was lying on the cold bathroom floor. Her head was splitting, pounding. She slowly raised her hand to her brow and could feel that it was sticky. She held up her fingers in front of her and saw that she was still bleeding.

Despite the pain, she was glad she was alive. Jack had struck her head with the handle of the knife and she must have fainted. Although the pain was shooting through her head in waves, she was alive. That was what mattered most.

"You should have killed me, Jack," she muttered.

She calmly wondered why he hadn't, and hoped her father wasn't waiting somewhere close by. She couldn't think about that now.

She got up on unsteady legs, supporting herself on the sink, and examined her wounded and swollen face in the mirror.

Jack.

And David.

Both of them were going to get what they deserved. The fact that Jack had the photo that proved Julienne was alive was a disaster. But she would retrieve it. He wasn't going to rush to the nearest police station brandishing the photo. There was still time. Her temporary downswing—when she had wanted to give up and escape it all—was over. That wasn't her. Faye never gave up. She gave as good as she got.

She screwed her eyes shut tight, remembering the photos of Julienne she had found on Jack's computer. Photos of Julienne undressed and vulnerable. Abused by the person she loved most. That was what had triggered it all. It was what had made her do what she did best. Take care of the people she loved. And defend herself. No matter what the cost was.

She had lulled herself into a false sense of security, in the hope that Jack was gone forever. That had been naïve. Innocent. She wouldn't repeat that mistake. Now she was going to put a stop to Jack. Permanently. For her own sake, but above all for Julienne's. He was never going to be allowed to get close to her again—he was never going to be allowed to hurt her again.

It was just past midnight and Revenge's offices were dark and empty. The only light that was on was in Faye's office, and as Faye looked up she could picture Henrik sitting there working. On Revenge. Her Revenge. She drove past the building quickly. She didn't want to see it. Instead, she carried on through the darkness toward Lidingö. The asphalt glittered black following a gentle evening shower that had come and gone in the space of ten minutes. She had to go to Alice's to speak to Ylva.

So much depended on Ylva. And Alice.

If Ylva refused to help Faye, she wouldn't be able to stop Jack. The best outcome would be that she'd end up in prison, the worst case was that her father would murder her first. He was out there somewhere. Jack too. And she needed both Ylva and Alice to win back the company.

She rang the doorbell and Ylva opened up. Ylva's eyes widened when she caught sight of Faye's face. She opened her mouth but then shut it again.

"Alice isn't home. Are you okay?"

Faye took a couple of steps inside the hallway.

"I'm okay," she said briefly. "But I need to speak to you."

"What's happened?" said Ylva, leading her to the guest room where she was staying.

Faye had wondered how honest she could be. She had decided to tell Ylva everything. No more lies. At least not for Ylva. If she suspected Faye was lying, there was a risk she wouldn't trust her. Faye couldn't take that risk.

"Jack."

Ylva put a hand over her mouth.

"He attacked me at the apartment. Beat me unconscious. I woke up on the bathroom floor."

Faye sat down in an armchair and reached for the picture of Nora on the nightstand. She examined it, thinking about the picture that Jack had taken from her: the one proving that both Julienne and Faye's mother were alive. It made her pluck up courage.

"There are things about Jack I haven't told you, Ylva. Things that I haven't told anyone. I lived with him for almost my entire adult life, but I never saw those sides to him—didn't understand them. Not until near the end. That's why I doubt whether you will have seen them, even though you also know Jack and shared a life with him."

Ylva's eyes widened.

"What do you mean?"

"I should start by saying that Julienne is alive. She's living safe and sound in Italy with my mom."

Ylva's jaw dropped.

"So it's true what she said, that policewoman who came to talk to me? I sent her packing and said she was crazy."

"Yes, Yvonne Ingvarsson is right. I framed Jack for a murder that never happened. It was never about me, or my ego because he left me, or because Jack denied me money that I was entitled to. You know the two of us—you know that I was there and helped to build what would become Compare."

Faye stroked her chin. She found it hard to say the words aloud.

"It was all about some photos I found of Julienne. Jack had taken highly detailed, nude pictures of her. She was completely at his mercy. He's a sick man, Ylva. I realized I had to protect Julienne from him."

Faye stared down at the floor. She struggled to summon the words.

Ylva stared at her, her face white.

"Thank God Julienne is alive," she whispered. "But what she went through at the hands of Jack is dreadful. What he put her through."

Faye blinked away the tears. Her voice was stronger now.

"You have a daughter with Jack too. And for as

long as Jack is alive, Nora will be in serious danger. Other children will be, too. He's a pedophile. I need your help. As a friend, as a woman. Because there are some things that the justice system doesn't look kindly upon, even if the politicians always claim it does."

"What do you need help with?"

Faye contemplated Ylva. She had put her life in her hands. If Ylva betrayed her confidence, then Faye would end up in prison. She would be one of the most hated women in Sweden. Which was strange, given that all she had done was act the way any responsible mother would have. Society hadn't been capable of protecting her—it never had been. Not when she had been raped and assaulted at home as a young girl. Not when she had been conned out of the money from the company she had created. Not when she was chucked out like an old rag because her husband had met someone new.

She trusted Ylva precisely because she was a woman, because she could understand that vulnerability and powerlessness. Although they might never have faced it, every single woman could **feel** that emotion. And she trusted Ylva because she too knew Jack. She had seen the monster behind the mask. And she too had loved him once.

"Jack has to be eliminated if our kids are going to be safe. And Henrik is going to pay royally for trying to take away something that belongs to me."

Ylva looked at her hands, which were clasped on her lap. She didn't reply. They were interrupted by a cry from the next room.

Ylva stood up hastily.

"Go. See to her," said Faye.

Ylva nodded and went into the room next door. A few minutes later she returned with Nora in her arms, her sleepy face red and bloated, her hair tousled. When she caught sight of Faye she burst into a smile that showed her tiny milk teeth. Ylva kissed her head. She looked at Faye with tears in her eyes. Then she nodded.

"I'm in. And I'm guessing it's time for plan B?"

"It's definitely time for plan B. And I've also got an idea for Alice."

"What?" said Ylva curiously, cradling Nora in her arms.

Nora shut her eyes and fell asleep. Faye said nothing—she merely got out her phone with a smile. When Alice picked up, Faye could hear the sound of traffic and laughter. She must be having a drink out somewhere.

"Hasn't Sten Stolpe always liked you?" said Faye.

"Liked?" Alice chortled. "That's putting it mildly."

"Would you be up for contacting him?"

"Sure, no problem. What did you have in mind?"

Faye explained while Ylva cradled her sleeping daughter, her lips forming a grim smile as she listened.

FJÄLLBACKA—THEN

As the weather changed and the nights closed in and grew cooler, it was time for me to return to school.

I was starting seventh grade, and tradition dictated that a big party was held, where all the local youths gathered in the woods the weekend before the schools went back. High schoolers were drinking, listening to music, sneaking off to fool around, fighting, and hurling into bushes.

I went and sat alone at a slight distance, mostly because I had nothing else to do. Sebastian was there. He'd achieved some sort of celebrity status, thanks to having been on TV, in the papers, and on the radio all summer talking about how great his friends had been.

I usually never went to parties. I didn't want to be there. But I had to make sure that no one asked, no one wondered, no one knew. I felt no regret at what I had done, just anxiety that I would be found out. I wanted to hear what people were saying—I wanted to hear what gossip was going around Fjällbacka. I needed to be among my peers to make sure I was safe. And I wanted to keep an eye on Sebastian.

When he caught sight of me his eyes flashed. He came staggering toward me. Clearly drunk. He stumbled across the rocks, almost fell, but managed to keep upright.

"What the fuck are you doing here, you whore?" he hissed, sitting down next to me.

He stank of booze and vomit.

I didn't reply. The balance of power between us had changed. Now it was only when he was drunk that he dared treat me like this. Otherwise he seemed almost scared of me. Just the way I wanted.

"Go away, Sebastian. I don't want any trouble."

"You can't tell me what to do."

"Yes, I think I can, actually. And you know why."

I moved away and was getting ready to stand up and leave when he grabbed hold of my arm.

"I'm going to tell them—all of them—what happened that fucking night. How you killed them."

I regarded him calmly. He hadn't touched me since the rapes on the island. But he drank too much. And when he drank he talked. Got angry. Lost control. I detested him and his weakness. There was way too much of Dad in him. Sebastian was a lost cause, and now that the attention around him had begun to die down, he was going to find a new way to be seen.

"Witch," he sneered. "You fucking disgusting witch. I hope you're raped again. You do too, really. I know you liked it."

I sighed, got up, and left him.

While walking through the woods, I could hear the music, the laughter, and the hoarse voices of the partygoers. I knew I would have to silence Sebastian. Mom loved him, but she didn't know him like I did. She didn't know what he was capable of.

The world didn't need more men like him. Men who hit, terrified, and raped. One day, he would marry, father children, and have them in his violent grip. I didn't intend to let that happen. I didn't intend to let Sebastian treat his future girlfriend or his wife the way that Dad treated Mom. I wasn't going to let a little boy or girl grow up and have to see what I had seen. I was the only one who could break the cycle.

But most of all, I wasn't going to let him ruin everything for me. He'd had his chance. He was the one who'd opted not to take it.

I had intended to let him live. For Mom's sake. Despite him hurting me in ways that weren't visible from the outside but that on the inside made me lie awake, night after night, suffering from phantom pain as a result of what had been done to me. We'd held each other's safety in our hands, and he'd robbed me of the small shard of something beautiful that had existed between our four walls.

He had taken away from me those memories that had helped me to retain a small, small belief that life contained something that was good and right.

But he hadn't just let me down. Mom loved him too. She saw nothing but good in him—none of the darkness and the evil that he had inherited from Dad. He had been given a chance, thanks to Mom's blind love for him. And now he had proven that he hadn't deserved it.

Mom's heart would break the day she realized that Sebastian was just like Dad. That the horror would continue in the next generation and that her love hadn't been able to change that. That was why he had to die. To spare Mom that sorrow. She would never find out what he had done. And who he really was.

The red summer house was in a desolate location at the top of a cliff not far from a lake and surrounded by dense forest. It belonged to Ylva's parents, who had long ago become too elderly to use it. It had been years since they had used the place.

Faye examined the metal handle on the front door with satisfaction before nodding and closing the door behind her.

In the setting sun, she could see contours, shadows of old furniture, could smell the dampness. She fumbled for the light switch and found it. The sound of the switch flicking was not followed by light. A fuse had probably blown, because Ylva had told her the power was usually on. She would have to find the fuse box. Fortunately, she'd brought a flashlight with her.

The floorboards creaked as she entered what appeared to be a living room.

Faye put down the jerry can on the floor, and

let both herself and the old house fill with silence. She massaged her right arm, which felt tender after dragging the jerry can all the way there.

This was where she and Jack would finally part ways. Only one of them could leave alive. There was a lot that could go wrong. She might just as easily be the one who lost the battle.

How long did she have before he arrived? An hour? Two? In order not to leave any digital traces, Ylva was taking care of her mobile. Faye glanced at her wristwatch and saw it was a little after ten o'clock in the evening.

Ylva had called Jack on the mobile number he had left when he had visited her apartment. She had said in floods of tears that Faye had turned up and taken Nora away. That she had been acting crazy, muttering that she was going to take away the last thing Jack had—his youngest daughter. That she hadn't said where she was going to take Nora, but that after she'd left Ylva had discovered that the keys to her parents' cabin were missing.

Faye pulled the flashlight out of the bag she'd brought, switched it on, and swept the beam around, searching for the basement door. She examined the framed black-and-white photographs on the walls. The people in them looked old. They were probably dead. Other pictures showed Ylva as a child. Ylva without front teeth. Ylva on a horse. Her stomach did a somersault. How well did Faye actually know Ylva? What if she was on Jack's side? Had she been all along?

Faye had underestimated Jack. And David. Ylva too? No, there was no chance.

"Stop it," she murmured.

She opened a door that turned out to be the right one and she began to descend the stairs to the basement.

She caught sight of the final rays of sunshine across the treetops through a small rectangular window. When it returns, I might be dead, she thought to herself. The stairs were steep and protested at every step she took.

The smell of damp was stronger the farther down she went.

Once at the bottom, Faye managed to locate the fuse box, and she flicked the main circuit breaker. Using the flashlight, she found new fuses and managed to replace the blown one. When she turned the power back on, the ceiling light came on. She checked her watch and quickly went back upstairs. In the living room, she selected a lamp.

Faye pulled the cord out of the socket in the wall. She quickly unscrewed the plug and made the necessary adjustments using the screwdriver she had brought. Just like in the video she had watched. You could find everything on the internet, if you knew where to look.

She got out the steel wire and wrapped it around the front door handle. Loop after loop. Tightly. Then, from the 1.5-liter bottle she'd brought with her, she poured water onto the top step. It formed a small, shallow puddle.

It wouldn't be noticeable in the dark.

By the time she was done, she had been in the house for forty minutes. She turned off the light, sat down on the sofa, and waited in the darkness. She kept an eye on the illuminated figures on her watch, squeezing the screwdriver in her hand. Jack wouldn't turn up unarmed, and if something went wrong she would have to defend herself against him.

Fight for her life.

Perhaps she would die. But she intended to die free—not as a hunted, terrified animal.

Exactly nine minutes later, she heard the rumble of a car engine.

The rumble of the engine died away and silence descended. Faye got to her feet. She carefully took off her shoes, left them on the sofa, and crept to the lamp she had positioned beside the door. She plugged it in and glanced nervously at the door handle.

She sank down to the floor with her back to the wall.

She could hear footsteps outside the cabin. She licked her lips. She felt her nerves tingling, a fluttering in her stomach. Beyond the walls, Jack was tramping about. What if he didn't pick the front door but went through a window? Or via the basement?

But why would he do that? He knew she was waiting for him. He thought Nora was in the house and in mortal danger.

"Faye," Jack called out. "I want my daughter."

She saw his silhouette outside the window and pressed herself closer against the wall. He couldn't see her. The next second, he switched on a flashlight and directed it through the window. The beam of light passed inches away from her right foot. She stopped breathing. Did he suspect anything? Was that why he was circling around the house?

She pictured him out there. Once upon a time she had loved him more than anything, perhaps even more than she loved Julienne. Now she just wanted to destroy him for what he had done to their daughter, and for the humiliation he had heaped on Faye. For all the women who had been in her place, suppressed, feeling worthless, who had taken their lives, been deprived of their dignity. Who had been kept as serfs. Exploited. Women who were still shackled, even if the appearance of those shackles had changed over the centuries.

Faye was going to strike back.

She wasn't going to be a statistic, one more woman killed by her husband or ex.

"Come out now," he called out. "If you've hurt her, I'll kill you, Faye."

She heard the suppressed rage. The voice was behind her now, close by, on the other side of the wall. That meant he was heading for the front door.

Faye swallowed.

"She's here." Her throat felt tight, her voice hoarse. "In here."

Jack shifted his weight from foot to foot on the steps outside. He didn't seem to be able to make up his mind about what to do. He was scared. He knew what she was capable of. That she was smarter than him. That she was dangerous. And that he was the one who made her dangerous.

"Bring her out," he shouted.

Faye didn't reply. She gritted her teeth and screwed her eyes tight shut. She didn't want to do too much to tempt him in case it made him suspicious.

"Do it," she whispered. "Do it."

The footsteps had stopped. He was probably standing still on the steps, two feet or so away. She could feel his presence, his hesitation, his fear.

Her legs trembled with anxiety. Faye dug her nails into the palm of her hand.

"Touch the handle, Jack," she murmured. "Open the door. I'm right here waiting for you."

A second later she heard a sizzling sound.

She smiled and opened her eyes.

"One, two, three," she counted before reaching out and turning off the light.

She heard a heavy thud on the other side of the door. She got up slowly, sniffing the air. There was a burnt smell seeping in from outside.

Faye slowly opened the door, but it soon jammed because Jack's body was lying in the way. She saw his legs through the crack in the door. He had fallen backward. She kept pushing and eventually made enough of an opening that she could squeeze through the gap.

She bent down and examined his face. His eyes were wide open. Empty. She leaned forward and put two fingers to his neck. There was no pulse.

She looked at the man she had once loved more than anything else on earth and tried to understand what she felt.

The forest loomed before her like a wall around the house, shutting out the world.

The silence was dense.

It was as if they were in another dimension—where there were only Faye and Jack.

The story that had begun at the Stockholm School of Economics so many years ago was over.

The one that had brought her tears. Thoughts of suicide. Humiliation. Abortion. The women he had cheated on her with. But it had also brought her Julienne, the takeover of Compare, the creation of Revenge. Her liberation. Was there anyone more free than a person who had been imprisoned? How else could you recognize the scent of freedom? A person could be someone else's prison—their rage or contempt could be the shackles that kept them fettered.

Faye grabbed Jack's wrists and dragged the heavy body across the threshold and into the living room. His head hit the floor.

Jack was left in the middle of the floor while Faye, panting with effort, sat down on the sofa and looked at his body. She got up. She went over to him and kicked him. The sound was muffled. No reaction. She took aim. Kicked him again. Thought about the pictures of Julienne on Jack's computer. His face when she gave him the plastic wallet with the photo.

She leaned over the dead body.

"You should have let me go. You shouldn't have been so stubborn. So proud. You should **never** have humiliated me. Used my daughter to threaten me. And you should never, ever have done what you did to Julienne."

Faye got to her feet. She picked up the jerry can, stood behind Jack, and unscrewed the cap. She moved in parallel with his body, drenching his clothing in gasoline.

Then she opened the door, lit a match, and let it fall. The next second, fire exploded next to Jack's body.

FJÄLLBACKA—THEN

I caught a whiff of the familiar smell of smoke from Sebastian's bedroom and heard the clanking of bottles. He was playing music at a low volume so that Dad didn't wake up. Mom had just gotten home. Yet again, she'd been driven to the hospital by Dad. With excuses about having fallen down the steps, slipped, gosh she was clumsy, so unfortunate. Excuses that no doctor could reasonably believe, but that no one dared to question.

Mom had made the mistake of saying she was planning to visit her brother Egil, and Dad had pushed her down the stairs right from the landing. Time was beginning to run out. Dad's rage was escalating. This time she had landed on her arm—next time she might land on her head, and then I would be alone for real.

It was just after midnight now. Mom and Dad were asleep. He was always a bit calmer just after Mom had come back from the hospital. I knew I'd never get a better chance.

I wanted to protect Mom. I didn't care what Dad felt. I'd deal with him later.

I slammed the book shut and placed my bare feet on the floorboards. I had already planned how I would act, what I would do. I put on the thin white nightie that I knew Sebastian liked. I had noticed that he couldn't keep his eyes off me when I wore it. I found the three sleeping pills I had stolen from Dad and crushed into a powder three days earlier.

I left my room and took a deep breath before knocking on his door.

"What is it?"

I pressed the handle down and stepped inside.

He was sitting at his desk, but he spun around and stared at me. His turbid eyes caught sight of my bare legs and slowly worked their way up.

"I was thinking about what you said."

Sebastian furrowed his brow. The black eye from the last time Dad had hit him was very prominent.

"What the hell are you talking about?"

"At the party in the forest. About me liking it when you all did me. You were wrong."

"Oh?" he said indifferently, turning back to the screen.

I took a step into the room, standing below the bar that was positioned above the door for pull-ups. I'd never seen him use it.

On the walls, there were posters of scantily clad women with boobs spilling out of tiny pieces of fabric. The room was untidy, with plates of leftover snacks, heaps of clothes everywhere, and a musty smell of sweat and rotten food. I wrinkled my nose in disgust.

I carefully put the small bag onto the floor and shoved it with my foot so that it ended up in a corner.

"I didn't like it when **they** did it with me. But I like it when **you** do it with me."

He froze.

"Do you want me to leave?" I said. "Or is it okay if I stay awhile? Mom and Dad are asleep."

He nodded, not looking at me. I interpreted that as meaning that he wanted me to stay.

"Can I have a beer?"

"They're warm."

"That doesn't matter."

He lay down on his front by the bed, reached underneath with his hand, and produced a bottle. He opened it and passed it to me. He still had the scars on his arm from the time Dad had cut him with a broken bottle.

I sat down on the edge of the bed and he sat down next to me. We each took a swig in silence. I glanced at his bottle. It was almost empty. Before long, he'd want another. That was when I'd have to add the sleeping pills. Four empties were standing on the desk, and I hadn't heard him go to the bathroom even once.

It would soon be time. Best to be ready.

"Do you like it when I struggle?" I asked softly.

His face went red, his gaze fixed to the wall.

"I don't know," he said.

His voice was thick.

"I just want to know what you like, what's best for you. You can do whatever you want to me."

"Mm."

He fidgeted. Through his tracksuit bottoms, I could see his penis swelling. He noticed that I had spotted it and seemed embarrassed.

"It's okay," I said.

I reached out with my hand and placed it clumsily onto his crotch. I felt vomit rising into my mouth but I quickly swallowed it.

He moved on the bed.

"I need the bathroom," he said.

I nodded.

"I'll wait here."

Faye walked through the forest naked. Behind her, the house was in flames. She had thrown her clothes into the fire—they would be destroyed together with Jack.

The orange flames licked up into the night sky, the smoke climbing high.

She didn't turn around, she just kept going, away from Jack. She was filled with a newly won and strong sense of freedom—it possessed her body.

The car headlights illuminated the narrow forest track at exactly the spot where she and Ylva had agreed to meet. Her friend had been close by all along and had been instructed to drive to the meeting point as soon as she saw smoke rising from the house. And just as promised, she was there.

Ylva smiled faintly at her from behind the wheel. Faye opened the passenger door without any expression. The car was red, old, freckled with rust, and had no GPS. Ylva had borrowed it from a guy she knew, no questions asked. He wasn't the sort to talk to the police. No one would be able to prove they had been here.

"Is it done?" Ylva asked.

"It's done."

Ylva nodded and reached into the backseat. She passed over a black bag containing clothes. A clean set. No trace of Jack.

"Do you want to get dressed before we go?"

Faye shook her head and climbed into the passenger seat with the bag on her lap. The smell of smoke was beginning to fill the inside of the car and Ylva coughed.

"No, just drive."

Faye saw the inferno in the house between the tree trunks at the very moment that the roof caved inward with a crash. Ylva, who had been about to start the engine, froze and slowly lowered her hand.

They sat in silence for a while as they watched the old house burn. Then Ylva put the car into gear and they slowly rolled forward.

"What do you feel?" she asked.

Faye thought about this for a bit.

"Nothing, actually. You?"

Ylva swallowed, then looked at Faye.

"The same."

When they reached the highway, they passed four fire engines going the other way at high speed, their sirens blaring.

The morning sun shone through the window of Alice's guest room. It illuminated Ylva, who was holding Nora in her arms. The little girl had just woken up and was rubbing her eyes sleepily.

"Are you okay?" Faye asked, putting her head around the door. She had spent the night wide awake on one of Alice's sofas.

She looked searchingly at Ylva.

"I'm okay," Ylva said, but her words and tone were contradicted by her viselike grip on Nora.

"We did what we had to do."

"Yes, I know," said Ylva.

She buried her nose in Nora's hair and closed her eyes. Her daughter's chubby little arms were wrapped tightly around her neck.

Alice came into the room, looked at them, and smiled.

"Breakfast is served."

When they had returned home during the night, Faye had told Alice everything. That hadn't been easy either. Naturally Alice had been very shocked.

Faye's phone rang and she hit the green button when she saw who it was.

"Hi, sweetheart," she said when Julienne's face filled the small display. "I can't talk right now, I'll call you later. But I'll be home soon. I promise. Really, really soon. Kiss kiss! Love you!"

"Okay, Mommy, bye!"

She hung up.

"Does she miss you?" said Ylva. Nora blinked her eyes slowly. She was at the point of falling asleep again in Ylva's arms.

"Yes," Faye said briefly.

She didn't feel up to talking about Julienne right now. Jack was gone. Forever. And no matter how much she had hated him, how much she realized that there had been no place for him in Julienne's life, she was still grieving. For the fact that Julienne would go through life without a dad.

The guilt was a heavy burden on her shoulders. Not because she had killed him, but because she had picked so poorly. But without Jack she would never have had Julienne. It was a mental equation she found hard to balance. She just wished she still had that picture in the plastic wallet. It had been her talisman, giving her strength and reminding her of what was important. But it was gone, just like Jack.

"What's the next step?" Alice said.

She looked strong and decisive.

Faye looked at Nora, at her soft eyelids and her long eyelashes.

She was so similar to Jack sometimes.

"We need to use the video and photo evidence. It's time for Ylva's plan B."

Alice smiled.

"You mean we're going to turn the screws on Eyvind?"

"Yes, we need those papers from the Patent and Registration Office."

"It needs to be the right papers and they have to be worded the right way," Ylva said, cradling Nora in her arms. "I've done a spec of exactly what we need."

Alice smiled again.

"When he sees the pictures and the footage, I guarantee he'll do everything we ask. Otherwise we'll send it all to his wife."

"Good," said Faye.

She looked at Nora again; she had fallen asleep against Ylva's shoulder. She looked just like Julienne when she was asleep. For a moment, Faye wanted to cry. For Julienne. For Nora. For Ylva. For herself. For them all.

FJÄLLBACKA—THEN

By the slimmest of margins, I managed to do it all. I fetched the bag from the corner, got on my front under the bed, and pulled out a new beer, opened it, and emptied the powder into it before Sebastian returned.

I passed the new bottle to him. He accepted it without a word, then sat down on the bed and raised it to his lips. He took a big swig.

He was still cautious—as if he couldn't believe that I had suddenly given in and was going to let him sleep with me without putting up a fight.

"Could you change the music?"

"What?"

Now I needed to get him to drink the rest of the beer, to keep him away from me for as long as possible. The mere thought of what I might have to do with him made me want to vomit.

"Maybe Metallica?"

He nodded. Got up, went to the stereo, took out the CD, and ran his finger along the row of CD cases until he found Metallica. He inserted the disk and pressed play. He turned the volume up slightly.

Then he stood in front of me.

"I need to be more drunk," I said. "I know what we're going to do is wrong, but I can't help liking it."

"Let's play catch-up," he said.

I smiled.

"Good idea."

I tipped my head back and we downed our beers simultaneously. I held my breath to avoid the taste. I gasped when I had finished it all. Sebastian wiped his mouth. He looked at me hungrily and an unpleasant shiver ran through my body. How long would it take before the tablets took effect?

"Have you got any porn magazines?" I asked.

I knew he had a stash. Sometimes he kept them behind the radiator, sometimes under the mattress. He turned and stuck his hand under the mattress.

He passed me a magazine. The cover showed a woman with enormous boobs parting her legs for the camera. Her pussy was shaved.

I opened the magazine and leafed through it.

"What do you like? Is there anything you want me to do?" I said, my gaze firmly fixed on the magazine. Anything to delay, to give the sleeping tablets time to take effect.

He shrugged.

"There must be something you like more than other things?"

"I don't know," he said quietly.

"I'd like bigger boobs. Don't guys like big tits?"

Sebastian didn't answer.

I carried on turning the pages.

"If you'd said you liked being with me, I would never have let them touch you," he muttered.

I looked up from the magazine. He didn't meet my gaze.

That's a lie, I thought to myself. You would never have stood up for me. You're too much of a coward.

Instead, I said: "I know."

"That means it's my fault they're dead."

You're right, I thought to myself. And soon you'll be dead too. I'm never going to shed a tear for you. Because I know what an awful, cowardly excuse for a human being you are. You're never going to ruin anyone else's life.

"Don't think about that now."

Sebastian yawned and his eyelids fluttered. He leaned back, resting against the wall. His eyelids began to close.

"Lie down," I said. "And I'll make you feel good."

I closed the porn mag and put it aside. I crept closer to him and put the pillow under his head. Sebastian already seemed to be asleep, so I curled up next to him and contemplated his peaceful face.

I lay still for a while to make sure the tablets had

definitely taken effect. When I was certain that he was deeply asleep, I got up from the bed carefully and went to his desk. There was already a sheet of paper in his typewriter, so all I had to do was type up a suicide note in which Sebastian said that he missed his two friends and felt so guilty that he hadn't been able to save them. Since I was a better writer than he was, I kept the language simple and made a few deliberate spelling errors. It took some time, since I was using two of his lighters on the keyboard in case anyone dusted for prints.

I left the letter where it was so that whoever came into the room would quickly find it.

And then it was time for the heavy lifting.

Moving mechanically, I went to the wardrobe, opened the door, and found a belt. I remembered to position the chair. I lay down behind Sebastian with my legs on either side of his body, put the belt around his neck, and pulled. It was hard. Harder than I'd expected.

I stood up on the bed, pulled harder, bracing my legs. His face went blue. He gasped for air. But his eyes remained shut.

I carried on pulling with all my might for at least five minutes before I finally let go. Then I reached out with one hand and touched his neck. No pulse. No life.

The body really was heavy. I squatted on the floor and slowly dragged him across the room.

Once there, I heaved him onto the chair under the pull-up bar. I struggled to attach the belt to the bar. Then I kicked the chair so that it fell onto the floor. Sebastian was left hanging loose-limbed from the belt.

I looked around the room. What had I missed? I had run Sebastian's fingertips over the bag I'd kept the sleeping tablets in, to make sure it had his prints on it. No one would suspect me. Suicide would be the logical consequence of the difficult summer Sebastian had dealt with after two of his best friends had died.

I looked around the room one last time before taking my beer bottle with me and padding back to my own room. I considered going outside to throw it away, but settled for hiding it under the bed.

I lay awake until six o'clock in the morning, reading, thinking, and trying to decide whether I had a guilty conscience. I didn't. Not one bit.

At around six, I heard Dad's footsteps on the landing. He must have noticed Sebastian's open door as he was heading for the bathroom, because he came to a halt. A second later I heard him cry out.

The first part of my plan had been completed. It had been relatively easy to execute. Now all I had to do was save Mom.

"Is it morning at home?"

Faye nodded. Kerstin looked rested. Happy. That pleased Faye. In the middle of all the chaos that reigned, Kerstin's happiness brought her hope.

Kerstin's face came closer to the screen. The fine lines around her eyes were visible. The concern in those eyes warmed Faye's heart.

"Are you okay?" Kerstin asked.

"You know what? I actually am. I've learned my lesson. I'm never going to hand over power to anyone else again. Never going to be vulnerable."

"You can't promise that. I don't want you to promise that. We all have to be a little bit vulnerable."

Faye sighed and thought about Julienne. The future she wanted to give her daughter.

"Yes, I suppose you're right. But it'll be a while. I'm not sure I can cope with having my heart broken any more times."

Kerstin suddenly laughed—the warm laugh that was always such an unexpected pleasure.

"Stop being such a drama queen, Faye. You're stronger than that, you know it. It's not like you to feel sorry for yourself. There are a lot of us who love you. And you may have lost the battle, but you'll win the war. Never forget that."

"I haven't won yet."

Kerstin placed a hand on the screen and Faye could almost feel the caress on her cheek.

"No, but you will win. Call me as soon as it's over."

"I promise. Kiss kiss. Miss you."

"I miss you too."

Faye ended the FaceTime call on her computer. She realized she was smiling, despite the tension she felt about what was to come. She missed Kerstin, but it was wonderful to see how happy she was with Bengt in Mumbai.

She reached for her mobile and called Ylva.

"Hi, Faye, I was about to call you."

Ylva's tense voice made her pulse race so much that it pounded in her ears.

"Is the investment done?"

"Yes, the wife is in on it. The investment is secured."

"God, what a relief!"

Faye shut her eyes. Her pulse slowed down and for the first time in ages she felt the feeling of pleasurable expectation spreading through her. The final piece of the puzzle was in place.

She looked at her reflection in the mirror and applied a bright red lipstick. Then she folded the white Max Mara coat over her arm, picked up her Louis Vuitton briefcase with her other hand, and left her suite. She had checked back into the Grand. She felt safer there after everything that had happened. It was on the borderline between walking distance and taxi distance, but she decided to opt for a pair of her comfiest heels and walk. She needed the fresh air to gather her thoughts.

Beside the quays the water sparkled. It was a perfect day. The sun was shining and there wasn't even the slightest breeze rippling the waters around Stockholm. She smiled at the people she passed.

Then she came to a sudden stop. Something at the corner of her eye had caught her attention. She turned toward the big window of an art gallery. A female bust with tears of silver. Faye was entranced by the sculpture. She put her hand to her breast where the charm given to her by her mother so many years ago had hung. Before it had disappeared during those dark days on Yxön island.

She moved closer. The artist was called Caroline Tamm. Faye checked the time and then went inside.

"I'd like to buy the sculpture in the window. The one in silver."

"Don't you want to know what it costs first?" said the woman sitting at the table inside in a tone of surprise.

"No," Faye said, handing over her Amex Black. "I'm in a bit of a hurry. I'll pay now, but please send the sculpture to this address."

Faye handed over her business card.

While the card was being processed, Faye went to the sculpture and examined it from the other direction. The tears streaked across the face and fanned out into the air behind the head like wings, transforming sorrow into flight. It symbolized strength like nothing else she had ever seen. It symbolized the new. When she had thought she was going to lose Revenge to Henrik, she had felt as if she had waxen wings that had melted because she had dared to fly too close to the sun. Now she felt like she could fly as high as she wanted. With her wings of silver.

When the gallery door closed behind her, Faye knew she was ready.

Faye put her head back and studied the beautiful nineteenth-century façades. When she had first arrived in Stockholm from Fjällbacka, she had been wide-eyed at all the beautiful old buildings. Now, almost twenty years later, she was rich enough to buy a whole block of the city. It was a strange feeling.

She shifted her gaze to the left, toward Stureplan and Biblioteksgatan, where the nightclub known as

Buddha Bar had once been. She remembered that enchanting summer night in 2001 when she had met a lovely, kind boy called Viktor. Too kind, she had thought back then. How might her life have looked if she hadn't chosen Jack? If she'd let Viktor live and killed Jack instead?

She looked up toward the window again. Up there on the fifth floor, David was waiting. And Henrik. Each in a separate office.

Alice and Ylva had texted to say that everything was in place and that neither of the men had seen the other arrive. The scene was set. Faye tried to make out what she was feeling—whether she was nervous, angry, or upset.

But no, deep down she felt only happiness. Wild, pure happiness. Everything might have been so much worse if she hadn't had Ylva and Alice in her life. They had saved her. They had saved each other.

She keyed in the door code and waited for the elevator. A little while later, she passed between the empty desks in Revenge's open-plan office, taking delight in the smell of freshly brewed coffee. The lights were on in the conference room. She saw the back of David's neck and his broad shoulders as he chatted to Ylva and Alice. Alice's smiling mouth was moving, but the thick glass door deadened any attempt to hear what the conversation was about.

Faye opened the door and David turned around

and saw her. He stood up and held out his arms to embrace her.

"My darling, finally. I've missed you so much," he said. "Frankfurt was awful without you."

Faye walked past him without looking at him, pulled out a chair at the head of the table, and sat down.

She crossed her legs.

"Faye . . . what? What's going on?" he asked in surprise.

The smile on Alice's face was gone. She gave him a hostile stare. David seemed to notice the atmosphere in the room had changed.

"I've brought you here today to introduce you to our new investors," Faye began, stretching out her hand toward Ylva and taking a folder from her.

Faye opened it, examined the papers inside, and nodded.

"Yes, you may wonder what I meant by that, given that I'm no longer in control of Revenge. Partly thanks to information you passed to Henrik. But he's right here in the room next door. And believe me, Revenge will soon be mine again. If I were you, I'd take care to avoid being associated with Henrik Bergendahl in the future. You'll soon understand why. But until then, I think this says it all."

She placed the uppermost document on the table and pushed it across to David, who shuddered.

"This . . . I can explain," he stammered.

Faye snorted.

"You're not going to explain anything. You're going to listen."

For the first time, she fixed her eyes on him. She pushed three sheets of paper stapled together toward him. The heading said **Joint petition for divorce** and the names on the paperwork were David Schiller and Johanna Schiller.

"This is for you to sign."

"But what's this? I've been trying to get this divorce through for months. You know that."

Faye burst out laughing. Alice and Ylva chimed in. David looked from one to the other with his mouth hanging open.

"My dear, it's all over. You've spent your life deceiving women. That's finished. Trying to buy your way into Revenge with your wife's money while claiming you were in the middle of a divorce was . . . creative. And then covering yourself by feeding business secrets about the American expansion to Henrik." Faye nodded to the first document she had given to David. "I'll give you this, you're not lazy. But it's over now. Do you understand? You should be happy to avoid prison."

David swallowed. His face became redder.

"I . . ."

"Shut your mouth," Faye roared.

There was a knock on the door and she waved in a dark-haired woman wearing an elegant Chanel dress.

"Hello, dearest ex-husband," said Johanna Schiller, pulling out the chair nearest to Faye.

David's jaw dropped again.

He blinked furiously, looking between the two women.

"She's trying to trick you, Johanna," he said. "Don't believe her lies. She just wants your money. I had an affair, I had a moment of weakness, but it was never more than that for me. Never. It's you and me, Johanna. I love you."

Johanna began to titter.

"I would never deceive you," he went on, pointing at Faye. "She came on to me."

David suddenly slammed his fist onto the table. His face was transformed with anger. He looked like a furious little boy.

"Stop it," said Johanna, shaking her head. "Sign the papers and fuck off. We've got a board meeting."

David leaned toward her.

"Are you the new investor?"

"Yes, you're broke," Ylva murmured.

Johanna nodded cheerfully.

"Without you and the drama you brought to my life, I've got far too much time on my hands. And money. I'm sick of keeping your sinking investments afloat. When Ylva here explained the situation, I said I'd be delighted to invest in Revenge."

David turned to Faye. She contemplated him

with amusement and folded her arms. He opened his mouth to say something, but then closed it again.

"Sign the papers and get lost. Now, **darling**. We've got matters to discuss and then we're going out to celebrate this deal."

David grabbed the pen. With his gaze still fixed on Faye, he signed. Then he stood up so violently that the chair almost fell over. He began to back toward the door, his eyes wild.

"David Schiller," said a voice behind him.

David spun around. There were two policemen in the doorway.

Faye had seen them arrive but hadn't said anything.

"Yes?" he answered nervously.

"We'd like you to come with us."

"Why?"

His body language was defensive.

"We can discuss that outside."

David turned to Faye.

"What have you done?"

"Reported you for the crimes you committed against Revenge and against me. Corporate espionage should get you a couple of years' prison time."

The two police officers gripped David's upper arms and marched him outside. They could hear his loud protests echoing through the open-plan office. Ylva gathered up the papers and put them back in the folder.

Faye got up and went over to Johanna. She shook her hand.

"Welcome aboard."

"Thanks."

Faye took a deep breath. The champagne on ice would have to wait a little longer. She still had one more chauvinist bastard to deal with before she could celebrate.

Henrik looked up with a big grin when Faye stepped into what had, until recently, been her office. Ylva and Alice followed just behind her, and Alice closed the door.

"What might three former employees have on their minds? You should be grateful I'm giving you this time—I've got an enormous amount to do. We're in the middle of a major expansion in America and my patience for the complaints of former employees is limited, to say the least. We're complying with the contracts of employment that were in place to the letter. On the other hand, I must say it's a delight to see that you've apparently acquired a work ethic, Alice. That's a new side to you."

"Shut your face, Henrik," Alice said cheerfully.

He frowned.

"I don't have all day. Say what you've got to say and then get lost. You have no business being here."

He leaned back in the chair and linked his hands together behind his head.

Ylva placed a bundle of papers on his desk. Certain sections were marked with green highlighter.

"What's this?"

Henrik picked up the papers in irritation and began to glance through them.

"You own Revenge. That's absolutely clear. But you don't own the rights to our products," Faye said. "Here are the papers from the Patent and Registration Office that confirm it. It's going to be interesting to see what Revenge's partners in the USA have to say about that. Not to mention your financial partners. Owning a company but not its products means that in practice you don't own anything of any value whatsoever."

She nodded at Alice and Ylva.

"Together with these two, I've already begun to persuade the shareholders to come back to us. And all that stuff your private detective dug up to black-mail the shareholders, including Irene Ahrnell, into selling to you . . . Well, if you even consider ever using any of that information, we both know that Alice won't need the services of private detectives to dig up dirt on you . . ."

Alice crossed her arms with a smirk and nodded cheerfully.

"You fucking cunt! You're just making this up! My lawyers would never miss a key detail like that!"

Henrik stood up and glowered at Alice, his face bright red.

"Mmm, but apparently you did," she said. "Maybe it's time to change law firms? And I'd counter by calling you a fucking dick, but with that little thing on you it'd probably be more appropriate to call you a 'micropenis.' Then again, that doesn't have quite the same feel to it . . ."

"You fucking—"

Henrik made to lunge for Alice, but Faye stepped forward and fixed her gaze on him. She leaned across the table, pushed the documents toward him, and then spoke in a cool voice: "Without the rights to the products, this company is an empty shell. In other words, it's a huge financial loss for you. And your investors. So the best decision you can make right now is to sell your shares to me. For the same price you and your decoys bought them at. I hope you understand and appreciate the generosity I'm showing you right now."

"Why would I do that? I've got strong investors to back me up, I can afford to litigate against you, and I don't give a fuck about what you've managed to find in the small print of some stupid contract. I'm going to fight you until you haven't got a penny to your name . . ."

Henrik hissed and spluttered, making spittle fly, but Faye merely reached forward, calmly took the handkerchief from his jacket pocket, and wiped his face with it.

"Given that your biggest investor in the acquisition of Revenge—by far—was Sten Stolpe, I don't think I'd be so sure about that."

"Sten is one of my oldest friends and one of my most loyal clients and business partners. I think I can say with certainty he'll back me up unconditionally."

Henrik's voice was dripping with contempt. Alice had been studying her nails carefully throughout the discussion, but now she said casually: "You should probably check your phone. Something tells me Sten is trying to get hold of you . . ."

"What the hell?"

Henrik picked up his briefcase and pulled his phone out of it. Faye craned her neck to see the display. Then she turned to Ylva and Alice.

"Oh my, Henrik has apparently got forty-three missed calls and rather a lot of messages from Sten. I wonder what on earth he can want? He seems very eager to get hold of you . . ."

Henrik opened one message after another from Sten and the color drained from his face.

"What the hell have you done, Alice?"

Alice looked at him with innocent blue eyes.

"Me? I haven't done a thing. By coincidence, my phone was stolen yesterday, and I reported it to the police. You've got to do these things properly. And I have no idea what someone might have found on it and sent to Sten. Of course, it might just happen to

be a video of you fucking his underage daughter—
and our au pair—but what do I know? Like I said,
my phone was stolen yesterday. Did I mention that
I reported it to the police?"

Henrik roared and lunged toward Alice. But Ylva
stuck out a foot and he fell headlong to the floor.

He lay there shouting and waving his arms at them.

The three women left, but Faye turned around in
the doorway.

"I'd like your signature by tonight confirming
the sale of Revenge back to me. The papers are
at the bottom of that stack, under the contracts."

After they'd closed the door behind them, they
could still hear him cursing.

FJÄLLBACKA—THEN

Mom had been easily persuaded. It was as if she were in a fog after Sebastian's death, and Dad took out all of his grief and frustration on her. With each passing month, his madness became even worse. When I pressed down the front door handle after school, I would hold my breath. The first thing I always did was to call out for Mom, and every day I was terrified I wouldn't get an answer. I heard the cries and saw the black eyes, and, worse, I was forced to witness Mom fading away more and more. She barely ate any longer. I tried to coax her to eat something. I took over the cooking and learned the dishes that Mom loved. Sometimes she would take a couple of bites, but mostly she would just stare hollow-eyed at the plate.

I knew she was dying before my very eyes. I had always thought that Mom would die when Dad finally went too far in his desire to hurt her. But as the months passed, I realized she would die from a lack of hope. She could see no end. She could see no way out. I had wanted to free her through Sebastian's death—to save her from being crushed by the weight of our secrets. Instead, I was killing her, slowly but surely.

Every day, I pictured that time I had found her after she'd taken the sleeping pills. I pictured how I'd stuck my fingers down her throat and forced her to vomit. I had saved her then. But I was killing her now. I had to do something. I had to give her hope. A way out.

Once I'd made up my mind, I began to plan.

It hurt so much having to wait, having to be patient, while I saw Mom bloodied and bruised more and more often. But I knew that if I didn't help her get away for good, she would soon be dead. And I wouldn't be able to live with that.

Dad also needed to take his punishment. For what he had done to us, what he had taught Sebastian, the fear that he had forced us to live through.

There was only one person I knew could help me. Mom's brother. Dad didn't like Uncle Egil. Letting any outsider into the house was always a risk for him. A risk he didn't want to take. So to me, Uncle Egil was just a distant memory. But Mom often talked about him. And I realized that he would do anything for her.

Mom had his number in a tatty little contacts book hidden at the bottom of her underwear drawer. I didn't include her in any aspect of the planning. I looked at her glassy stare and I just wanted to wrap my arms around her and hold her tight, but it also told me that I had to be the grown-up now and take care of her. For the first time in my life, I was the adult and she was the child.

She was light as a bird, fragile, frail, and with every passing day she grew frailer. I called Uncle Egil in secret from school when the school phone was left unattended for a while in the office. It was important for me not to leave any trace. I told him what I needed and he immediately promised to help. Unconditionally. No questions. His voice was so similar to Mom's and it made me feel reassured.

One evening late in summer, I decided that everything was in place. I called Egil again from school and gave him my strict instructions. I knew he would follow them to the letter.

Once Dad had gone to bed and fallen asleep—with a little help from some sleeping tablets in his evening whiskey—I got to work. Mom was absolutely loose-limbed, like a rag doll. She was so broken, so small, so weak, that she didn't say anything, didn't ask any questions, just did everything I told her to and let me lead her. I didn't dare pack anything for her. Nothing could be missing. It couldn't look like she'd taken anything with her, as if she had left home voluntarily.

It was a fairly chilly evening. There was no sun to warm the skin as we slowly made our way down to the water. I had Dad's boots on my feet. In one hand, I was holding his hammer. I was using my free arm to lead my mother to the water's edge. Dad's gloves were big, so I had to keep pulling them up over my far smaller hands. Mom slipped and I caught her, and I took the opportunity to smell the scent of her hair as she leaned against me. I was going to miss her. Dear God, I was going to miss her. But to love someone was to set them free. And I was releasing Mom right now.

Down by the water, Uncle Egil was waiting in a boat with the lights extinguished. He knew exactly what I was going to do. I hadn't excluded him from any part of the plan. He hadn't protested, even if the silence at the other end of the line had been heavy with unspoken words. But he knew I was right.

I hadn't said anything to Mom. I considered it more compassionate to wait until this moment to seek her approval. But I knew she would agree to what I wanted to do. She was used to pain.

"Mom, I have to hit you. I have to hit you hard. With the hammer. It's Dad's hammer. He's going to pay for what he's done. We have to get him out of our lives. Do you understand, Mom?"

Mom didn't even hesitate. She nodded. I had greeted Uncle Egil when we got down to the boat, but now I didn't even dare look at him. I hugged Mom. I felt her thin, brittle shoulders pressed against my rib cage.

I was so scared of hitting her too hard. Scared to see her shatter like a crystal bowl. But there was no going back now. I took the hammer. Raised it. Shut my eyes. And brought it down. I took aim for a soft area where there was nothing to be broken. But not a drop of blood ended up on Dad's hammer. I needed blood. I realized I would have to strike a harder area of the body. Something would have to break and pierce the skin so that blood was smeared on the hammer.

I took aim at her shin. I raised the hammer high above my head and swung it, hard. All that came out of Mom's lips was a quiet groan. I saw out of the corner of my eye that Egil had turned away. I looked at the hammer. Blood. Mom's blood.

I put the hammer down three feet or so from the water's edge. Far enough from the water that it wouldn't reach the hammer if it rose before the police found it. I tenderly led Mom to Egil's boat. She couldn't support herself on the leg I had hit. But her body against mine was warm and soft. I reluctantly handed her over to Uncle Egil, taking the last of her scent into my nostrils. I knew it would be many years before I saw her again.

After seeing them disappear across the water into the pitch-dark moonless night, I slowly turned around and returned to the house again. From the corner of my eye, I saw the bloodied hammer.

When I got back to the house, I carefully left

Dad's boots in the hall. There were drops of blood on them. I took off the gloves—they too had drops of blood on them—and carefully put them on the hat rack.

The house was silent. Now it was just me and Dad left.

After tomorrow, it would just be me. I could hardly wait.

I went to bed. I thought about Mom. I remembered the sound of the hammer smashing into the bone.

I loved her. And she loved me. We loved each other. That was my final thought before sleep took over.

Beside the circular table at Riche there was a bottle of Bollinger peeking out of a silver ice bucket. Alice, Ylva, and Faye raised their glasses in a toast. This was their second bottle of the evening. They had told the waiter they would order food later, but they had long since forgotten that. Faye felt intoxicated, but decided that it might be worth flying to Italy a little hungover in the morning, given this was the last time for three months that she would see Alice and Ylva.

They had planned together how to divide the work in the future. In early October, they would all meet again at the new office in New York for the launch of Revenge in the USA. Johanna would also be joining them. She was recently divorced, happy, and apparently enjoying regular sex with her personal trainer. Given how quickly she'd ended up in bed with him, Faye strongly suspected it was no new relationship. But that wasn't something for her to be bothered about.

David was on remand, waiting for the prosecutor to charge him for corporate espionage. The last they'd heard of Henrik was that his company was on the verge of bankruptcy. Rumor was that there had been a schism between Henrik and Sten Stolpe and that Sten was now doing everything he could to crush Henrik.

The waiter, a handsome guy of about twenty-five, with broad cheekbones, ice-gray eyes, and the body of a Greek god, cleared his throat.

"Would you like anything else, or are you all happy?"

He smiled at Faye, and she felt a shiver run through her body. She was free and happy. Ready to move on. A brief but intense little adventure as a mark of farewell to Sweden wouldn't be amiss.

"It could be better," she said gravely.

He looked taken aback. Ylva and Alice looked at her in surprise.

"Yes," said Faye, signaling that he should come closer.

He bent forward.

"It would be **perfect** if you told me what time you get off, so that I can have a car waiting outside to bring you to my hotel room," she whispered.

His facial expression switched from surprise to amusement.

He straightened his back and said with feigned seriousness: "One o'clock, madam."

Alice and Ylva now realized what Faye had asked, and laughed. The waiter adjusted his shirt and disappeared with a wink.

They raised their glasses in another toast.

A movement from the corner of her eye made Faye look out of the window facing toward Birger Jarlsgatan. Through the pane of glass, she saw a familiar face. A face that filled her with horror. Her hand shaking, she set down the glass.

There was no doubt about it. The man was her father. He came closer to the window, met Faye's gaze, and held the photo of her mother and Julienne against the glass.

Then he was gone again.

ACKNOWLEDGMENTS

When you write a novel, there are a lot of people to thank. I'd like to start by explaining who Karin—to whom this book is dedicated—is. Karin Linge Nordh has been my publisher ever since my second book. I wouldn't be the author I am today without Karin and her knowledge, wisdom, and passion for literature. Since my last book came out, Karin has moved on to new pastures, but what she taught me will always remain a part of my work. And I have the benefit of getting to keep Karin in my life as a close friend. Massive, heartfelt, sincere THANKS to you, Karin!

During the genesis of this book, I've had the privilege of working with John Häggblom and Ebba Östberg. I can't praise them enough, and this book wouldn't be the same without their affectionate touch. They are stars in the publishing sky and I am eternally grateful to have the opportunity to work with them. I'd also like to

ACKNOWLEDGMENTS

thank my editor Kerstin Ödeen and everyone else at my publisher Forum/Ester Bonnier. There are so many of you who do a fantastic job—no names, but none of you are forgotten. You know who you are . . .

A very important person to my work on both this book and the previous novel about Faye is my friend and great colleague Pascal Engman. He has contributed both brilliance and dedication to brainstorming ideas, and I'm incredibly grateful that he was willing to give me his time. Thank you, Pascal!

I also have a supremely competent team behind me that I worked with day in, day out ahead of the launch of **Silver Tears** in Sweden: Christina Saliba, Joakim Hansson, and Anna Frankl, as well as the rest of the team at Nordin Agency, in addition to Lina Hellqvist and Julia Aspnäs.

Facts are incredibly important when a book comes into existence. Emmanuel Ergul has been a tremendous source of information for the financial parts of this book, in addition to Martin Junghem and Sara Börsvik.

In my personal life, there are so many people to thank. Without my family, I wouldn't get a single sentence written. My husband, Simon, whom I love above all else, and my wonderful, amazing children, Wille, Meja, Charlie, and Polly; my mom, Gunnel Läckberg, and my parents-in-law, Anette and Christer Sköld. Thank you for being you and for being my safety net.

And, as ever: thank you, Dad, for giving me a love of books.

Camilla Läckberg
Stockholm, March 2020

A NOTE ABOUT THE AUTHOR

CAMILLA LÄCKBERG is the prizewinning, best-selling author of the Fjällbacka series, which has sold more than twenty-eight million copies worldwide. Her books are sold in more than sixty countries and have been translated into forty-three languages. She lives in Stockholm.

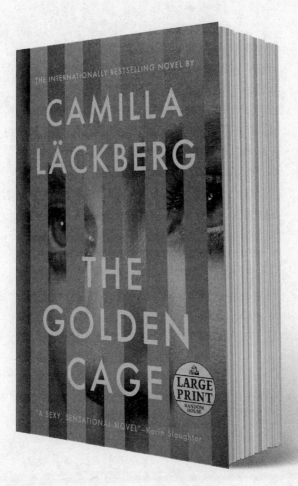